AND WHERE THEY STOP

AND WHERE THEY STOP

A NOVEL OF THE 1950S

ROBERT HILLIARD

IBSN: 978-0-9842489-9-5

BOOK AND COVER DESIGN BY MAGGIE MAY ROGERS

PARLANCE
PO Box 1144
Sanibel, FL 33957

REMEMBERING THE CHILDREN AND FAMILIES

OF THE GREAT DEPRESSION,

FOR SOME THE BEST OF TIMES

IN THE WORST OF TIMES:

IRVING, EDA, ROBERT, NORMA

PREFACE

And Where They Stop was my first novel, written in 1951 when I was 26 years old. I was offered a contract by one of the popular publishers of the time. Just before I signed it I learned that the publisher was a strong supporter of McCarthyism, the term applied to Wisconsin Senator Joe McCarthy's intimidation of freedom of speech and belief, turning virtually our entire nation into abject fear of guilt by accusation of Communist subversion as the Cold War against the Soviet Union became hotter. A spoken word or an anonymous letter could result in a given target losing his or her job, many victims going to jail for refusing to name friends and acquaintances as "Reds" before the House Committee on Unamerican Activities. Teachers were required to sign loyalty oaths to keep their jobs. Hollywood, television and radio blacklists destroyed the careers of many performers and other film and media artists. It took television producers Edward R. Murrow's and Fred Friendly's courageous profile of McCarthy, live with his own words, to reveal to the entire nation McCarthy's paranoia, contributing importantly to his eventual downfall. I could not align myself with supporters of what to me were clearly neo-fascist practices and policies and I turned down the publishing contract that might have been a significant career starter. The manuscript was put into a filing cabinet where it remained until now, over 70 years later.

This novel is a story of young people in their 20s whose beliefs and behaviors were formed by two major factors: They were the children of the Great Depression and the teenagers of World War II. In both periods there were unwanted restrictions, economic and physical, on individual and group ambitions and plans for life. The years following the end of World War II offered and facilitated profound changes in society, young people seeking new freedoms, breaking from cultural, economic and moral traditions, embracing the explosion of arts in New York City, interacting with each other while dealing with their individual demons and angels. I was part of that society.

As a writer—more accurately, as a young would-be writer—I sought new approaches to my art. As a reader I had long been put off by the passive "he said," "she said" third party approach to writing, making the reader an observer rather than an intimate participant in the lives of the characters. I wanted the reader to experience what the characters were experiencing through sharing their thoughts even before reading about what they said and did, to feel as they did against the background of the sights and sounds of New York City in the early 1950s.

Robert Hilliard
Sanibel, Florida
June, 2022

"The wheel of fortune spins…round and round she goes and where she stops nobody knows."

(The Original Amateur Hour opening, Major Bowes on radio, 1934-1946, and Ted Mack on television,1948-1970.)

PART ONE

THE STATEMENT

CHAPTER 1
WALTER

Julia poured another drink. She hated liquor. She poured another. Her husband would be coming home soon and she hated the son-of-a-bitch.

Even the name Walter sounded big and fat and sloppy to Julia. His sex was insurance. When he lay next to her in bed at night she didn't think of him as a man but as an insurance policy.

When you look at liquor in the afternoon it looks dark, like some distasteful medicine that you force yourself to drink because it takes the edge off something else that you hate even more.

"Dinner ready?"

That was Walter. Big, brusque, the smiling fat boy. All the world loves a fat man. If only he discovered he was a homo and kept away from her in bed at night. Wishful thinking.

"No. Let's go out tonight, Walter dear."

"Like to, honey, but I have a couple of clients gotta call on. Besides, there's nothing like good old-fashioned home cooking. And I love your cooking, baby. Some wife I got, hey! Let's have a great big kiss."

Is security really worth it? Are three meals a day, a home, clothes, money worth it? Would picking up men on 45th Street two or three times a week and being independent of Walter be better security?

"All right, Walter. Come on, I'll make you something to eat."

Where is the beginning of frustration and where is the end of sickening? When you prostitute yourself to one man for three years under the guise of security, how do you know what frustration means and whether sickening is real or imagined? On 45th Street in Manhattan, in this year 1950, they know. For twenty dollars they take off their clothes, feel warm, wet, dirty, heavy, take a hot shower, put the money in their purse and finish another day's work. Supply and demand. They have to make a living, whether they like the man or not. But when you sleep with a man for three years you don't like because you promised, of your own free will, gratis, no charge, easy come, easy go, take it, it's yours, you're my husband, till death do us part, which one is the prostitute?

That night, any night, for a thousand and one nights and more, count 'em, three hundred and sixty-five plus three hundred and sixty-five plus three hundred and sixty-five, Julia lay on a bed. Life was nothing for Walter except insurance policies and Julia laying on a bed.

"C'mon, Julia. It's been three years. I'm making good money now. How about a baby?"

"It's too soon. Let's wait a while. Let's enjoy ourselves before we get tied down."

Panting like an ox. Walter the ox. Walter the overgrown bull.

"Why not now, honey? You'll be my little mother."

"Let's wait, Walter. Let's enjoy life first."

"But what more enjoyment is there in life, Julia, than having a baby?"

Vicious thoughts: For you, Walter, probably nothing. So why don't *you* have it? Murderous thoughts: The carving knife in the kitchen. Instead:

"No, nothing more, I suppose."

"Then, c'mon."

Has he any soul?

"I'm tired now, darling. Not tonight. Let's just go to sleep."

If he would only make her want him. Not like an ox, but like a man. Make her love him. Make her want babies.

"All right, Julia. You shouldn't make me get like this. If you don't feel like it, not tonight."

The stupid, ignorant, fat ox of a fool, Julia thought to herself. Always thoughts to herself. There was no one to think out loud to. She closed her eyes, pulled her body into herself. I wish I had insisted on twin beds.

She didn't sleep for a while. Ugly, fat, pawing flesh poked at her from the opposite side of the bed.

Julia Mitchell was a young woman. You know her. Look at the young woman next door. Look at the young woman you met on the subway or the bus. Look in the mirror and you know her life. Family background? It doesn't matter. Her father could have been a doctor, lawyer, storekeeper, bookkeeper, engineer, factory worker. Her mother could have been, and was, a housewife. Julia never starved. She always had enough of what she wanted. Not too much, but enough. She finished high school. She started college.

If I've got to be out in the world, I may as well wait a while before doing it. The family can see me through a few years of college.

She met Walter, a nice, happy, successful young man. She was twenty. Walter was twenty-five. He had a college degree and a good job with an insurance company.

"Majored in business administration, Walter?" the personnel officer said. "Good. we need young men with a solid foundation. Don't want any of these young kids who come out of college with fancy, new ideas. They think they know it all. They think too much."

Walter thought just enough. In three years up to over $10,000 a year, a substantial sum in 1950. He spent a lot. Flowers, candy, jewelry. If I'm going to fall in love with anybody, it might as well be Walter, Julia thought. He can do so much for me. He wants to do so much for me. I guess I must be in love with him.

"Of course, I love you, darling."

"You're sure?"

"Walter, you know me well enough to know I wouldn't say what I didn't mean."

"Then you will marry me?"

"Of course, I will."

"Darling, darling Julia. You're going to have the most wonderful life any woman can have. I'm making over ten thousand a year. You're going to have anything you want. I'm going to buy it for you."

New York is a big town and a small town. When you go to college in New York you know a lot of people and you know few people. The lot of people were mostly like Walter. They let life walk by, taking a little of it at a time, if they had the time, money, and energy to do so. They strive for all three, with money the key to the other two. Let the rich get richer and the poor will reap the overflow. The few people Julia knew, knew better. They didn't want to lose any of life. They didn't let it pass them by, but hurled themselves into it. Some went into it too hard. If there were twenty-four hours a day, they wanted twenty-five. They went to theatres, to concerts, to museums, to galleries. They made friends with people who wrote and painted and composed and acted, and those who could did those things themselves. Some found that there weren't twenty-five hours in a day and went to shrinks to find out why.

Julia found, too, that twenty-four hours in a day and seven days in a week weren't enough. She wanted things. She could have been an actress or a painter or a writer. Not because she especially wanted to act or paint or write, but because she wanted to feel life and give to life. Walter wasn't particularly interested in those things. He might not encourage her, but she was sure that he wouldn't interfere. Live and let live. After a while she might even interest him in the arts. Plus, she needed the security. She needed the physical and economic security so that the quest for food and clothing and lodging—and a car—would not distract her from doing what she wanted and being with whom she wanted.

"Do you have to go out again, honey? What do you want to spend time with all those...bohemians for?" If there was a more contemporary term for her friends, he couldn't think of it. "You know, Julia, I don't begrudge you your friends. But why that type? They have no idea of propriety. I didn't mean it that way, honey. I mean, well, I think if you'd give my friends from the office a chance, you'd really be happier with them. They're nice, proper people. No, I don't mean your friends are improper. They're, well, they're different. We should have the Ellises over for dinner and bridge. Mack Ellis, the guy at the desk next to me. He knows the most hilarious jokes. And Jerry Thompson. You know, the guy who I sometimes co-write policies with. He does the best imitations. You've never seen anything like it. Cary Grant and Charles Laughton and even FDR. You'll really love these people. Good upstanding business people. And they'll be on top of the heap someday. People you ought to know. And, if you really want to go, maybe next week I'll take you to one of those Broadway shows you always talk about. Now, let me tell you about Mack Ellis... ."

Is it really obscene to think about a carving knife?

A fat sloppy man who wanted her to cook for him. And sleep with him. And have babies. She refused to have babies.

"Yes, goddamn it, Walter, I want to have a baby. I love babies. Since I first learned what could happen when I went to bed with a man, I've wanted a baby."

"Julia, why then…?"

"Oh, hell, Walter, I mean…"

"I'm sorry, Julia. I don't mean to upset you. Did I do something wrong?"

"No, Walter, you didn't do anything wrong. Just stop bothering me about babies."

"But if you say you like them…"

"I like them. I love them. I want to have one."

"Then why not? Why not?"

"Don't you understand? Not by you, Walter, not by you…oh, god, I'm sorry, I'm sorry, I didn't mean that…I'm just tired…I don't know what I'm saying. Please Walter, let me go to sleep, let me go to sleep now."

"Not by me?"

"I don't know what I'm saying. Maybe I'm sick. I do want your babies, Walter. Yes, I do."

"Then why not now, Julia? Now."

"We've been married only a year. Wait a while, darling. Another year. Let's enjoy life without responsibilities a while. It's…it's because I love you, I want to enjoy life with you alone. Let me sleep now, darling. Let me sleep."

Walter meant well. Julia meant well. In their different visions of what well meant. In their different visions of what security meant. Julia at first thought she had found hers. Later she knew she hadn't. Walter was sure he had found his. But he sometimes wondered. For Walter, security was job, home, wife and…hopefully…children. Julia went out looking for her security.

She went for long walks in Central Park. She envied the lovers paddling the boats in the Central Park lake. Walter had never taken her on a boat ride. She laughed as she imagined him in a three-piece suit, watch fob dangling from his vest, folded handkerchief in his jacket pocket, sweating profusely as he rowed, rowed, rowed the boat… .

"I'm going out for a drive, Walter."

"Where will you drive in New Rochelle at this hour of night?"

"I don't know."

In an hour she was walking on the sidewalks of Manhattan. She was all alone and she was part of teeming humanity. People, people, people, vibrating, moving, living.

"Excuse me, miss, but I notice you walking all alone, and wonder if I may accompany you?"

"I'm meeting a friend."

"Sorry, excuse me."

"Hey lady, you're all alone, I'm all alone…"

"Go fuck yourself."

Rockefeller Center. A multi-million-dollar tribute to success in America. She admired millions of dollars.

"Hey, babe, how much, huh? C'mon, I ain't no cop. I'll treat you right. I got dough."

"Beat it before I call a cop."

Fifty-ninth Street. Fifth Avenue. The Plaza. Tiffany's. The center of life. Music from open windows. Parties on penthouse terraces. Midnight strollers with theatre programs in one hand, the other clasped with a partner's. Glistening monuments of glass reflecting from the Steuben shop window. In New Rochelle they put the kids to bed at eight, play bridge or watch television till 11, then lay down in bed and have more kids.

"But it's security isn't it? It's what any girl would want. A home. A family. What's wrong with it? What's wrong with me?"

"Jack, this is Julia. I'd love to come and see the gang again...no, I hate it...a big fat slob...I'd say it anywhere. Do I need somebody to sleep with? That was four years ago, Jack. I've learned a lot since then. I hope you have, too...seriously, darling, when are you having the gang over, I just got to get away from here...he's really all right, maybe it's just me...that's sweet of you...no, don't call me here...just don't, please. I'll call you next week. I'd love to get together with everybody again."

"What's the matter, Julia, aren't you feeling well again?"

"I'll be all right, Walter. Maybe the sudden spring weather."

"It's three years next month, darling."

"Yes, Walter. It is, isn't it?"

"Tell me what's wrong, Julia."

"Nothing."

"Going out again?"

"I have another meeting."

"You've been having a lot of meetings lately."

"You wanted me to get interested in something so I wouldn't be alone when you work late or are out of town on business. So, I got interested in the Children's Welfare Society. And they have meetings. And I go to meetings."

"Okay, Julia. No reason to get upset."

"I'm not upset. Just stop annoying me about meetings. You spend evenings with your clients. I go to meetings. That should make everybody happy."

"If we had a baby, that would give you something to do here."

"Please, Walter, none of that now."

"It's always 'none of that now'."

"I'm going out."

"And I'm going upstairs to bed. Good night, Julia"

"Good night."

At some parties you sit and gossip. At others you play cards. At others you drink. Julia went to parties to be with people. Old friends. Friends who Walter would call "bohemians." She liked the new world of the second half of the century's Allen Ginsbergs and Jack Kerouacs better. Hippies. It sounded much freer. She liked to be with friends who she couldn't be seen with at any self-respecting insurance executive's party. People who stimulated her, gave her something to think about, who she argued with and laughed with. Who she learned from. Men and women who she loved. Maybe because they didn't have what she had but had something she didn't. They couldn't afford her clothes or fancy food. None could buy a new car each year. Or any car at all. She had financial security, but they were more secure.

How long can the circle go around and around before it turns and twists and winds up in little knots that you trip on and try to untangle and get caught in and wrapped in. Where it stops nobody knows. What is faithfulness other than being true to oneself? Above all, to thine own self be true. Good rationalization. Lean over backwards trying not to hypocritical. But it hurts to be honest with one's own feelings. Almost any old tenement has a gas pipe on the wall. A bottle of iodine doesn't cost more than twenty-five cents. A modern kitchen invariably includes an oven.

Do you keep walking on the thin edge of the circle, waiting to finish a lifetime passing the same points, arriving nowhere, feeling nothing? Or do you cut the rope someplace and begin to walk anew, in new directions, feeling new things? Does part of you die while you are still alive or do you live because part of you dies?

CHAPTER 2
JACK

If you ask a dozen people what fate is you'll get more than a dozen answers. Is it taking the plane after the one that crashes? Is it finding a wallet on the street with a thousand dollars? Is it making a "Cross of Gold" speech at a political convention? Is it picking the right horse at a Mutuals window? Is it crossing a slippery street as a huge truck comes barreling along? Is it walking down a corridor and meeting someone you've known for a thousand years and never met?

For Julia Mitchell, Joe Templeton and Ben Stevens it was meeting at Jack Evans party.

Jack Evans was an ordinary writer. He didn't make a living at it. He paid the rent by writing radio commercials for ad agencies who sold them to clients for five times more than they paid Jack for them. Jack was only the writer, the raw material. Raw material was worth only as much as the producer and distributor decided it was worth. In Jack's scheme of life there were very few producers and distributors. But there was plenty of raw material and most of it, like Jack, lived in cold-water flats on Manhattan's lower east side.

Jack Evans was born in New York, raised in New York, went to school in New York, and loved New York. Someday, he kept telling himself—as did every painter, artist, actor, writer, musician struggling to make it big in the City—he would own New York. At the moment he owned three bottles of scotch and two of them were consumed in his apartment by friends, acquaintances and others who knew there would be free liquor. He also owned a check he was waving proudly among his guests. Three-hundred dollars. A small fortune. More than enough to live on for a month. His first big fee for writing a script for one of radio's premiere programs, "Cavalcade of America." Most writers, the good ones and the bad ones, send scripts at one time or another to the DuPont sponsored "Cavalcade of America," one of the few shows open to freelance writers. No matter how good you may be, no matter how bad the program may be, if you don't have an in, a contact, or a good agent, you don't have a chance.

"Imagine that. Me, a socialist, taking a check from the DuPonts, the fucking capitalists."

"Why, Jack, how you talk. After all, they are sharing the wealth."

"My conscience tells me one thing. My stomach tells me another."

"How are you going to beat the capitalists, Jack, unless you got money to do it with?"

"You know what I wrote about? William McKinley. Do you know how he beat William Jennings Bryan for the presidency in 1896? He got Mark Hanna to order his industrialist supporters to close their plants and told the workers that they'd stay closed unless McKinley won."

"Aw, fer Chrissakes, we didn't come here to talk politics," another voice protested.

"We always talk politics."

"I'm a lousy bastard for taking that money," Jack complained.

"Okay, Jack, so you're a lousy bastard. Where's the liquor?"

In 1937 Jack was 14. He knew nothing about politics. Then he began to read about the Spanish Civil War. In New York you grow up to either love war or hate war. Half the time Jack hated it. Half the time he loved it. When Franco's fascist Insurgents won a battle he hated it. When the Loyalists won he was happy.

If you leave your senses open and spend a moment every now and then thinking about something other than the Brooklyn Dodgers or the New York Yankees you begin to feel as well as think things. You begin to feel what you want to be right but what you know is wrong.

Killing people was wrong. Putting people in concentration camps was wrong. Letting people starve because their politics, race or religion was different was wrong. Hitler and Mussolini were wrong. Franco was wrong.

Going to join the Lincoln Brigade in Spain, Jack? I'm not 18 yet, my folks wouldn't let me. And they think the Lincoln Brigade are Communists. I hope the Loyalists win. Best those fascists. Sure, I'll contribute two bucks. Didja hear that Jim Connelly, from down the block, died in Spain fighting the fascists with the Lincoln Brigade?

"Someday I'm going to write the great American novel. About democracy and fascism. We don't have real democracy here. This depression. Families homeless. Kids starving. People dying because they can't afford to go to a doctor. While the rich people live in big houses and drive fancy cars.

"That's everyplace in the world, Jack."

"Not in Russia. They share the wealth."

"Are you a Communist, Jack?"

"Maybe."

"Maybe?"

"They do better for the people than we do here. This isn't a real democracy."

"They got a dictatorship. What about the purges?"

"Necessary."

"No political freedom."

"I don't know about that."

"People are starving there."

"No more than here. Maybe less."

"No freedom of the press."

"Necessary for the ideal."

"No freedom of speech."

"They have forums."

"They got rid of religions."

"They got rid of mind-controlling superstitions."

"Well, I'll take the democracy here anytime. America for me, Jack."

"I like the Russian system."

"They ain't got nearly half the freedoms we got here. You're no more communist than I am, Jack. You don't even know why you want to be one."

"Well, I just think it's better. They don't discriminate against people because of the color of their skin."

"Wait till you grow up some more, you'll see the light. See ya' around."

Jack read the newspapers. Hearst, McCormick, Patterson, Scripps-Howard, and "All the News That's Fit to Print." He listened to the radio commentators. Fulton Lewis, Jr., Lowell Thomas, Walter Winchell, Boake Carter. He watched his friends go off to C.C.C. camps and relief payments go up to $14 a week if you had four children. He watched bums in the Bowery begging a few cents from cars stopped in traffic and the New York Yankees win the World Series over and over again. He watched crowds going into theatres on Broadway and shoeless kids on the waterfront at the East River. Rockefeller Center and the Empire State Building made New York the greatest city in the world. No, I'm not even 18 yet, my folks won't let me go to Spain.

But then America went to war, World War II, barely a generation after America went to war in World War I, the war that was to end all wars.

Jack went into the army.

"A writer, huh? Okay, we'll put you into the communication section. You can put your writing into Morse Code. Up on the line with the combat infantry. Haw, that's a good one, soldier, ain't it."

"Yes, sir, Sergeant."

"Son, we got a bad report on you. Hope it isn't true, but that's what Intelligence reports. You knew some commies, maybe even tied up with some commie groups. Report says you even had some nigger friends. We can't take a chance with anyone like that in

Officers Candidate School. Sorry."

"Yes, sir, thank you sir."

"Damned commie. Nigger friends. I thought he was a good soldier."

"Private Evans, it gives me pleasure to grant you this honorable discharge. You have served your country nobly and well."

"Thank you, Major."

There are thousands of Jacks in New York city and every one of them tells the same story. Or almost the same story.

"Didn't you have this same seat last Tuesday?"

"I always try to get the same seat for these Lewisohn Stadium concerts. Feel more at home that way."

"My name's Jack Evans. I'm a writer."

"A writer!"

"Got a bunch of rejection slips home."

"My name's Julia. Julia Harris. I go to Brooklyn College."

"Know Sally Rosen?"

"Only my first year there."

"You like this music...Julia."

"Yes, especially when Kostelanetz plays."

"I've got a collection of Gershwin and Kern at home."

"I'd love to hear them."

"I'd ask you up tonight, but I have a gang coming up."

"Private party?"

"No, sort of...a meeting."

"Tomorrow's all right...Jack."

Sometimes you start walking the circle and think that it's a straight line. You get tired of the circle, not realizing that you could have made it a straight line and you jump onto another circle.

"I'm marrying Walter Mitchell, Jack."

"We've had a terrific year, Julia."

"I'm decided. He has everything I want and need."

"Everything?"

"Money."

"I could fight for you."

"My mind's made up."

"When?

"In three weeks."

"You didn't tell me it was serious."

"I wasn't sure. And I haven't slept with him."

"Does he know about us?"

"No."

"Won't change your mind, Julia?"

"No."

"Can't stop you? One more night?"

"No. Good night, Jack."

"Good night and…uh…Julia…good luck."

What is the square root of two? Can one circle become two? Can two circles become one? You meet five guys on the street and under the proper circumstances you can fall in love with four of them. Or with none of them. How far can you walk on the edge of the circle without falling off?

"Hey, I can get two tickets to *Death of A Salesman*? Who wants to come with me?"

"Who doesn't! You gonna spend your three hundred bucks in one fell swoop, Jack?"

"I can get a couple tickets from a friend who can't go."

"One script he sells and he's got that kind of friends already?"

"Wanna go or don't you?"

"It's too morbid."

"You some kind of existentialist?"

"Julia will go."

"Will you go, Julia? Come over here."

"In a minute. I need another drink."

There's not much room in a small Barrow Street flat where you sit and talk quietly during a party. Jack and Julia really didn't have to. Too much can happen in a year that needs talking about. Little things, a few words can say enough. Sometimes too much.

"Any better, Julia?"

"Same."

"I'm still here."

"Not that way, Jack."

"Why don't you leave him?"

"Haven't got the guts."

"Regret our year together?"

"Never."

"Remember that first evening?"

"I was scared to death."

"We didn't listen to Gershwin."

"We sat together and read …you still have the book on that table… *This is My Beloved.* Damn it, Jack, I haven't got the guts. Sorry."

"It's okay. Let's get back to the party."

At parties of young people with endless hopes and, for most, unknowingly, hopeless ends in their quests for Broadway dressing rooms or Pulitzer Prizes, people come and go, some from their jobs selling shoes, others to their jobs waiting tables at all-night hash houses.

"Hey, Joe, Ben, I want you to meet a special friend of mine. Julia …uh…Miss Julia Harris."

When two young men in their mid-twenties meet a young lady they both think of two things. Whether she looks interesting enough to consider considering her seriously. And whether she would consider considering them not seriously.

"If Jack hasn't mentioned you to us before, he certainly should have. My name is Joe, Joe Templeton."

"My buddy here took my opening line. It's no less a pleasure for me, Miss Harris. I'm Ben Stevens."

CHAPTER 3
WHAT IS LOVE?

What is the line of demarcation between love and affection? Between affection and sex? Between sex and feeling? Does sex stop because people look up the meaning of love in a dictionary? Is there really something that means love? Is "I love you" only a polite way of saying "I want to have sex with you"? Is there love without sex? Are sex and love interchangeable?

After three unhappily married years Julia began to think so. Unhappy because sex wasn't love and love wasn't sex. It was that confusing.

When Joe Templeton, young, brash, candid, stood in front of her with a bourbon in his hand and stripped her clothes off with his eyes, it was that simple. Joe wanted Julia. Julia wanted Joe. Who wanted the most? How long does it take for two bodies to move into each other? A minute, an hour, a day, a week, two weeks…?

"It's been two weeks, Joe."

"Will have to write a book one of these days and dedicate it to Jack Evans. It was at his party, wasn't it? Come closer, Julia."

"You don't remember when?"

"A joke, baby. When I don't remember when I first laid eyes on you I'll be over 90 and spending most of the time alone in bed and not because I want to."

"At the rate we're going, you won't last much past 30."

"It's nice to know I'm appreciated."

"If you're not, then I've been misjudging my husband for the last three years."

"Like the kid who wears a tight shoe just to see how good it feels when he takes it off. Do you have to mention him, Julia?"

"Just so you can see that I really don't give a damn about him."

"Frankly, my dear, I don't give damn whether or not you give a damn."

"You don't mean that, Joe?"

"I'm broadminded, baby. Any gal I sleep with can think whatever she wants of her husband. I'm not possessive."

"Jesus, Joe, I'm getting out of here."

"You're pissed-off?"

"Of course, I'm pissed-off. You think I'm some kind of whore?"

"You're too sensitive. You know I like you."

"Like me?"

"Well, what the hell do you think I am? Just because we met at a party. It's not like I picked up some dame at a corner bar and turned her loose as soon as I got my rocks off. We've been seeing each other for two weeks. And, as I said, I like you."

"Like me? You sound like it's just sex and nothing else."

"Don't knock it. Our sex is great. But it's more than that. Kind of an understanding, a closeness."

"And that's it? Well, it's nice to know I don't cost anything, isn't it? Good night, Joe."

"Look at this way, Julia. The moment I saw you at Jack's party I knew what I wanted. And I knew what you wanted. I got it and you got it and I like it and you like it. Maybe women look for a different 'l' word right away, but fer Chrissakes, it's been only two weeks, Julia. And I do like you. I like you a helluva lot."

"Turn out the light, Joe. It's awfully distracting."

Sometimes something you want to be there seems to be there because you want it. Sometimes if you want it hard enough it becomes real. Sometimes no matter how hard you want it, it never becomes real. Sometimes you just think it is.

"It's been three months, Joe."

"A terrific three months, baby."

"Do you really think so?"

"Ever know me to say anything I didn't really mean?"

"I was hoping you meant it."

"You ought to know by now."

"I want to be sure."

"That I like you or love you?"

"Both. I need to be sure."

"Haven't I been here for you whenever you wanted to come in from New Rochelle?"

"Yes."

"Then what is it? Something's wrong. What's wrong, baby?"

"Nothing's wrong, Joe. Everything is ok."

Ben Stevens was a nice guy. No smart mouth, no clever repartee. Just a nice guy. But more than just being a nice guy, he thought about things. A lot of things. He thought about where he was going in the world. He thought about how he was going to write and what he was going to write. How he would write his first novel and then another until his name would be on the New York Times best-seller list. But Ben was afraid. Afraid that he had no talent. Afraid that he didn't have the strength to face the world. Not by himself, anyway.

"Damn it, what am I afraid of? There's nothing to fear but fear but fear but fear but fear. I don't want to write like Gertrude Stein even if I could. Nobody'll understand it. Gotta write for the people. But to publish, who are the people? MacMillan, Harper, Prentice-Hall, Little-Brown, Viking, Random House. Those are the people."

But those aren't the people for whom Ben wanted to write. Can you write for one and not for the other? Are they mutually exclusive? Or can you write for both? Or for millions? Or for two billion different, separate people? Do you write about workers and sell it to Russia or do you write about lovers and sell it to France or do you write about money and sell it to America? Do you write about heaven and hell and find a pristine spot on top of a Catskill mountain or the Empire State Building or the Brooklyn Bridge? Are those the people? The ones with a shovelful of stars, with a bucketful of coal, with a pocketful of money? How do you know to be born and live? Why don't you know how to die? It's over, it's finished and you step out of the circle forever as long as there is a forever and who the hell knows the difference except for fear. Nothing to fear but fear but fear but fear.

Is it qualitative or quantitative? Take a vote. How many of you two billion want to read about sex? The hell with sex! How many of you two billion want to read about yourselves? There's no such thing as yourselves. You're all different, every one of you. How many of you two billion will pay me for writing whatever you want? We pay only for bread to put in our kids' mouths, a bed for our wives and mistresses and husbands and paramours. You, with money in your pockets, will you pay me to write? Sure, we'll pay you to write. Write us a story of a woman with fifteen different lovers and describe in detail. Write us a story of a man who becomes a millionaire through business dealings and don't describe in detail. Write us the story of our lives, our biographies, our autobiographies, of our pet dogs and cats and stables of horses. Call it philanthropicality. And keep on thinking that someday we're going to pay for your writing.

"Hey, Mac, where's the highest point on this here Brooklyn Bridge? Is it still for sale?"

Write about the two billion. Write about what they think, feel, want. Write about what they want you to think they think, feel, want. Then write about one of the two billion. Or two of them. Or three of them. Truthfully. Enough people have more than just bread and butter and less than penthouses on Park Avenue to understand what you're writing about. Write what you want to and to hell with the Brooklyn Bridge.

"Whaddya mean publish this? What the hell country do you think you're living in? Go back where you belong."

"Hey, mister, I'm a good writer. How about a job with your advertising agency? I got ideas for terrific ad writing."

"Kid, do you know the way to the Brooklyn Bridge?"

It's lonely when your alone. Lonelier when you have to deal with two billion people alone. And every damned one of them different, every damned one of them living in themselves and only in themselves. No, that's not true. Not every one of them. How many, then?

"Hey, Mac, which way to the souls of two billion people?"

You're in the middle of two billion people and you're alone. You're next to just one person and you're not alone. Two is twice as much as one. Sometimes two into one is a half. Sometimes two into one is one. Sometimes two into one is two. Sometimes nothing.

"Hey, babe, come and sleep with me. That'll make two or one or one-half." Maybe Joe knows the answer.

"Is that the answer, Joe? So, I wake up in the morning and I'm limp. What does that help?"

"Ben, m'boy, you're young. You've got a lot of living to do before you can really understand these things. Get a babe, throw her into bed, and you feel like a new man."

"Is it all sex, Joe? Like a machine?"

"What the hell are we but machines? We're born, we live, we die. You've got enough food, eat it. You've got enough shelter, live in it. You've got enough sex, enjoy it."

"But that pleasure's only for the moment. You turn on the light and wonder what you're doing there."

"An unceasing, infinite moment. Ben, never stop as long as you're strong enough to keep going. You don't think beds were made for sleeping, do you?"

"Okay, wise guy. I'll be having kids at 80, and you'll be worn out at 35."

"And am I going to love these next ten years!"

"Go to hell."

"What's wrong, Ben?"

"The whole world."

"Writer's block again?"

"Again? Still!"

"We've both been writing for four, five years since college. And we've both got enough rejection slips to…but they ain't soft enough."

"I was going to write big things, Joe."

"Me, too. But the world doesn't want big things. They want crap. So I think I'll go into that new purveyor of crap, television. You continue to write big things and I'll write crap and I'll drive a Cadillac. With a blonde in it. Make that two blondes."

"You've got the stuff, Joe. You've got the talent. If you'd be more serious about your writing, you'd make it."

"So, someone'll have the privilege of writing my epitaph on a grave in Westminster Abbey someday?"

"That's only for British writers."

"That's what I mean, Ben. No Westminster Abbey or Pantheon for writers in this country, Ben. Nobody gives a shit about them, about us. Except the entrepreneurs who can make a quick buck off our sweat and tears."

"Who's trying to cheer up who? I keep thinking about Steve Brodie."

"You're tired. Go home and go to sleep."

"Can't sleep, Joe."

"You're lonely, Ben. You need to find a babe. Sleep with her. You'll feel better. You won't be lonely."

"Yeah. Maybe that's the answer."

Ben thought about a lot of things, including women.

Ruthie Green was the girl who answered the phone and if you were part of the would-be artists world of mid-century Greenwich Village you said wrong number. She should have been Ruthie Mitchell. Not really. But if you had to put two people together, Ruthie and Walter were the two. Put them together from birth and if neither found out what was outside of themselves they would live happily ever after and celebrate their golden wedding anniversary with a drink of insipid white wine and dozens of grandchildren.

But Ruthie never met Walter Mitchell. Instead, she met Ben Stevens.

She met Ben Stevens because she wanted to meet Ben Stevens or John Brown or Bob Smith or Harry Jones. Provided John or Bob or Harry had a college degree or read the News and Theatre supplements of the Sunday Times or went to art galleries on 57th Street or knew who wrote "Faust" and "Madame Butterfly" or could recognize Shostakovich's "First" or was anything more than an 8:15 commuter train or a five o'clock whistle or the Sunday afternoon ride in the country or the cozy nook by the babbling brook. She wanted to meet what she thought were the right people because she didn't know that for her they were the wrong people.

"That Ruthie, she's a swell kid, you know, Bud."

"Yeah, and just about the best-lookin' kid in the junior class."

"Maybe the best-lookin' kid in our whole high school."

"Shame, ain't it?"

"Yeah, I don't know any guys who even say they have."

"She doesn't, Stan, and probably wouldn't."

"I dunno, Bud. Get her in the right place under the right circumstances and I bet she would. A girl would if it's the right time and place."

"Don't get hot pants. Maybe any other girl in school, but not Ruthie. She's the kind who'd make a good wife. You know what I mean? The kind you'd like to marry."

"Yeah, I guess you're right. Shame, ain't it?"

Sometimes you find a guy to take you out to the theatre or maybe to a concert or to a night club in the Village. Greenwich Village is exciting. Especially at night, stopping to see friends and acquaintances in coffee shops. Most of them working as waiters or waitresses. Or walking up mid-town Broadway with the crowds. Sometimes too many people, too many crowds. Too many night clubs and the music in Carnegie Hall makes you sleepy. Walk up Columbus Circle and into Central Park. Walk with someone. The grass is soft and bushes are heavy and no one will see. Or a taxi will get you quickly back to an apartment on 10th Street and a fifth of scotch. Or a ten-minute walk to a room in a brownstone on 76th Street. Music hath charms and Broadway has bright lights. Sometimes too loud and too bright, flashing on and off in crescendos of different colors.

"Sure, I know about sex. I took a course in biology in high school. I graduate in June. Maybe I'll go to nursing school. That's a good profession. No, my mother would never let me go to Europe. Not alone or with somebody she…oh, you're not really asking me. I do love music. No, I don't play any instrument. But I'm a good cook. Well, to tell the truth I haven't read very much about the Marshall Plan so I don't really…well, you seem to know so much about these kinds of things. Yes, I'd love to go out with you again. No, I've never been to a flat in the Village. Oh, I couldn't. No, I'm not afraid. It just wouldn't be…proper. Oh, I believe you, you wouldn't do anything like that. Is something wrong? Well, yes, I can get home alone on the subway to Queens."

Is Bohemian the antonym of platonic? Is Bohemian the synonym of culture and art? Are culture and art and Bohemian synonyms for confusion? Is platonic the antonym of pleasure?

Where does understanding of love start? Of sex start? When you know there is something you want? When you want it only because you know it is there It doesn't come easy. Maybe it isn't supposed to come easy? Maybe it isn't supposed to come?

Sometimes you find a guy to go out with to dinner and a movie.

"The real estate game is big, Julia. Right now, with the GIs from World War II beginning to make good livings and starting families. Real big. I've been in it only two years and I've bought this car and saved a coupla grand."

"I'm sure it's really interesting, Walter."

"Now, if you sell a house, for example, for over 25 thousand…"

"There's a concert at Carnegie Hall next week."

"Yeah. I went to one coupla months ago. Fell asleep."

"People ought to go to concerts."

"Why?"

"Well…they should."

"In another year of two, if my commissions keep up, I'll have enough to buy a house."

"You do make a lot of money."

"It's a game, like everything else. Now, if I …"

"This isn't where I live."

"I know, but there's a streetlamp in front of your house. It's dark here."

"I think I'd better get in."

"Sorry. I hope I didn't insult you."

"It's okay."

"How about next Wednesday?"

"All right. Can we go to the theatre?"

"Yeah. Just what I was thinking. There's a new picture out I want to see. A murder mystery."

"I meant…oh, never mind."

It's not easy to even begin to wonder why. For many the circle has a high wall around it and when you peek over it you see both stained glass windows and neon lights. But anybody can open the door.

"Gee, Ruthie, you really jitterbug, kid."

"Thanks, Andy. I had a swell time."

"Just like back in high school. You really should have gone to the senior prom with me."

"Stan asked me first."

"Yeah, well how about we go out again next week?"

"I don't think so. I have an appointment."

"Then may I kiss you goodnight?"

"If you'd like. . ."

The wheels begin to spin and you don't know whether to catch one of the prongs or let the wheel spin and see where it stops. But suppose it doesn't stop? Second floor: furniture and kitchen ware. Third floor: curtains, draperies, bedspreads, linens. Fourth floor: women's clothes and trousseaus. Fifth floor: music, books, arts, and crafts, watch your step, please. Be careful, Miss, watch your step.

Which floor do you stop on? Only one? Or do you try for all at the same time? The media won't tell you. There's "Li'l Abner" and "Dick Tracy" and "Little Orphan Annie" and Errol Flynn's escapades and the "shot heard round the world" and another Gloria Vanderbilt marriage and Jack Benny and "The King and I" and something new called "Off-Broadway" and, oh yeah, something going on in Asia, rah, rah, rah, save the ass of our corrupt South Korean ally, Synghman Rhee, from a revolt of his own people and call it a police action, not a useless war. Where do you find the real reality of life, the more of life than the reader-seeking headlines? How do you know when you've reached more or when you've reached enough?

"A party down in the Village, Ruth. Want to come?"

"With a flock of wolves?"

"Why Ruth darling! They're my friends."

"Yeah. And you?"

"Me? Sure. But that's because you're the most beautiful, sexiest woman in New York."

"Someday I'm going to meet a guy who says it and really means it."

"And I've got just the guy. Talented, charming, and as harmless as he's sincere. My buddy Ben will be at the party."

"Okay, but I have to be home early. And up early to get to work. My boss complains about my typing, as it is."

"With your looks and for someone who likes to hang around with theatre people in the village, you should have been an actress."

"Maybe I should of? You got liquor at the party?"

You watched girls like Ruth grow and hoped she'd make it. But you wondered.

Maybe money isn't everything? Maybe there's a world beyond a home and children? Maybe you can get off on the fifth floor and find yourself on the second? Or vice-versa. Maybe you can be Rosalind Russell and Rita Hayworth without passing through the cold-water flat or the brownstone rooming house or the bushes in Central Park? Maybe you can meet guys like Ben Stevens who are quiet and sincere and lonely and honest and really do just want to talk? Maybe you can meet guys like Ben Stevens who are creative artists and are sober, calm, and intelligent? Maybe you can meet a guy like Ben Stevens who will help you walk on top of the circle without falling off? Maybe you meet a guy like Ben Stevens who gives you everything he can because he needs you and you want him to have you. Maybe you find that sex isn't just sex but part of love? Maybe you do, once in a million years?

Maybe you find a girl like Julia Harris who is beautiful and vivacious and will look good in front of any insurance company vice-president you invite over for dinner? Maybe you find a girl like Julia Harris who will make a good wife and good cook and good mother? Maybe you find a girl like Julia Harris who will be a perfect companion and press your golf pants and clean your lodge uniform and tell your friends you're a 33rd-degree Mason and join the Eastern Stars and hand you your pipe and slippers? Maybe you find a girl like Julia Harris who will give you a perfect body and warm sheets and a hot bed? Maybe you find a girl like Julia Harris and prove to yourself that love is not either amorphous poetry or unbridled passion, but good old-fashioned solid tenth-generation red-blooded one hundred percent Rock-of- Gibraltar love honor and obey and obey and obey? Maybe you do? Walter Mitchell didn't.

Love could be an imaginary ideal. It could be a picture of a movie star. Cary Grant? Marilyn Monroe? It could be the prose of Thomas Wolfe. It could be springtime in the Rockies. It could be autumn in New York.

For a college girl who had never known love, it could have been a concert at Lewisohn Stadium and an apartment on 72nd Street.

"Love? What is love? You are, Julia. I love you."

"Jack Evans, you keep telling me that. But you never look me straight in the eyes."

"You don't believe me?"

"I don't know what to believe."

"Then believe in me and the heavens shall open and out shall pour diamonds as big as two-ton trucks."

"I'm serious, Jack."

"So am I. What's the matter, Julia?"

"Nothing's the matter."

"Then…?"

"Do you love me, Jack?"

"Don't change the subject."

"I'm not."

"I don't care whether I do or not. That's not true, Julia. That's what I would have said six months ago. Now I do care. A helluva lot. I don't know what I'd do without you."

"Poor little lost Jack. Six months ago I was the little lost girl."

"I'm not lost. I know where I am. And, damn it, I love you."

"Okay."

"Just 'okay', Julia?"

"Do you want to marry me?"

"I… I can't."

"But if you love me …"

"I got things to do. Big things. A lot of things."

"And no place for me, Jack. You've got no time for anything or anybody but your damned political meetings."

"They're my life. That's what I've got to do."

"You've got to eat. And you've got to love."

"Maybe I don't take much time to eat, Julia. But I do love. You sure as hell ought to know that."

Love could be now or it could be something out of the past that keeps taking your body and soul and wrapping them in newspaper headlines you grew up with in the 1930s. "War in Spain." "Lincoln Brigade Fights." "Franco Gaining Ground." "Hitler Sends Arms." "Loyalists Surrender."

"I do love you, Julia. I've told you. What more do I have to do? You're beautiful and I love you."

Beauty is only skin deep. Does love go any deeper?

CHAPTER 4

WHERE SHALL I RUN TO?

You run and you run and you run and where do you run to? Into the valley of the circle and each time you take a breath you drown as your tears become the flood waters of the unknown. High on the edge of the precipice and you look back and see the inundation and you look ahead and see an insurmountable high wall and you look again and see nothing because it is blank with no beginning and no end.

Ben Stevens was about to step onto the sharp prongs that made the transition from being to doing. Ruthie Green was feeling the bitterness and then the fullness and then the richness and still looked up into blankness. Joe Templeton washed himself in the torrent and the more he washed the more there was to cleanse. Julia was caught in the whirlpool, a dry whirlpool, struggling to free herself, but not knowing in which direction was freedom. At Jack Evans party, putting Walter and New Rochelle completely out of her mind—well, almost completely—she made her first choice. Joe Templeton.

Joe Templeton felt like freedom to Julia. A freedom from security, the security of four walls in New Rochelle. A freedom from mediocrity. Like the song says, the blacker the berry, the sweeter is the juice. You didn't have to be a St. Louis woman to know that. You could be Julia Harris of New York. You didn't have to go to gypsies. You could go to an apartment on Eighth Street in the Village that had a bureau, a stove, a table, a desk, a typewriter, and a bed. Especially a bed. You could go there and wait for Joe Templeton, not because he asked you to wait. You had to wait because if you weren't there, he'd pick up the phone and ask for Mable or Millicent or Marilyn and in twenty minutes he wouldn't care whether it was you in bed with him or not.

"What a hell of a life for a woman to lead!"

"What's that, baby?"

"Nothing, Joe, just thinking out loud."

"Sorry I'm late, Julia."

"No, you're not sorry."

"No, but I wanted it to sound like I was."

"What if I wasn't here."

"I'm only a half-hour late."

"I repeat, Joe, what if I wasn't here."

"I'd go to sleep."

"With whom?"

"The garbage collector. I read the Kinsey Report."

"Okay, forget it."

How secure can you be when you keep running away from things. When you escape reality with a joke, a pun, a barb? When you can't be your real self, your thoughts, your ideas, your actions. Is bluff a good substitute for security?

"Maybe Ben is right? Maybe I ought to wise up?"

"About what, Joe?"

"About everything. A new look. Maybe I really could be a good writer?"

"I know you can. If nothing else, you've got…experience."

"I'm serious. I want to talk."

"How do you like it?"

"Like what, Julia?"

"Oh, Christ, you don't know?"

"I want to be serious and you're playing word games."

"Don't make me feel sorry for you, Joe"

You never feel sorry for Joe. Not like you'd feel sorry for a man. More like you'd feel sorry for a little boy. But not often. There's was too much excitement with Joe.

"Hey, Julia, guess what?"

"What?"

"Tonight we make a night of it."

"Who did you rob?"

"The Saturday Evening Post. It was easy. Just say sex enough times without using the letters s-e-x. If you use those letters in today's hypocritical society you shock somebody. But if you describe it in detail without using the verboten words, they think it's wonderful."

"They bought a story."

"Two hundred bucks worth."

"Put it in the bank."

"The writing approach, yeah. But the money? What am I going to do with a bank account of two hundred dollars?"

"Pay the rent."

"I manage to do that, anyway. Nope. Tonight, Princess Julia, the Prince shall call for his magic carpet–where did I put that taxicab company number?– and you shall float majestically above the clouds, a night on the town, lord of all your heart cares to survey. Have a palace, Your Ladyship."

"Joe, you're wonderful."

"Of course. It isn't everyone who can make two hundred bucks, more than a month's salary if I was still working in that shoe store, by writing about sex so that even the ladies of the DAR can read it out in the open, away from their secret little piles of erotic literature."

"Be serious."

"I am, Julia, my love, my heart, my devotion. I would marry you except for one thing. You're already married."

"Joe…"

"I'm sorry. Besides, that line was from a lousy True Romances magazine story."

"It's okay. Sometimes I feel guilty. Walter doesn't have the slightest idea."

"What he doesn't know won't hurt him. Ooh, how trite! Why the hell don't you leave him?"

"And do what?"

"Get a job. Do anything. Live here, in the big city, in New York, live your own life. Really live."

"On what, Joe?"

"Who cares? On anything. On love. You've got to make the break. You can do it."

"How do you know? How do you know if I have the guts to do it? How do you know that it would be the best thing for me?"

"Are you happy in that life, Julia?"

"Would I be happy in this life?"

"I am."

"Are you, Joe. Really, are you?"

How much do you really know about yourself? Sometimes when you're off your guard you may learn more than you want to. But don't let it sink in. Toss it off. It's hard to face the truth when you've tried so hard to avoid it.

"C'mon, Julia baby, we're going out on the town. Up to two hundred bucks' worth. Ever been on top of the Empire State Building?"

"Joe, are you serious?"

"You know, I've lived in New York all my life and I've never been to the top of the Empire State Building."

"Neither have I."

"We're typical New Yorkers. But after today we shall not be typical New Yorkers. We'll pretend we're typical tourists. From Oshkosh or wherever typical tourists come from. After the Empire State Building we'll take a ferry ride. The Staten Island ferry. To wherever and whatever Staten Island is. Do you think there really is a Staten Island or is it a figment of Robert Moses imagination?"

"How prosaic can you get?"

"Much more, Julia. After that, we go to the Statue of Liberty. And tonight to the Village for a midnight dinner. An orchid for you and a fifth of Calverts for me. And with another fifth for good measure we head back here to our sweet little apartment, our cozy little nest built for two."

"You know something, Joe?"

"What?"

"I love you."

"Naturally."

"If I leave Walter, will you really marry me?"

"Let's go, baby. With a stop at Sardi's on the way to the Empire State Building."

You overlook the things that slap you in the face and look for meanings in things that have no meaning. You call Walter and tell him you won't be home that evening, that one of your woman friends is ill and asked you stay over in case she needs emergency care. And you wonder when he is going to stop being the good, trusting husband and wonder how there could be so many meetings that you so often have to stay in the city overnight. Poor frustrated Walter. Maybe you could hire an equally frustrated cook or maid and she and Walter could alleviate their frustrations with each other? You had to find something that would free you to find the something in yourself before you were 40 and, you thought, doomed to a life in a house in New Rochelle with a Walter, maybe Joe was the something? So much inside of him that you couldn't help, but want it all to come out, to explode inside of you. Divorce Walter, live with Joe. Live the life you really wanted. But what if Joe wouldn't marry you? Where would security come from when you were 40? Isn't there a different kind of security? The kind you'll never find with Walter? And who needs Walter's security, anyway? With Joe there'd be no need for security. Joe would be all you'd need. Joe was everything. Except sometimes.

"Shhh, baby, whatever your name is. Julia might be sleeping. Shhh. Wouldn't want her to find me drunk".

A short skirt where everyone else wore a long one, clipped blonde hair, big lips, big bust, add a bar and a bartender and you've got a saloon and some women waiting to make a living. Add an Eighth Street apartment, a guy named Templeton, a woman waiting inside for him, and you've got a triangle.

"Hey, Joe—is that your name? You didn't say you were married. Who's this Julia?"

"Shhh. Just a friend. She's Walter's wife, but she doesn't like Walter, so she stays with me sometimes. I give her what she wants. You want some too, baby? Come on in."

"I don't like this."

"Julia, you're up. I want you to meet a friend of mine. Uh, what's your name?

"Francie."

"Where are you going, Julia? Don't leave. I'll do Francie and then it'll be your turn. For the whole rest of the night. Hey, Julia, don't go. Shit, she's gone. Hey, Francie, she left."

"I told you I didn't like this. What the hell kind of a shit are you, anyway?"

"Yeah, that's a good question. What the hell kind of a shit am I, anyway? If I wasn't a shit I'd stop chasing fantasy shadows and look at myself for what I really am. Oh, shit, I'm drunk."

"You sure are."

"Over there, baby, or whatever your name is. Over there you'll find the bathroom."

Can you love a man like Joe so desperately that there seems to be nothing without him even if too often there is nothing with him? You love and you hate and you love and love and time becomes lost and there is no night or day and no calendar, no New York, no New Rochelle, but just Joe and more Joe. Sometimes you feel that you're going to fall off the edge of the circle into a bottomless bottom that you let swallow you up.

"Joe, I love you, I love you, I love you. What more can I say?"

"Julia, you're pushing me into a corner. I don't know what to say."

"Tell me that you love me, that you want to marry me. Take me away from Walter. Can you imagine how I feel when I have to go home to him and feel his flesh crawling over me and my stomach tightens into knots when I know that it could be you instead of him inside of me?"

"What the hell can I say?"

"Say you love me. That you'll marry me."

"Julia, if I told you I loved you I honestly wouldn't know if I were lying or telling the truth. And I can't marry anyone."

"Why not? All we've had together. Doesn't it mean anything?"

"I don't know if anything means anything in my life. I'm not being evasive. I really don't know. Life to me is ephemeral. I live it moment to moment. For the fun, for the excitement. I run from the serious. The idea of permanence scares the hell out of me."

"And what happens when you can't run anymore? When the fun is gone? When you're 60 or 70?"

"If I'm not dead yet, I'll commit suicide. Well, what the hell do you expect me to say? All I know is that I don't know what's going to happen. Sure, I want you. And I need you. Right now. This minute. Maybe for this hour, this day, this week. But if I meet a sexy blonde in a bar, I mentally turn off everything else and satisfy myself and I don't know if it's you or her."

"But you say you need me."

"Yeah, and I also need nine out of ten women I happen to see on the street. Julia, the best thing for you is to forget about me. And maybe I'll curl up and die. Outside of you and inside of you."

"I love you, Joe, don't you know that?"

"I know it, I know it, I know it."

And you know, too, what happens when you touch the top of a hot stove or a cigarette burns too close to your fingers or you're standing too close the edge of the subway platform when a train rushes by. And you know about a tenement house on the east side and never having quite enough to eat or a new pair of shoes on your feet and when you did get something of your own it didn't stay long enough to become part of you. It was part of the pattern. A baloney sandwich for lunch and an empty stomach after recess.

A nickel for carfare and if you wanted an ice-cream or a bubble gum with a baseball player's picture card you walked back home from school instead of taking the trolley. A good thing lasts only as long as you hold on to it. But it always goes. A steady stream of people pouring out of the tenement toward the lone toilet that stood in the back yard. And even if you have the key, so has the guy next door. If you steal a milk bottle from the corner grocery and cash it in for three cents at the next corner grocery and buy three cents worth of candy, unless you eat it all before you get home your brothers and sisters and neighbors and friends will take almost all of it all away. Eat while the eating's good. You don't need a slide rule to transpose that to an Eighth Street apartment. Fuck while the fucking is good.

"Hey, Joe, let's hook from school today."

"Might as well be in school as not be. What the hell can we do outside? No money for anything."

"We can go to Prospect Park. Watch the animals at the zoo. More fun than watching the teachers. I got fifteen cents extra. Carfare and a bag of peanuts. We can feed the elephants."

"The hell with elephants."

"You comin' or not?"

"Okay, might as well get a little sun."

The boy going through high school can become big or stay little, depending on how much he needs to become big or how much he's afraid to stay little. It depends on whether it's worth it.

"Hey, Joe, let's go try out for the baseball team."

"What for?"

"You're a good first baseman. Best one in the neighborhood."

"Like I said, what for?"

"You'll be a big shot in school."

What if I don't make the team? That makes me a little shot, small fry, a loser."

"You'll make the team."

"And have to take orders from some teacher with a cap and a

whistle who probably can't play any better than I can."

"You'll have a big name in school, Joe."

"I'd rather watch the animals in the zoo. They can't tell me what to do."

Sometimes the boy does reach out and gets his psyche burned and decides not to reach out again.

"You know, Templeton, you've got a nice style of writing."

"Thank you, Mr. Estrin."

"This story you submitted to the school magazine, it's got a lot of good stuff in it."

"Thank you. I worked especially hard on it."

"Good character delineation. Good dialogue. Except in places."

"You're going to print it, aren't you, Mr. Estrin?"

"I'm only the faculty adviser, not the editor. But that's what I'm getting at."

"Getting at what?"

"You see, Templeton, you've got good promise as a writer, but you've got to be more careful with language. Hell and damn are acceptable if you don't overuse them. But some other words you use, well..."

"I use words only where they are necessary."

"Indecent language is never necessary. And some of these four-letter words...it just isn't done, Joseph, it just isn't done."

"There weren't any other words that better expressed what the characters were thinking and feeling."

"Don't you see, Joseph, people don't talk that way."

"Which people, Mr. Estrin? The people I hear on the streets and in my mind talk that way."

"I'm trying to help you, Templeton. But I can't help you if you won't listen. There's too much unacceptable language in your writing. And too much sex. Your characters...well, too much suggestion of perversion."

"Perversion?"

"I mean eroticism. In any case..."

"You're telling me you're not going to publish my story. Is that right, Mr. Estrin?"

"Well, you see, I'm not the editor, I'm just the faculty adviser... Templeton, where are you going."

"To the zoo. To watch the animals."

The tiger, we are told, is really a more ferocious animal than the lion. The lion, however, is king of the beasts, we are told, because it lords it over the jungle with its ferocious roar. The hyena laughs, we are told, because it is an animal that takes no responsibilities or allegiance, even to its own pack. Some lions and hyenas could make millions of dollars in the political and economic society of 1950s America.

"Sure, I love you, Doris. You don't see me saying much around school. That's because when I say something I say it loud and strong and mean it. I think you're the prettiest girl in our class. Sure, I love you."

"You've got to tell me you love me, Joe, or I'll feel real bad. I've never done this before, Joe, you know that, it's the first time and I'm doing it because I love you, and if you didn't love me back, I think I'd just die!"

Who needs a big name, who needs fame when you can roar and laugh at the same time?

"Grace, you are without doubt the most beautiful girl I've ever had the privilege of making love to."

"I want to ask you something, Joe."

"Go ahead. Your wish is my command."

"What will you do next month, after we finish high school?"

"I dunno. Why?"

"Let's get married."

"Married?"

"Well, we practically are, you know. All this last semester. Wouldn't Mr. DeSantis the janitor be surprised if he knew we were doing it every afternoon down by the big boiler!"

"Yeah, we've really had a great time, Grace."

"You didn't answer my question."

"Well, it's this way, Grace. I'm going to college. That's four years. Then I'm going to medical school. That's another three years. then a couple of years internship. It'll be a long time before I can support a wife. You better just forget about me, Grace, and get yourself some nice guy who'd be able to support you right away. You're a swell kid, you know that Grace…"

After a while, the roaring and laughing are not so easy.

"You knew I was a heel, Jackie. I told you that right off. I told you that all through our junior year. I'm sorry. Maybe it should never have happened. But as far as I'm concerned, I have no regrets."

"You never did promise to marry me, did you, Joe?"

"I'm a college senior and I should have known better. I'll take all the blame."

"It's my fault just as much as yours. But we did have fun."

"More than fun."

"We're still friends, Joe?"

"We'll always be friends, Jackie. You know how I'll always feel about you."

"And I about you."

"And when I publish my first novel, I'll dedicate it to you."

"So long, Joe."

But the roaring and laughing never really stops.

"Operator, get me Sunset 1-4748. …Hello, Sue, this is Joe. I know, but if you'll only let me explain…Jackie? …she's just a good friend… you know I wouldn't do that to you. …Of course, I still love you…tomorrow night?…great …see you at 8:30 … in my room."

Sometimes the lion sleeps and the hyena remains awake, howling at the moon. Occasionally he finds a stray lamb. He laughs because he's got to know that he still has control of his part of the jungle.

"Look, babe, if you don't like it, I'm sorry for you."

"You told me you couldn't see me this afternoon, Joe, because you had an appointment with a publisher. So I come over to wait for you and find you in bed with another woman."

"She was just a casual friend. Doesn't mean anything. Forget it."

"Forget it? After all these months? You tell me to stay home today so you can go to bed with somebody else."

"Let me explain something to you, Mary Lou. When we first met I told you I was neither the type of guy who falls in love or the type of guy who gets married. I asked you if you wanted to be with me anyway and you said you did and we did, and that's all there is to it."

"But you made me fall in love with you."

"I didn't make you do anything. You want to go home or stay here tonight?"

"Why don't you love me, Joe?"

"Why don't you go home tonight and we'll talk about it tomorrow!"

"You don't give a damn about me, do you?"

"You're a nice kid, Mary Lou."

"You really don't give a damn for me, do you?"

"As a matter of fact, no. I'm tired, babe. I'm going to bed. Are you staying or not?"

"Can't you understand, Joe, I'm in love with you."

"And can't you understand, I'm not in love with you. But we enjoy each other. So let's forget all the angst. Come to bed. Where are you going?"

"Goodbye, Joe. Get somebody else to be your whore. You're alone, Joe, you're afraid and you always need someone to take to bed to prove to yourself that you're not alone and afraid. You don't have the guts to face life so you forget it in bed."

"Now, wait a minute."

"Not anymore. Goodbye."

You grow up and go to school and finish college and go into the Army and get out of the Army and keep searching for something and the moment you think you have it in your hands it disappears. There is no security and the only way you have it is imagining it. If you have enough food your stomach is full. If you have enough shelter you're warm in the winter and dry in the summer. If you have enough sex there is no time to think of anything else and when there is time there's always Calverts or Seagrams or Four Roses. You try to make sure that there isn't time. And you keep walking around the circle and you follow the signposts that all point in the same unending direction. Major Bowes was right. Around and around you go and where you stop nobody knows. When you're moving continuously it becomes impossible to stop and look at yourself. A mirror always seems to reflect too strongly. Especially if there is too much light. Sometimes there is too much. Sometimes you get weary of the circle and try to step outside of it. For a while, maybe. Maybe for always.

"Julia, I haven't known another woman since I met you. Almost a year now."

"Except at least once."

"I'm sorry about that. I was drunk."

"I've forgiven you."

"What am I going to do, Julia?"

"You ask me?"

"I need your help."

"I want to help, Joe, but you won't let me."

"You mean marry you? Save you from Walter? I can't marry you because I don't know if I really love you because I don't know what love really is. I should love you but I just don't know."

"You'd know if you tried."

"I've been trying to know who I am and what I feel for years. Nothing that I try works."

"If you stop talking in circles, Joe. You know you want me."

"I already have you."

"Is that it? All right, I won't sleep with you anymore."

"It's more than that, Julia. I need…something new. Somebody new. Innocent. Fresh. Young."

"And you think that will automatically erase who you are and make you innocent, young and fresh?"

"Maybe?"

"Somebody like Ruthie?"

"Maybe?"

"You want to use her, too, Joe, and then throw her away like all the others? Like you're trying to do with me."

"I haven't touched her. Nobody's touched her."

"Not even Ben?"

"She's not that kind of girl."

"But I am?"

"Oh, hell, Julia, this is crazy. Let's not argue. Come to bed."

"No."

"What do you mean, no?"

"Just what it sounds like. It's taken you a long time, but I think you're beginning to learn, Joe. If you won't love me, you can't have me."

"I told you, I don't know. I'm not sure. What the hell can I say if I don't know?"

"Then good night, Joe. I don't want to leave, but I love you so much I have to. I may be your whore, but I'm still a woman. You're beginning to learn, Joe, and I think you're going to learn a lot more. Goodnight!"

You cover the circumference and find yourself at the starting point again. You can stand on the precipice and look down into the valley far below and step over the wall. Or you can turn up your collar, close your eyes, and start all over again.

Have you ever watched cats grow up out of the same litter? Same mother, same father, sometimes even the same markings. If they remain in the same neighborhood, the same block, the same house they will likely play with each other, drink from the same cup, eat from the same bowl, use the same litterbox. Some will be frisky, some will sleep. Some will be friendly, some will run. Some will be rough and tough and fight to live, others will be weak and hide and barely survive, if at all.

Joe Templeton and Ben Stevens were born out of the common

weal. They could have been alike or they could have been different. They were both. Joe had to fight for everything. Ben had to fight for nothing. Joe had to protect himself from everything. Ben had to protect himself from nothing.

Joe was afraid. Ben was afraid.

Joe had to fight for a dime to buy penny cigarettes at the corner candy store. Ben got a new pair of shoes every year. Joe had to fight for the hand-me-down clothes of a father or brother or uncle. Ben got a new outfit at Easter and more new clothes at Christmas. Joe had to fight for a slab of butter on a piece of bread. Ben had a turkey dinner every Thanksgiving. Ben wasn't rich, but he wasn't poor. Joe had to cover himself from the elements, from hunger, from the teenage gangs, from people, from the world. Ben was given the protection of three-square meals a day and clean sheets and a roof that didn't leak. At the age of eight Joe was facing the world. It took Ben ten years longer.

Have you ever seen kittens pushed away from their mother's teats, afraid to be old enough to look for food for themselves, but doing it because they had no other choice? Is there some instinct in cats that tells them they have to? Is there some instinct in humans that told Ben and Joe they had to?

You first, Joe.

You're born, you grow up, you become a man, you fight the world. Can you find a life without fighting the world? You want to write because for you it's the easiest thing to do. Too many guys walking around with big businesses and ulcers to match. Too many guys getting up at five in the morning to open up some two-bit mom-and-pop store and not getting home to bed until one the next morning. Too many guys drying up in offices from nine-to-five, pushing a pencil back and forth over the same pages, making the same marks and never getting to a new, different page. Too many guys bringing in big sales to add up to big promotions, adding to columns until there's no room left. Hey, Mac, I paid a whole two grand in taxes last year, made over ten grand myself.

Paid more in taxes than I made the whole year just a few years ago.

A Cadillac in the driveway and a house in the country. What's happening tonight at the country club?

We'll have to cut out a movie this week, the kid needs a new pair of shoes.

A house in Florida and house in Maine. We've really made it!

Some guys go to work at five and get home at one and some guys go to work at one and get home at five.

But what if your old man doesn't own a factory or a fleet of trucks or a lumber yard or doesn't have an office on Wall Street or even a nine-to-five job? Hey, Joe, we're gonna pull a job at that furniture store next week. Want in? Hey, Joe, after that we might tackle a loan agency. You could get a big cut. Hey, Joe, we've got a big outfit now, gonna knock over a bank. Can use a coupla more guys. Hey, Joe, how long is ten years at Ossining?

Tell about it, write about it, put it down, let everyone know what you think and feel, get it out of your system. What kind of a profession is it where you got to practically die for ten years before you begin to live? What kind of profession is it where you get three meals a day and a Cadillac in your driveway, but die eight hours a day, five days per week except for two weeks every summer when you worry about dying the rest of the year? What kind of profession is any profession? But you got to pay your rent today, not ten years from now. Hey, babe, I got a fifth off liquor in my apartment, want to help me forget something?

If you're Ben you try to make a place in the world. You never had to do it before, but you have to now. Not in front of a dozen people or a hundred or a thousand. There are two billion in the world. Talk to them, one at a time and all at the same time. Tell them that it's you, Ben Stevens. Tell them what you know, what you want them to know. Hunger? Don't know what that is. Do you know what that is, but don't care? A new suit? Had lots of new suits when I was a kid. Don't need one now. What I need is to prove that I'm me. That I'm somebody. All two billion of you, sit back and listen. Sit back and read. But I'm afraid. Afraid they won't publish, afraid they won't buy, afraid they won't read, afraid they won't get to know who Ben Stevens is. I'll write you a letter and tell you all about him. Better still, I'll write you a book.

If Joe and Ben were both the same and different, Jack Evans was both a little less and a little more. Some people are afraid of being, others are afraid of not being. Others are afraid of not having been. Sometime in your life you should have done something. Whether you could have or not doesn't matter. Sometimes you miss the opportunity. It comes and you're afraid and it goes and for the rest of your life you wish it would come back, but it never does. Can you make it come back?

If you didn't do once what you should have done, you'll try to do it a hundred times now. And have others do it, too. Save the world! Make it a better world! You'll tell them. You'll write it in big bold letters, capital letters, letters four feet high. But Jack Evans was afraid that nobody will read them. Because the people who would bring your book to the world are afraid to publish it. It's the 1950s and McCarthyism stifles anything controversial. Anything that does not seek a Red under every bed. Yes, the world was afraid and Jack Evans was afraid.

The third floor of the NBC building in Rockefeller Center is a monument. A monument to everything that can give life and a monument to everything that will not give life. Inside you hock your ethics to get fifty bucks for a radio script or fifty bucks for three days work on "John's Other Wife" or fifty bucks to sing the commercials for a Pepsi-Cola ad or ten bucks to sweep out the third floor corridors when the fifty-dollar jobs are gone, or five dollars borrowed from some friend who sold a script, in order to pay this week's room rent, or two bits for a sandwich and free water at Horn and Hardart's, or a nickel to get a subway back to Bridge Street.

Another day, script in hand, at the third-floor elevator, with other wannabee writers and actors and singers.

"No luck today, bud?"

"No luck, couldn't even get inside."

"Me neither."

"You just don't have the knack. You don't do it the right way. "

"What have you sold?"

"Nothing."

"I've got the solution."

"Shhh, not so loud. You want this thundering herd around us to torture it out of you?"

"You got to get the producers' attention."

"Yeah? How?"

"Jump off the Brooklyn Bridge."

"What's your name? Steve Brodie?"

"Ben Stevens."

"You couldn't be an actor. Must be a writer."

"What should I be named? Launcelot Fledermaus? And what's your name?"

"Joe Templeton."

"You must be a piano player."

"After pounding the not-so-ivory pavements day after day, I feel like a piano is playing me."

"Me, too. You guys couldn't get to see the script editor, either?"

"Who ever does?"

"You ever met Milton Berle?"

"He comes in the VIP entrance—with an escort."

"Tell me you're really Milton Berle."

"I can, if you insist, though I'm kind of modest about it, so I'll call myself Jack Evans."

"You write?"

"Yep."

"Selling anything?"

"Nope."

"Right now, I could use a cup of coffee."

"I've got a pot-full of almost-freshly made coffee at my apartment on Eighth Street. If someone will splurge on some donuts, we can have a feast."

"No sooner said than almost done. Jack Evans is no piker."

"Jack, Ben, we're off to the Templeton abode. And I don't have a piano."

When you feel a kinship, friendships can grow quickly. New York can be a very lonely town. There's a lot of glitter and a lot of Park Avenue penthouses and lot of cold-water flats on the east side. There are as many pushcarts as Cadillacs and as many pampered poodles as starving babies. Jack Evans had something to say about all that but didn't quite know how to say it. Maybe it didn't make any difference because he said it, anyway.

"I tell you guys; I saw all of it happen. I saw the thirties and saw how Roosevelt saved this country from complete disaster even while he saved all his fellow millionaires and a capitalist system that some president is going to have to save again someday to prevent another possible people's revolution."

"You're no capitalist, I see."

"Hey, capitalism looks good until socialism has to bail it out."

You can't see the faces of the people on a bread line and not care, not feel you've got to at least try to do something. Because nine times out of ten, even if you don't know it, its you on the bread line, one way or another. Why was that happening? Jack began to read. Philosophy, psychology, history, and, finally, economics. He found confirmation. Do you know that whatever economic principles you apply, capitalism is a corrupt and oppressive system? Under it you can't avoid depressions and bread lines. The rich get richer and poor get poorer. And everyone wants to be in the middle class, which will be the first to be screwed by the rich when times get tough. Even in the so-called good times you've got a bunch of cattle working in the mines, in the factories, in the sweatshops while the guys employing them are vacationing in hundred-dollars-a-day hotels down in Florida. Look at employment figures and look at the incomes of the bosses and of the workers who make their bank accounts possible.

You got a bank account, Ben? You got a bank account, Joe? Are the guys on NBC's third floor making it possible for you to have one? We go to that ivory tower and outside we see that statue of the guy holding up the world. Inside you've got a bunch of people sitting on chairs plusher than they've ever had before, given to them by their bosses who are in Florida. You know how that guy holds up the world and that whole Rockefeller Center. On the sweat and blood off the asses of those people who sit on plush all day as small compensation for their sweat and blood. And they've got it a helluva lot better than the ones giving their sweat and blood in the mines and factories.

"You sound like a communist."

"You sound like a McCarthyite."

"Hell, no, I'm on your side. Just wondering."

"I sure as hell ain't a capitalist. And you guys sure aren't, either."

"You got that right."

"Joe, Ben, we're all in the same boat. Writers dependent on the largesse of guys in three-piece suits. We want to contribute to society the best we know how. Writing. If we can write stuff as good as the next guy, shouldn't it have an equal opportunity to be read? Have you ever seen anything in print that you knew wasn't as good as your stuff?"

"Too many times."

"Then why was that published and why wasn't yours?"

"Where are you going with this, Jack?"

"To the system that hits us as hard as it hits the guy in the blue collar and the overalls. How many Naked and the Dead books do you think were written in this last war? How many South Pacific and eath of a Salesman' plays in the last few years? They're great works by terrific writers. But I bet there are dozens of equally terrific manuscripts stuffed in filing cabinets and closets all over the country by people like us who can't get the guys in the three-piece suits to read them. You stand in line, manuscript in hand, in their offices and hope a secretary comes out and says, 'Mr. Big Shit will see you now'. But unless you're lucky enough to find a hot-shot agent or your uncle knows somebody in the publishing business, Mr. Big Shit never sees you. It's the system."

"So, you don't like and I don't like it, Jack, but what the hell can we do about it? That's been my life. Growing up fighting for every piece of bread I wanted to put in my mouth."

"So, you don't want to do anything about it, Joe?"

"I take what I want wherever and whenever I can get it. I'm not going to waste my time and energy on something beyond my control. Watch this apartment about two in the morning and you'll see a different babe going in or out every night."

"Okay, so you lay pipe with a different babe every night. That'll sell your stuff? That'll make you a big author?"

"That'll make me happy."

"Joe's got a one-track mind, Jack. But I know what you mean. I've thought about the system, too, but I don't go as far as you. Sure, I hate all those bastards who won't give me a chance. Some of us break through. We can go pretty far under our democratic system."

"Yeah, you can go real far, Ben, until they want to stop you. You can write all you want and maybe get it published, as long as they agree with what you write. More accurately, as long as you agree with what they believe. Look what happened to Paul Robeson. Howard Fast was put in jail. The Hollywood Ten are out of jobs and probably will go to jail. It was what they said and what they wrote. They stood up and said they wanted freedom for everyone. They stood up and said they believed in the Constitution of the United States. But the capitalist establishment didn't like the way they said it so they wind up in jail."

"I get the idea, Jack. All capitalists are bastards. So, if you can't beat it, don't fight it. Get out of life what you can."

"No, Joe, I'm not saying all capitalists are bastards. I'm not saying black is black and white is white. People and government are too complex for that. Ever hear of a publisher named Gaer? One of the capitalists I supposedly shouldn't like. He published some stuff that represented the side of the people making less than ten grand a year, like most of the people in this country. So, he gets called up before the House Committee on Un-American Activities to prove he's not a communist. Next thing you know they'll start picking on high school kids who wear red shirts or socks. Look, I'm not an economist, but I know this much. If you have a system where the workers who generate the profits get a fair share of them , where the writer gets a fair chance to sell his stuff and say what he wants, then you've got a real democracy."

"You may not be Joe Stalin, Jack, but you sure sound like a socialist."

"Socialist, Ben? Hell, I'm a communist."

"Oooh, I'm scared. Let me close the shades. What the hell am I supposed to do, crawl under the bed? You don't have horns."

"Joe, you'd be surprised at how many people would be surprised that I don't."

"Jack, Ben, let's cut out all this bullshit and get something to eat. I'm hungry."

Hey, Mac, about that Brooklyn Bridge. What's on the other side?

CHAPTER 5
CONFIDENCE OR SECURITY?

If you don't have confidence in yourself, you can be the best writer in the world and never know it. And if you don't know it, no one else will know it. If you have a woman to talk with and sleep with and get respect from, you begin to at least think that you have some confidence. If she's a woman of the world, the kind of woman you haven't known before, a woman you have to build yourself up for, you begin to feel you have even more confidence. With that kind of woman giving you her love, your ego climbs to where it tells you that you can do anything and everything.

If you have a nice girl, a sweet girl, a girl who tries hard to please you, a girl who would make a good wife or, rather, a good housewife if you ever wanted to get married, you would find security, but not the ego-driven force that you need to be a good writer.

If you had a woman like Julia, your head tells you that even the sky might not be the limit. Even if you don't really know all you should about Julia, you can believe what you can imagine. Writers have to have good imaginations. If you had a girl like Ruthie, you could be happy and secure. How high a price for security? Ask Julia.

"You're lonely, Ben? Get a woman. Sleep with her. You'll feel better. You won't be lonely."

Sometimes you can be with a million people and be lonely. Sometimes you can be with one person and be lonely. Sometimes you can be by yourself and not be lonely.

"Hey, Ben, stop moping around like you lost your last friend.

I want you to meet a charming young lady. Ruthie Green, Ben Stevens."

Sometimes you can be with one person and not be lonely anymore.

"You've never been at one of Joe's parties, Ruthie?"

"No. I've met him at parties at other friends. He's very nice."

"Is he?"

"Why, yes. Unless you're being very subtle."

"I'm never subtle. That's one of my problems. Really, I like Joe, too."

"What are your other problems, Ben?"

"I've got a lot of 'em."

"Maybe you need someone to talk to?"

"Maybe. Is that an offer, Ruthie?

"You can talk to me."

"Maybe I will."

As time passes so do many other things. The weather, the tide, the seasons, even loneliness.

"I had a wonderful time, Ben."

"Only wonderful? I thought it was spectacular."

"Was it for you, Ben? I'm glad."

"Sometimes you seem unsure of yourself, Ruthie, like a high school girl."

"In some ways I still am like a high school girl."

"Ruthie, you're very nice. I enjoy being with you."

"I've enjoyed being with you, too, Ben."

"When I'm with you, Ruthie, I forget about a lot of things. Like being afraid of a lot of things. Of being insecure."

"What are you afraid of Ben, what are you insecure about?"

"The world."

"I know. I am, too. And people. When I was a kid I used to cross the street not to have to meet people, even nice people who I knew. Are you afraid of things like that, Ben? …Ben?"

Sometimes it's better to be alone than have questions asked of you that you're afraid to answer. What if someone is afraid? If you tell yourself not to be afraid, will you still be afraid? If you're not afraid, would you then be able to do anything you wanted to do? And would doing anything you wanted to do make you happy?

Joe did what he wanted to do. Joe said he was happy. Joe was lost.

When you wanted to write you couldn't write. When you could write, you didn't want to. Does only an artist understand this? Maybe you didn't know what to write? Maybe you knew, but were afraid to write? What if you weren't alone and had someone by your side who helped you not be afraid?

"Ben, why do you go to those political meetings? You don't agree with those Reds, do you?

"No, Ruthie, not altogether. But Jack asked me to go with him."

"Bad things can happen. You could even go to jail."

"Bad things can happen if you're just crossing the street. I may not believe in a lot of what they say, but I do believe they've got a right to say it and I've got a right to hear it."

"That's what they're firing people for, putting people in jail for."

"And that's why I insist on going to those meetings if I want to. If we can't speak freely and listen freely, then maybe we ought to let the Reds take over. Those people trying to stop McCarthyism, well maybe some of them are Reds, but most of the ones I meet are like you or me, they want the freedom to think and speak and write and they're not afraid to stand up for it. That's important for a writer."

"You're a good writer, Ben. I understand what you're saying. And I'll even go to those meetings with you, if you want."

Is a good woman all a man needs? Why turn to a woman if she doesn't give you what you need? Some women can be bought. But not even a bought woman will necessarily give you what you need. Herself. Her strength. If she depends on you, you have to be strong enough to give her what she needs. If she is stronger than you, does make you weak and afraid? If you have to lead, can you? If you share your strengths, then you both can be strong. Really strong, and you have nothing to be afraid of.

Some women are named Julia.

"Yes, Ben, I left Walter. For a week. For a lousy week. And then I went back. If I was really strong I would have stayed away. But Joe won't marry me. All he wants is to sleep with me. I love theatre and music and art and literature. And the people who make them. I love to be around them. I'll lie to Walter and I'll stay in town and I'll sleep with Joe. But it's all a sham. I'm barely reaching out. A little serious encouragement and I'd do more than just reach out. I can't just leave the security of one life for no security in another. A little encouragement and I'll go as far as the rainbow. That's what you need, too, Ben. The right encouragement. You've got the stuff to go all the way. I know, you've told me you love me, Ben. So why the hell didn't I fall in love with you! I should have. With you, I could go places. We could go places. We'd climb right up to the sky. That's what so shitty, Ben. I'm in love with Joe."

Some women are named Ruthie.

"Sure, Ben, I want to help you all I can. I don't know very much about a lot of the things you care about, but I'm willing to learn. I can help you in a lot of ways. I'm a good cook. I love children. And I'd love to travel with you. Westminster Abbey and the Eiffel Tower and the Colosseum in Rome. And all the different people we could meet. Well, I don't suppose we'd really want to meet all of them. Isn't that funny, I'm talking as if you had asked me to marry you or something."

Sometimes you get so lonely and afraid that you need more than you have ever needed.

"I need you, Ruthie. I need you more than you can imagine. Right now the whole world frightens me. I know I'm a good writer and I feel I could write some of the best things ever written. But I need somebody. I'm not asking you to marry me, but I need somebody to be with me and you're here right now, so I'm asking you."

"I love you, Ben. What do you want me to do?"

Sometimes you begin not to be afraid.

"Here's a present for you, Ruthie."

"Oh, Ben, it's wonderful. You shouldn't have."

"It's wonderful, you shouldn't have? Is that an oxymoron?"

"You know what I mean. How did you know?"

"How did I know what?"

"You're teasing me, Ben. My birthday."

"I have an infallible memory."

"You're wonderful."

"That's transference of affection. I thought it was the gift that was wonderful. It's also a double celebration. That short story I've been working on, that I've been reading to you. I finished it. It's one of my better efforts. Maybe it's worth some big bucks from Esquire."

"I want to read it."

"That's why I have it in my hand."

"You are such a good writer, Ben. I want to see you write more and more."

"Keep talking like that, Ruthie, and I will."

Encouragement, like love, doesn't necessarily last forever. Or solve all of life's problems. You can't use it like a shot of bourbon or a Benzedrine pill. You can't send fear away for the moment and not expect it to return. It's got to be sent away for at least a millennium.

"Damn it, Julia, I don't know what the hell is wrong."

'Is it Ruthie, Ben?"

"Ruthie's good. She's great."

"You don't love her?"

"I like her a helluva lot."

"I thought she was what you were looking for, Ben. Encouraging you. You've been doing some good writing."

"She is. But something's missing."

"Good sex? Don't look like a kid caught with his hand in the cookie jar. Are you afraid of me asking you questions?"

"You're the only one I'm not afraid of being totally open with, Julia. No, it's not about sex. It's about love."

"Is she in love with you?"

"Probably."

"But you're not in love with her?"

"You already know the answer to that, Julia. I'm in love with you. When I'm in bed with Ruthie at night, I pretend it's you I'm making love to."

"If I thought it would do any good, Ben, I'd sleep with you. But it would only hurt you more. Stop thinking about me. I belong to another guy."

Ruthie didn't.

"I love making love with you, Ben. It makes me cry with so much happiness that I think my tears could write the most beautiful words in creation."

"I'm glad I make you happy, Ruthie."

"I was sorry at first. I swore to myself that I wouldn't until I was married. But I had to, Ben, I just had to. I love you so much."

"I'm glad, Ruthie, I'm glad."

"Will we get married someday, Ben? I know you don't really love me now. But someday you will. I just know you will."

"Sure, Ruthie. Someday."

If you had a girl like Julia, even the sky wouldn't be the limit. If you had a girl like Ruthie, you could be happy, encouraged, secure. Can security be as high as the sky? Maybe, if you knew how to use it. Ben didn't know how. He thought about Julia and had Ruthie.

CHAPTER 6
TWO INTO FOUR OR FOUR INTO TWO?

What happens when your best friend falls in love with the woman you're sleeping with? Do you throw your woman out of bed and send her to your best friend? Do you tell your best friend to get the hell out of town before you beat him to a bloody pulp? Or do you just ignore the whole thing? Joe Templeton ignored the situation. He could afford to because he knew Julia wasn't in love with Ben. He knew she was in love with him and would continue to love him as long as he wanted her to. Only he wasn't sure how much longer he wanted her to. Then he'd need a replacement. Maybe he should get to know Ruthie better?

He had known Ruthie for several years. She was a good kid. Too good. She never succumbed to any of his offers. Just the kind of woman for Ben. They got together frequently. Joe and Julia and Ruthie and Ben. At parties, at dinner, Ben would invariably gravitate to Julia, sit near Julia, talk to Julia, dance with Julia. Joe didn't care. He didn't have to warm up Julia by dancing with her. She was already a fixture in his bed. Joe and Ruthie were often left with each other. What do you talk about? How lovely Julia is and how talented Ben is? Do you talk about nothing? Do you sit and stare into space? Or do you talk about yourselves? They talked about themselves and about each other. When you've walked around the circle enough times with the same person you begin to wonder whether there's something more in another lane. More than what you've had: Going to the theatre and to art exhibits and concerts and reading manuscripts aloud and laughing at parties and changing gears with a fifth of whiskey and watching the lights of New York at night and the smoggy sun in the morning and sleeping with the man you love and the woman who loves you.

"Ruthie, what's between you and Ben?"

"Right now a woman by the name of Julia, Joe."

"Not to worry. She's not into him."

"But I can tell that he's a lot into her. Ben isn't easily discouraged."

"Neither is Julia. You didn't answer my question, Ruthie."

"What question, Joe?"

"Playing word games with me, Ruthie?"

"Maybe?"

"I like that. Gives you… another dimension. What's happening between you and Ben? I sense a…discomfort?"

"You're not being very subtle, Joe."

"I'm not trying to be subtle. I'm interested."

"Why? Because you're a writer?"

"Because I like you."

"Are you coming on to me?"

"Do you want me to?"

"Ben needs me. I need him. He can go places. I can help him."

"Are you in love with him?"

"I am. Very much."

"How do you know if you're really in love with a person? You can say they're intelligent, you can say they're sexy, you can they're caring. You can say a lot of things, but how do you really know?"

"You've never really been in love, have you, Joe?"

"I don't think so."

"You sound like you might want to be."

"Maybe? Maybe not? That's very personal. I never talk to people about personal stuff like that."

"You're talking to me."

"I guess I am, Ruthie. Somehow, you make it easy for me."

"I always thought you were just bluff and blunder, Joe. But in these talks we've had lately…something's getting you down?"

"Things have been getting me down for years. But I don't let them. I keep running away from them. Is Ben in love with you, Ruthie?"

"I wish. And I don't know why I'm telling you my personal stuff, either. We'll have to talk more often, Joe."

"How about this weekend? Julia's got to be at some kind of business party Walter is having in New Rochelle and I'll be alone in my apartment…"

"Same old Joe!"

"It won't hurt to think about it."

The old becomes older and the new becomes old. When you're dissatisfied just turn to the next page or turn at the next corner or cross the street. Don't bother looking to see if you're on the right street. You might have to stop and think and start all over again. The precipice looks pretty high. Sometimes it takes only a little baby step. Do you know that they're tearing down parts of the Great Wall of China? Needs only a few blasts of dynamite.

"I like dancing with you, Ben, but we shouldn't leave Ruthie and Joe alone at the table like that for such a long time. They're so different, they won't have anything to talk about."

"When I'm with you, Julia, I don't want to think about anybody else. Even when I'm not with you."

"I know, Ben. And I'm sorry that I can't feel the same way. It's funny. When I look at you and Joe, sometimes you both seem so much alike, you both want to write, you both feel so much inside that needs to come out. You both keep trying and neither of you really knows what you're trying for."

"I know what I'm trying for, Julia."

"But I'm in love with Joe and I'm not in love with you."

"How can you keep loving Joe when you know he's just using you? You know he can't be in love with anybody but himself. There's no future for you with Joe."

"My head tells me I shouldn't love him. But I can't help it."

"Leave him, divorce Walter, and I'll marry you. I'll marry you in a minute."

"What about Ruthie? She's very much in love with you. You'd break her heart."

"I've got a heart, too."

Sometimes a dance is over not soon enough. Sometimes it's over much too soon. You want to talk more. You've got so much to say and you want to say it with the right words, the words that will have some effect. And then when you've thought of the right words and you've gotten up enough nerve to say them, the orchestra stops playing.

"Julia, come up to my apartment. I need you to talk to."

"Okay, Ben, just to talk."

"And we won't tell Joe about it."

"No, Ben. Or Ruthie."

You go home and you wait and you wait and you wait for something good to happen. It doesn't and you wonder why. But wondering makes you think and you don't want to think. About yourself, that is. You can think about somebody else but thinking about yourself can be too painful and you want to run away and hide and pull the blanket over your head. Sometimes you can stop thinking by talking.

"What are you afraid of, Ben?"

"Myself, Julia. The world."

"You've got talent, Ben. You don't have to be afraid."

"I can tell myself that, Julia. But if I don't feel it, it doesn't count."

"I thought I was afraid, Ben. Afraid to lose the security I sold myself for. Afraid to do a lot of things. But when I admitted it to myself, when I understood why I was afraid, when I knew what I really wanted, I wasn't afraid anymore."

"Look at Jack Evans. He thinks he knows what he wants, but I'll bet he's just as afraid of the world as I am."

"I don't think he is. Just listen to him talk. He knows what he wants out of the world and goes after it, like he's secure about himself and what he believes."

"So, what should I do, become a communist like Jack? It's all too confusing. It hurts to think about it."

"You can always talk to me, Ben."

"I need you for more than talking, Julia."

"I'm sorry, Ben, that's not going to happen."

"Think about it, Julia."

"Sure, Ben, I'll think about it."

Joe Templeton reluctantly began to think about things, too.

"I've been thinking, Ruthie. About you."

"In what way, Joe?

"I'm tired of me. I want something more. Something secure, that I know will always be there. Maybe that's why I feel lost."

Ruthie thought, too. She thought about being needed and not really being needed. She wanted something bigger and stronger than she had.

"I'm tired, too, Joe."

"Of Ben?"

"Maybe?"

"I thought you were in love with him."

"When you think you're in love, how do you know you really are?"

"I can help you, Ruthie."

"Not now, Joe, not now."

Sometimes you get tired of running around in the circle and you jump off. And find yourself going around and around again on another circle. And after that another circle, people moving from precipice to precipice to precipice. Will they ever stop to ask themselves why?

PART II

THE EVALUATION

CHAPTER 7
RHYME OR REASON

To drive to New Rochelle from Eighth Street in the Village you turn left onto Avenue C, pass several stop lights and end up on First Avenue. On First Avenue you continue past Bellevue Hospital to Twenty-third Street, turn right and then left on New York's East River Drive or, as tourists call it, using its official name, Franklin D. Roosevelt Boulevard. You can't imagine anything on New York's east side being called a boulevard, even one with such an illustrious name.

It's funny what a fistful of dough can do. In different ways.

The Village used to be a place where Bohemians lived. Union Square with political rallies, cold-water flats, long narrow rooms with limitless tin ceilings. The girl from Texas with long blond hair trying to get a job in a chorus no matter how many couches it takes. Only she really wants to be a singer. The kid from Long Island who couldn't live with his family because they couldn't understand his lifestyle, thinking gender preference meant that one arbitrarily could determine the preference. If you're out on your own, you can't afford much. One room with a sink will do. The guy from Ohio who wants to act. Only he can't get to see an agent, no less a producer. So, he gets a job hopping trays at Horn and Hardart's and finds a room in the East Village. The young woman from Saint Louis who wants to play her violin in Carnegie Hall. The young man from California who will have a one-man exhibition if he could ever get an art gallery proprietor to look at his paintings. The sisters from Maine who just want to experience New York. The girl from Kansas who decided any kind of living was better than physically and culturally starving on an arid farm. The boy from Chicago who is positive that he will soon be dancing with Martha Graham. The tough guy from the East Side who decided to become a writer because it seemed like the easiest thing to do. He didn't come to New York from anyplace. He just stayed.

When does genius take over? When does success come and how do you know if its success? When does your name go up in lights, get printed in the gossip columns, make Red Channels' subversive list and you get blacklisted in good company with authors and publishers and composers and actors and directors and scene designers and dancers and musicians and practically the entire Group Theatre and much of the Theatre Guild and Tin Pan Alley?

How many got the break, knocked 'em dead, got rich quick? One in a million? One in ten thousand? Genius row? Tiled baths and glass showers and Baby Grands and form-fit chairs and friends and even homes in the Hamptons. Somebody knew somebody, somebody slept with somebody, somebody was lucky enough to be in the right place at the right time. Some made it the hard way.

Pounding pavements all day, waiting tables all night, cattle calls and barred office doors. They lived in garrets and cold-water flats on spaghetti and rice. Most didn't make it at all.

Not much of the Old Village remained, the Village of the 1920s and '30s and '40s. The war changed both perception and reality. Some of the Old Villagers remained there. Newcomers were making the Old Village into a new village. Everyone tried to hold on to the Old Village. Or at least the aura of it.

Julia thought about all of this as she drove her Cadillac to East River Drive. Reluctantly going home to New Rochelle. She loved the Village. At least she thought that she loved it. For a year now. Two nights, sometimes three and even four nights a week with a self-styled tough-guy writer on Eighth Street. This was one of the nights that Walter expected her home. You can't get a new Cadillac each year unless you play hostess to some old guy who wants to buy a couple hundred thousand dollars worth of insurance. The best-looking mausoleum in Woodlawn Cemetery. She shuddered at the thought of the old guy leaving and Walter climbing into bed with her, shifted the Cadillac into second at the stop sign, and entered the Drive.

"Darling, I wish you'd come home more often. If you'd really miss the auxiliary meetings I'll drive in and pick you up at night so you won't be afraid of driving home alone and won't have to stay over."

"But where would I leave my car and how would I get in the next day, Walter? It just wouldn't work. And you wouldn't want to deprive me of my few little pleasures, would you, Walter?"

Along the East River you pass a panacea of living quarters for those who cannot afford to buy a house or the increasingly steeper rents of new housing in New York or the munificent bribes needed to even be considered for a rent-controlled apartment. A panacea for the moment, perhaps the slums of a future generation, occupied now by some of the people who lost their two-room railroad flats, torn down to make way for these new skyscrapers of modern apartments, of cooperative housing opportunities built by unions for union members, built by obscenely wealthy insurance companies for privileged low- and middle-income residents. "I know this guy whose sister works for the Metropolitan Insurance Company and he thinks maybe she can get me on the list for an apartment. I'd give anything to get Met housing. No, he didn't ask me to sleep with him or for money for his sister." High-rise after high-rise after high-rise, becoming virtual cities in themselves, creating their own suburbias from the east side to upper Manhattan and the Bronx. Julia didn't think about them now. They were familiar sites, not even drawing a bare glance. A few years ago, she would have thought about them. Jack Evans made her. You couldn't stay in Jack's apartment night after night and not read the red-underlined newspaper articles and the dog-eared book pages on money and people and power and not begin to think about them. You couldn't go to a party with Jack Evans and not admire, although not necessarily agree with, his passionate even violent arguments on democracy and capitalism and how the powers-that-were owed it to the public to build those new housing icons to capitalistic democracy. That was one of the reasons why she couldn't really fall in love with Jack, at least not on a permanent basis. His devotion to his political beliefs and his need to constantly argue them. He loved them with more devotion than he could ever give to any woman. During the past few years Julia learned to talk about things, too. You couldn't live with Jack Evans and Joe Templeton and even Walter Mitchell without thinking and evaluating and talking. About a lot of things. Now, as New Rochelle loomed closer, she thought about Walter.

"I'll even give up some of my clients here, Julia darling. We'll move into the city so you can do the things you want and we can be together every night. We can afford a hotel apartment, a nice one, even on Fifth Avenue. We can have a maid. And we won't need two cars."

She'd have to tell him that she would do nothing that might hurt his career. That his career was most important. She'd continue to commute back and forth so he could continue to see his contacts and makes his sales in Westchester County, where his big New Rochelle house enabled him to have client parties that would be much more difficult to have in a New York apartment. Then Walter would suggest, not forcibly—no, Walter couldn't do anything forcibly, damn him—that she have a baby. A baby would keep her at home, replace her interests in New York. Walter's words would make her feel sick again, not butterflies but pains in her stomach. She needed some Anacin, some aspirin. Get me some, Walter. And Walter would carefully sleep in a corner of the bed and if she were lucky she'd wake up in the morning not feeling that she had to rush to take a bath.

The Cadillac stopped for a light. Why was it taking so long? She waited. What was she waiting for? A baby. She wanted a baby.

Certainly not Walter's. The only one she wanted was with Joe. It shouldn't be too difficult to have a baby with the man you sleep with. But Joe didn't want a baby. Nothing that would give him even the slightest sense of responsibility. Condoms aren't 100% safe. But Joe tried to be. If she couldn't have Joe permanently, she could have his baby. Try and get it.

If you stand at 72nd Street in Central Park you can see the New York skyline. Not the skyline you see from the Hudson River. Not Wall Street, cramped and jaded to those on the outside, munificent and golden for those on the inside. Not the paunchy buildings vying with each other to see which could grow fatter, stifling the air of the smaller and less affluent buildings underneath them. They were a tribute to those who built them. Not the architects, but the owners. The Rockefellers, the Astors. They were also a tribute, although try and find an owner who would admit it, to the little guy, to the 99% of Americans whose sweat and toil made it possible for the 1% to build their pyramids to the almighty dollar. Doesn't everyone live in a penthouse with a grand piano and mirrored bedrooms and platinum bathroom faucets? Yes, sir, Mr. Astor Junior the Fourth. Anything you say, sir. Your great great great grandfather was one of the most successful crooks of them all. All hail the crooks who made America their fiefdom. Oh, hell, let Jack Evans go to jail for preaching this kind of subversion. I have a Cadillac and a home in New Rochelle. Why didn't Walter buy a house in Scarsdale?

The Empire State Building and the Waldorf-Astoria and Rockefeller Center and the Chrysler Building stand out high and proud from the East River Drive. Julia looked at them as she passed, then glanced at them through the rear-view mirror. She thought how impressive they were. Why think anymore? It only leads to confusion. Wonderful drive, except it's going the wrong way. Few traffic lights, lots of scenery. The only scenery I want is in a bed in an Eighth Street apartment. Oh, hell, Julia, you are confused. Sex on the brain. Drive the car and shut up those inner thoughts. But some things you can't shut up. They creep through your senses, your head, your mouth, your ears, and they keep coming. Like those people from Ellis Island. You can see Ellis Island from the West Side Drive. A tight little island. Are you a relative of a pure 100% American with at least 200 shares in a corporation or a steady job on an assembly line? Step in. If they kept their mouths shut—damn those books and pamphlets of Jack Evans—and were obedient, quiet, non-thinking citizens, they could stay. Maybe if Julia would learn not to think, she wouldn't have to go back, either. Maybe if she learned not to feel? Or to feel more? Or to think more? Who the hell knows? Somebody's got to know. Here I am in this fancy expensive Cadillac and I don't know. I'm poor stupid Julia Harris Mitchell. Does the name Mitchell sound fat and sloppy and grimy to anyone else but me?

Poor stupid Ben. He isn't stupid, but right now he is. He thinks I'm smart. He thinks I've got guts.

Walk out of the house, tell Walter you've got to get away, move in with Joe, no steaks for dinner, no martinis for breakfast, no fancy china or chic furniture or necklaces or I. J. Fox furs. Go back to Walter. I'm sorry, Walter, I wasn't well. I stayed with Elizabeth. You know, Elizabeth. She and I teach that children's class together or play bridge together or volunteer at that hospital together or go to parties together or make snowmen together. It doesn't matter. Oh, hell, I'm bored. Leave me alone. No, I won't go off like that again. No, I'm sorry. No, I'm all right. No, I'm not all right. No. No. No. No. No. Yes. Yes. Yes. Yes. Yes, Walter, I'll sleep with you tonight.

Islands in the East River passed by on her right. One was a prison. Another was a sanitarium. I think. You live in New York for years and you never get to know their names. They all look alike, anyway. You can live in New York a lifetime and never get to know a lot of things. Stuck and stifled in your own self-sustaining little corner of one of the city's five boroughs. Will you ever get to the Planetarium or the Museum of Modern Art or the Natural History Museum or the Cloisters or the Bedford-Stuyvesant section of Brooklyn or the Prospect Park Zoo or Ebbets Field or the Polo Grounds or going with Jack Evans to hear Vito Marcantonio at Madison Square Garden or Fritz Kuhn yelling Nazi rhetoric in Yorkville or Paul Robeson giving an impromptu private concert after being banned by a McCarthy-obeying ex-General President and all the moguls of the entertainment industry, and tens of millions of people in the 48 States having their heartbeats regulated by a tickertape in a large building on Grand Street. Some day some kids will occupy Wall Street and you'll pick up the Daily News and see red. Things begin to become part of each other in New York.

Julia thought how nice it would be if she could decide what was black and what was white. What she should do and what she shouldn't do. A kid ran out in the street chasing a ball and she slammed on the brakes. The guy in the car in back of her slammed on his, sliding till his front bumper touched her rear bumper. "Fucking woman driver," he yelled. Okay, smart ass, next time I'll hit the kid and splatter him onto your windshield. Why can't I be happy when I drive alone? Make up songs. Whistle. Happy-go-lucky like Joe. Like the guy in the cigarette commercial, "be happy, go Lucky." Joe always is happy. Except lately. Is it Ruthie? Maybe I could splatter her onto a windshield? Ruthie's a nice kid. Belongs to Ben. So why the hell doesn't Joe leave her alone? Joe doesn't know what he wants. He's confused. Like me. So, he's trying to find a way out. Like me. There, that makes sense. I know what I'm doing. But why am I doing it? What am I running away from? Running around and around in a circle. Ben's running around in a circle. Why am I thinking of Ben first? It should be Joe first. No, me first. Julia's running around in a circle. Ruthie's running around in a circle and Joe's chasing her. And Walter sits in the middle of the circle. Because he's the fattest. It's a good thing this car knows the way to New Rochelle. I'm so lost in crazy thoughts I don't even remember which way I've come.

You see New York's landmark buildings from the East River Drive, but you're not aware that you're seeing them. They pass in a mist as if they—or you—are in Brigadoon. The headquarters site for the United Nations, the Empire State Building, the taller hotels abutting Central Park, the posh east side residences along the water, the slum tenements right next to them, the Islands, the boats, the ferries, the barges. You finally come to a ramp which leads you up to the Triborough Bridge. Just before and underneath it is an island that holds Triborough Stadium, an athletic field to be used by the city's high schools and colleges. But you can't easily get there without a car so the schools might as well hold their athletic events in their school fields located next to subway stations, apartment houses, beer parlors and candy stores.

Julia looked at the track circling the interior of Triborough Stadium. That's where we should all be, going around and around and around. She turned the car up the ramp, three lanes wide, swung in a large curve that seemed to circle all of New York, high and free and smooth, and stopped at the toll booth. Fifty cents and you have the privilege of using the Triborough Bridge. A complicated entrance. To the tourist an exotic example of a complicated city. To the New Yorker unnecessary confusion.

Several tunnels, built for no apparent reason on top of this skyway, all appearing to go in the same direction and all looking alike. Like the Islands. But you didn't have to think about the Islands. They were now away from you. But you had to use the tunnels so you had to think about them. For Julia it was no problem, no confusion. She liked to solve confusions. Crossword puzzles, rebuses, word contests. It gave her a feeling of confidence, of achievement, working out a difficult puzzle. A substitute for her own puzzlements that didn't seem to work out. Choosing the right tunnel was easy, by now by rote taking the one that went into the upper Bronx and ignoring the ones that led to the East Bronx and to Queens. She always looked for another car that would stop, pause, confused, and then enter a tunnel slowly, unsure of itself. It made her feel superior, more capable, knowing where she was going. Did Joe and Ben know where they were going?

She turned off the bridge onto a road with the lopsided sign, "Willis Avenue," wondered who Willis was or had been, and headed north. She stopped for a light and noticed signs on nearby shops, "Joe's Sodas," "Ben's Laundry." She thought about them again, then deliberately thought instead about the tunnels and the Islands.

Even in a new Cadillac you hear the zoom-zoom-zoom as the wheels go around. Different ground at every zoom but the same wheel and the same sound. Like Joe and Ben. Different and alike. Men are all alike, anyway, aren't they? They think they want something and go out and try to get it. Money, sex, love. Or any of a dozen other things. When they finally get what they think they want they begin to realize that it's not what they need. Joe and Ben were like that. They each needed something but didn't yet really know what it was. So they searched for what they thought they wanted. Julia filled the gap for both.

Joe used her. A transition during a period of searching for permanence. Ben wanted her for the same kind of transition. But it really wasn't a simple as that. Too many variables, a mumbo-jumbo of ideas, flashing by like the telephone poles past a moving car. Julia wanted people, lights, life. Joe could give it to her. Because he was what he was. If Joe had a home in New Rochelle and a Cadillac she'd ask for nothing more. Even without them she'd ask for nothing more. But while she needed permanence, Joe wanted only transition. With her. Did he want more with Ruthie? Did Ruthie want more with Joe? Why the hell did Ben have to keep bringing her around? Around Joe. Maybe she would be good for Joe? Over my dead body! When I die I'll have as my epitaph: "Here lies a transition."

Have you ever been driving a car, gotten lost in thought, and the next thing you know you're suddenly conscious of the street you're on and wonder how you got there? Julia often got lost in thought and suddenly looked up and found herself a mile or two miles or three miles from where she last remembered being. Keep going to New Rochelle. She had to play hostess to the Ellises that evening. One of Walter's principal clients. If there were any people more stupid, loutish, or boring than Mack and Mitzi Ellis, Julia didn't know them. Only Walter could know them. She gritted her teeth at the prospect of Mack Ellis singing a version of "Mule Train" while Mitzi Ellis laughed uproariously and Walter bloated like a proud impresario.

If anyone could convey sloppy fatness as well as Walter, it was probably Mack. Or Bill or Mike or Oswald or Percival or any number of vice-presidents or members or clients of the hundred-thousand-dollar club that Walter brought home for dinners and parties. Stupid Walter. If he would schedule fewer of these parties she might be inclined to spend more nights at home and Walter wouldn't have to stare at some big-busted bleached blonde on the street and wonder why he didn't marry her instead. Poor stupid Walter. He'd never have the nerve to stop the blonde or brunette or redhead and ask her if she'd like to have a gourmet dinner, a Cadillac transport and a warm bed. It would be good if he did. Then I'd not have even the slightest twinge of guilt along with unfettered freedom. But plush is so comfortable. A woman can't live like a Bohemian. She can live among them and love it. But not like one.

Julia looked up, saw the sign "Westchester Avenue," wondered again how she got there without remembering the past few miles and drove on. Driving along the Parkway is driving through the typical life of New York apartment dwellers. The ones who live in the never-ending rows of apartment buildings for 20 years and never get to know who their next-apartment neighbor is. They get up, turn on the radio so that it wakes up the four families above, below and on either side, make some coffee, get dressed, take the elevator down, say hello to the doorman, walk a block to the subway, get downtown at 8:55, get lunch at the automat at 12:05, get back to the office at 12:55, leave the office at 5:00, buy the evening paper, struggle through the mass of people on the subway, get home, listen to the comedy shows on the radio after supper, once a week go to the movies a couple of blocks away, once a month go to a baseball game, every so often play bridge at the in-laws apartment, every summer go to Far Rockaway for two weeks, go to relatives weddings, relatives funerals, New Year's eve parties, take the children to the

Bronx Zoo, and get up in the morning and turn on the radio and wake four neighboring families.

Julia thought about all this, and not for the first time. She often told herself that she would never live like that.

Julia wanted parties that lasted until four in the morning. She wanted theatre and laughs and dancing and laughs and music and laughs and art exhibits, even if the galleries didn't allow laughs. Something more, something different than what passed for life in the apartment houses of the upper Bronx. Could it be found in a lovely home in New Rochelle? It wasn't here now. Maybe with Joe it could be? Maybe not? Maybe Walter was right? Lay down, spreads your legs and have a baby. She'd have to give a baby its own personal security and not continue to seek it for herself. Maybe? But what is security? Not Walter's ten grand or twenty grand a year. Maybe it would be easier to just have a baby than trying to figure it out?

You follow the Bronx River Parkway and along to your right you see streams and gardens and flowers. Eventually, along to your left you see two story homes and neat, large bungalows. Not the clapboard rural type, but with rambling architecture, stone facades, brick foundations, built up from basement garages and sloping rises. Venetian blinds and picture windows look out onto manicured lawns. Some houses are small, perhaps with only five or six rooms, others are large brick mansions, two floors, ten or fifteen rooms. New Cadillacs and an occasional Rolls Royce dot clean, meticulous streets. Some houses look like movie sets for bank presidents and Wall Street brokers, with a smaller house every so often of a super-successful insurance salesman. Not that New Rochelle was exclusive. You could live there on the modest salary of the upper-middle class. The biggest problem was keeping up with the New Rochellians. It was only half-true for the Mitchells. The externals had to be there, and were. Cadillac, catered parties, country club membership. "Didn't you know, Julia, that the biggest policy sales are made on the golf course?" Julia didn't play golf, but felt obliged to join Walter as the dutiful wife at the get-togethers of his golfing friends. After dinner, the men would adjourn to the club room to watch whatever sport was on television that day and the women would retreat to another room to cluelessly talk about kuche, kinder and kirche, the latest fashions, and the gossip about whoever happened not to be there. More than once Julia excused herself. Vacuous prigs. Bimbos in mink coats.

Julia turned the car into the driveway. Someday she'll get an automatic compressor installed so that the garage doors will open when she drives over a marker in the driveway. It was a nice day, a pleasantly warm afternoon. She stopped the car, left it in the driveway, and walked into the house.

Julia remembered the house where she grew up. A three-room apartment in Flatbush. Everyone is New York calls their apartment a house. "Hey, c'mon over to my house." An unconscious feeling of having, of suburban nicety contrasting with the cramped ten walls of the three-room apartment.

Julia's parents were well-off enough to send her to two years of college. Tuition was free at the New York City College system, but families that needed the new high school graduate to get a job to bring in money to a struggling household couldn't afford to send the newly-minted wage-earner to college. Julia always managed to be well-dressed, became popular as a good listener with an interest in the many and varied ideas and interests of a diverse group of going-on-twenty-year old's, attracted boys her age and men a few years older. She always dreamed of a house in that suburb-of-suburbs—second only to Scarsdale—New Rochelle. It would be like winning the sweepstakes and moving from Brownsville to Kings Highway. A fantasy difference, a difference that was a fantasy. Some houses are considered beautiful, some lavish. Julia's—really Walter's—was a step below: charming. Pretty. Not large, but not small.

Julia picked up a letter from the mailbox by the front door. Another financial report for Walter. Walter likes to impress himself. Leave it on the phone table just inside the door. Why did this "charming" house seem so distasteful this particular afternoon as Julia walked down the long hallway into the living room, past the Magnavox television set with its huge 19-inch screen, the Baby Grand Piano, and to the kitchen? She looked at the row of shiny steel cabinets, felt hemmed in by their faultlessness, opened the oven, looked in, took a breath of satisfaction, and called "Helen." An African-American woman in her early twenties came in. Julia told her to prepare salad and soup, that the guests would arrive at eight, that she was going upstairs to shower and dress and if she was needed, to call. The maid, who cleaned in the morning and cooked in the afternoon and then caught the New York, New Haven and Hartford train back to Manhattan where she walked from the 125th Street subway station to a three-room crumbling tenement apartment she shared with two parents and three siblings, answered politely, turned to the refrigerator and began to work again for her twenty-five dollars a week.

Julia changed the moment she entered the front door. Outside she was or at least thought she was what she wanted to be, what her inner body and soul told he she had to be. Inside she became a New Rochelle matron. The wife of a man who made thousands of dollars selling other men guarantees that they will be rich after they die. She was the woman of the house with a maid and institution to oversee.

At first she played a role. She posed her role. Now it pressed in on her as she felt it was almost becoming a part of her. Suburban respectability and stability. Did she no longer have a choice? She would prepare to be a good hostess for the evening. And wait for Walter to come home.

CHAPTER 8
SATISFACTION

It was two o'clock when Julia reached the house. Walter usually got home about five-thirty. Today he came a little earlier. Today was an important day. A big day in his life. Today he had been promoted. Today he had been given a raise, a title. Today he became an Assistant Vice-President.

Today he was coming home to his wife, to dinner with some of his best friends, and he would have to celebrate. He stepped into the elevator, gave the elevator operator a cheery hello. It's always important to be cheery. Especially to inferior people. Well, not really inferior, but people who clearly didn't have his brains and ability. And money. He stepped out onto the sidewalk and looked up at the building standing forty stories above him and thought how magnificent it was, how wonderful this world, this country, this system that could give a man such an inspiring building to work in, a home in New Rochelle, a new Cadillac every year, a state-of-the-art television set, and friends who had a lot of money and knew a lot of important people. He was proud and happy with the success of the world around him, with his own success. He turned away from the building, bumped against the old lady standing on the corner selling carnations for a quarter apiece, and began walking the few blocks to Grand Central Station for his commuter train. Walter was more than satisfied with himself, with what he had accomplished. Satisfaction in feeling that he had reached a goal, or at least finished an important step on the way to that goal. Each step was a special achievement for Walter until another goal presented itself and, when he reached that, still another. He didn't think too far ahead. Thinking in terms of a large future was for people who were born into one. The people with famous names, with large investments, who owned the office buildings he worked in. The people who founded libraries and foundations and fellowships. The people whose fathers were the crème de la crème of American enterprise. The people who were named Rockefeller and Ford and Astor and Edison. The people who had made America great and who continued to make America even greater. Of the people, by the people, and for the people. Exactly what Lincoln said. Walter knew how great and proud those words were. Great in industry. Proud in society. The top level of knowledge, education, culture, manners, taste, money. To make America the best nation in the world it should be run by the best people. Walter knew unequivocally that these were the best people. He was proud to be among them, work for them, strive with them for an increasingly stronger America. They were the wheels. He was just a cog. But it was important to be a cog. It was the cog that made the wheel go around. And today he became an even more important cog. It was the cog that brushed by the splinters and shattered the darts thrown at the wheel. And once they were shattered, the wheel ran over them and crushed them even more, with the divine right of acquired power.

Walter crossed Broadway, darted out of the way of a taxi that started before the green light flashed, stopped to glare at the driver who was beyond eye and ear distance, saw the chauffer-driven Lincoln Continental slow down as it came toward him, courteously allowing him to reach the curb before it passed him. He smiled to himself, repeating in his mind the mantra his economics professor in college had drilled into him: "class over mass." Apply any word in front of it, any descriptive adjective referring to America's economic elite, and you have a truism. It is the mass that creates the economic war, creating a jungle of divisiveness. It is the class that keeps a stabilization of economic society, enabling the mass to obtain a modicum of security through the trickling down of the largesse of the class. He thought of the taxi driver and the chauffeured limousine and applied the truism: class over mass.

Yessir, it was a great country all right, despite the masses that insisted on drinking and stealing and causing riots and talking communism and being dirty and having babies and cluttering up the street of the city. Something the class people, the big people, would have to get rid of. He pushed by several older men with ragged clothes, reeking of liquor, holes in their shoes and newspapers folded to long out-of-date want ad pages. He entered the vast brightly lit transition chamber between work and home, the Grand Central rotunda.

Walter said a silent thank you to his company's vice-president who had moved his department's offices from its Chambers Street location to mid-town, near Broadway. When he first started with his company he took taxis, but soon learned that the subway was infinitely faster, with traffic, particularly in the late afternoon, sometimes holding up taxis for an hour while the subway would get him there in less than 20 minutes. At first the subway depressed him. He had grown out of that plebian means of transportation. He tried to think of other things, things that elated him, like his weekend golf game at the country club. He turned his nose away from the stink of humanity. The mass. Little people going home to tiny apartments, to railroad tenements, to the stench of cabbage, the smell of seasoned fish, the reeking of fried cheese on spaghetti. And all around him garlic and more garlic with the occasional odor of whiskey. Newspapers with large print and small print and black headlines and red headlines. People reading the Daily Compass and, even worse, some with the Daily Worker. People pushing and pulling at each other and men squeezing themselves in front of women with protruding bosoms, smiling at them with a little shiver every time the train lurched or hit a sharp curve, throwing them against each other.

People talking in different languages, high nasal tones, gruff drawn-out phrases, staccato chattering, low emphatic whispers. White faces, light faces, brown faces, black faces, smiling faces, sad faces, pretty faces, ugly faces. All evolving into one mass. No distinction. No personality. No importance. The train slowed down, stopped at Fourteenth Street. Young men with boyish faces and books under their arms. Middle-aged men with screwed up smiles, pretending they weren't tired, depressed, or both. Women with hair cut short and horn-rimmed glasses, wearing business suits. Women with tight skirts that emphasized their undulating bodies as they stepped onto the platform. The masses. Not important. Barely interesting. They shoved their way out of the car, roughly, coarsely. So many of them going home to Greenwich Village. Radicals? Bohemians? The lunatic fringe? Sex perverts?

The train doors slammed shut, packing into the subway car another mass. He was pushed against an old lady guarding a package against her body, her sweaty face rubbing against his suit. He twisted himself away. He found himself in front of two young Black men in animated conversation. He consciously reached for his back pocket to assure himself that his wallet was still there. Although the two Black men ignored him, he managed to sidle away from them. The train raced past the platform, the station becoming a blur. The people, too. He shuddered at the thought of the government giving power to these people. Civil rights. Fair trials. Toleration of radicals and foreigners and perverts. Thank heaven for that Senator from Wisconsin who is protecting the country from the Red Menace. Walter was too important, too far along the path of elitism to be forced to live, even on a subway ride, with these people. He took comfort in knowing that in two more strops he'd be at Grand Central in a comfortable train car with people of his own class. Maybe it would be worth the outrageously high parking fees to drive his car to the office rather than commute by public transportation? He amended that thought: By mass transportation.

Walter didn't hate these people, he just felt sorry—and more than a little revulsion—for them. He had been one of them himself but had the fortitude to become more than that. He had ridden the subway when he came to Manhattan from Westchester to go to a museum or Broadway play or a first-run movie at the Roxy or the Paramount. He had ridden the subway when his mother took him shopping with her on Fifth Avenue or 34th Street or to see the Santa Clauses at Macy's and Gimbels and Saks before Christmas. Though not a New York New Yorker, he was a New Yorker. His father was a New Yorker. A contractor who made a lot of money and then lost more than he had made. He had little respect for his father and would have had none had his father not had the foresight to put aside enough money to send his only child to college. His father had let money slip out of his hands. Walter resented the fact that he himself wasn't but should have been a wealthy and influential contractor through inheritance of a thriving business from this father. His father, except for the fact that he had once made a pile, was clearly no different than the mass who surrounded him on the subway. He breathed a sigh of satisfaction that he himself was different. An important position in a forty-story building. But he couldn't hate his father. It just wasn't done. So, he didn't hate the people surrounding him. He shuddered, but only for the briefest moment, with the thought that maybe he feared them because they threatened his controlled, secure existence.

The doors closed on the 34th Street station, the car lurched forward, Walter edged toward the door so that he wouldn't be caught in the middle of the pushing crowd when he got off at the next stop, 42nd Street at Times Square. Out of the subway car window he saw the dull yellow tunnel lights flashing by. Zing… zing…zing…zing. For a moment, squeezed in the middle of the other passengers shoving toward the door, he felt like the dull yellow naked bulb.

From 34th Street to 42nd Street is a matter of less than a minute. Eight blocks at sixty miles an hour. Barely enough to think of anything seriously. Yet more decisions were made between 34th and 42nd streets than in the entire ride from Brighton Avenue or Pacific Street or South Ferry. On that final stop on the BMT, the express and local stop of the IRT, the stop of the Independent line, came the decisions. To see Clark Gable or Bob Hope or Louis Armstrong's band at the Paramount or the Rockettes at Radio City Music Hall. To go into a bar and drink or walk up and down 45th street until a bleached blonde picked you up. To go with your acting portfolio to Lieblings, Equity, Bloomgarder, and Helpburn or forget about making the rounds that day with a shrinking stomach and go to the employment office of Horn and Hardart or Schrafft's. To go to a lawyer or a psychiatrist. To look at the want-ad section of the New York Times or to walk up and down 45th Street looking at theatrical displays to take your mind off your depression. To go to a rally of the Arts, Sciences and Professions Council or to carefully avoid even being seen near there lest you lose whatever job you now have or end up on the blacklist. To stand in front of the penny arcade near Eighth Avenue where the cops won't bother you too often for panhandling or to stand on the corner by Nedick's where the danger from the fuzz was greater but so was the take. To go into Roseland or to an apartment on Second Avenue and ask her if she'd go out with you again. It wasn't simply yes-no, if-but, now-later, why-why not. Each decision is analyzed, reviewed, reconstructed, amended, all in a matter of seconds, and when that was done there still was uncertainty.

Sometimes, if you're smart, you realize you can't make a decision. Everything keeps rushing at you and past you, the pros and the cons. They swat at you for a flashing second, creating a dull haze, they swat you again and the haze becomes duller. Then they swat at you again. Walter felt like the dull yellow light bulbs. Zing… zing…zing.

Walter felt he was becoming big and important and making a place for himself. Except with Julia. In front of Julia he was naked. Like the dull yellow light bulbs, with Julia swatting at them.

Everything he did was wrong or, at least, not right. Nothing he did seemed good enough. In front of a millionaire he confidently sold ten thousand dollars' worth of insurance like a man. In front of Julia he was a boy with no confidence. He never seemed to find the right words to say to her. Even when he knew he was right and she was wrong, it was he who begged forgiveness. Running at her heels. When he was younger, girls had been digits. Ideals, physical bodies in a void, outside of the real world, the world of business.

When Walter was a young man he knew that he would marry someday. He wanted to marry a girl with a physical body meant to have babies. A home-type girl. The perfect housewife. The excellent cook. The gracious hostess. The ultimate mother. After all, that's what women were for. When he met Julia, he was convinced that she represented his criteria for womanhood. He imagined her getting his breakfast in the morning, cleaning his house, ironing his shirts, preparing his supper, sitting with him listening to the radio in the evening and, twice a night, when he would wake up, rolling over on her back as he gave vent to his manhood before he turned away and went to sleep again. Isn't this what women were for?

He couldn't understand it when he found that this wasn't what Julia was for. Julia wanted her own car to drive (well, it was nice to have a capable wife). Julia wanted to read the latest books (five dollars for a novel about romance and sex could be compensated by being blessed with a literary-minded wife). Julia wanted to go to ballets and operas and plays and art exhibits (culture is fine when it represents elitism, but only up to a certain extent; you don't sell insurance with culture). At the beginning he loved Julia despite his rationalizations. After all, she was his wife and it was right and proper to love one's wife. When what he considered her aberrations began to annoy him, he began to worry. When his worrying didn't change anything, he became afraid. Afraid that he'd made a mistake. But he insisted to himself that he loved her because divorce was unthinkable. It represented an admission of grave error, something that applied only to the masses, the bohemians, the amoral movie stars. He was a respectable middle-class man moving up the ladder toward elitism, honest, God-fearing, patriotic. His co-workers looked on him as a happily married man and he couldn't, wouldn't do anything to tarnish his reputation. If Walter was aware of the word bourgeois, it didn't enter his conscious thought.

There was nothing he could do except wait and hope that Julia would become the kind of wife he wanted. He couldn't make her into the kind of wife he wanted because you can't make people into your imagined image. If they haven't enough sense to be what they should be, then wait until they do. Julia someday would. In the meantime, he would indulge her and be the kind of understanding, caring husband that she would undoubtedly begin to truly appreciate. In the meantime, Julia played the role of the good hostess, was beautiful and intelligent and on rare occasions fulfilled his night-time manhood needs. But rare became even rarer. Was she really that often sick? Stomach pains, headaches, colds, overly tired? This hurt him most of all. But he didn't say anything about it. Someday, he was sure, she would fulfill his fantasy.

But now, on the way home with his promotion and raise, he thought maybe it was time to say something. He felt strong, even powerful. Nothing inflates a man's ego more than success, and his promotion certainly proved he was a success. Success in one endeavor should certainly translate into success in another. As the train doors opened at 42nd Street he had second thoughts. Would Julia just smile and say "that's nice, Walter" when he told her of his promotion and raise and make him feel as inadequate as she did before the promotion and raise? Maybe this time he wouldn't play the role of a dog at her heels?

Walter followed the green lights to the Lexington Avenue shuttle of the IRT, passed the soda machines and marveled at the progress of American know-how that could mix three different-flavored drinks into one cup for a nickel. He quickly calculated. A minimum of two cents net profit on every cup, five hundred people per day at each machine, 10 machines at a station. $100 net per day from a station Put them in 100 stations in the system and that comes to $10,000 per day. Better things for better living. Walter smiled in satisfaction, as if somehow he was part of the soda machine entrepreneurship.

He tried not to think of anything as the shuttle rumbled under 42nd Street for four blocks, pulled up at the Lexington Avenue station. He followed the crowd through the long corridors, went upstairs, turned left past the change booth, hurried up the marble steps and felt much better and cleaner and safer in the polished whiteness of Grand Central. It was a few minutes to five o'clock and he rushed to the platform marked New York, New Haven and Hartford, got on the train, found himself a red-cushioned soft seat by a window, breathed a sigh of relief at being away from underground rabble, thought how nice it would be to just ride on commuter trains with educated, intelligent, mannered people who knew how to dress well and behave properly, bought a magazine from the old Negro man who carried a basket of candies, juices, sandwiches, newspaper and magazines around his neck. watched him go into the next car shouting his wares for sale as he had done for forty years, settled back, comfortable for the first time since leaving the office, and opened the magazine.

He wanted to read because he didn't want to think. His last serious thoughts were about speaking to Julia on his terms and he knew that if he thought further about it he might well back down and change his mind. He would probably change his mind, anyway, but he would try to be secure in his courage as long as possible.

Walter tried to read, but couldn't. What he lacked in life nagged at him. Some men of twenty-nine couldn't afford a baby, but he could and he wanted one. Sometimes Julia responded to his insistence on having a baby in a way that he thought she agreed. But when actually tried, she'd say no. Not now. Later. No way. There's only one way, goddamn it, and I'm man enough to do it. Only he would never say that to Julia. Maybe that's what's wrong? Maybe he needs to do as some of the guys at the office say. If a woman isn't acting the way she should, throw her on the bed and give it to her till she decides that's what she really wants. Give what to her? C'mon, Walter, just because your stomach is beginning to bulge, don't pretend you don't know what we're talking about. Walter blushed when he thought about it. He didn't like to be made fun of at the office. I should know better than to talk about personal things. Give it to her. He thought about that often. Maybe that was all right for them, but not for him. He was more refined than that. Still, there was only one way to make babies.

Walter switched his train of thought. Another thing that bothered him was Julia spending so much time in the city. Another thing he should talk to her about. Again. Whenever he raised the subject, Julia would accuse him of being insensitive and selfish. After all, Walter, you spend many evenings seeing clients, so why shouldn't I have the same privilege of doing what I want. He wanted to tell her that it was different because she was a wife. Like in that damned literature course he was required to take in college, a wife is a wife is a wife. Confused. Unintelligible. Insoluble. Yet, he knew what it meant to him. It meant something entirely different to Julia. He turned back to the magazine, began to read about whether Ted Williams was a better ballplayer than Rogers Hornsby.

The germ of the decision that began between 34th and 42nd Street resurrected itself by the time he reached New Rochelle. In this modern world of men like himself, nothing was really insoluble. Confused, perhaps, but not insoluble. When he reached his home he would, with much bravado, tell Julia about the raise and the promotion and what she must do from now on to be a good and proper wife. He got off the train, found where he had parked his car that morning, and drove home. He stopped for a moment at the front door, reaffirmed his decision, and walked in. He started toward the kitchen, called for Julia. The maid told him that she went upstairs to take a shower and nap, but if there was anything urgent she, the maid, should wake her. Walter hesitated a moment, looked at the dim yellow bulb inside the open refrigerator door casting shadows that strangely looked like subway pillars, told the maid not to bother Mrs. Mitchell, that he had nothing particular to tell her, got his business report letter off the entrance hall table, went into the living room, turned on the television set , and sat down on the couch to read about the latest trends in the wholesale and retail sales of dog foods.

CHAPTER 9
JOE

Walter tried not to think about Julia. Julia tried not to think about Joe. Joe tried not to think about Ruthie. Walter was busy with business statistics. Julia tossed uncertainly trying to sleep. Joe sat on the cornice of the roof outside his apartment window. He looked down at the people walking in the street eight floors below. He looked at the workers in the commercial buildings, in the offices, the stockrooms, the steamed-up workshops. He looked at the apartment windows with the shades up, at the men and women in the apartments and wondered if Ruthie was sleeping with Ben at that moment.

Joe could look up at the sky, at the little upright sticks of people below, at the hundreds of smeared windows, at the dozens of open ones, at the skirts and dresses that flowed back and forth across walking hips and thighs and tell himself that he owned the world and could have every and any skirt or dress or hip or thigh that passed and that he didn't give a damn. But he did. And that's what confused him.

It was dog eat dog and, in the jungle, it was the first one to the water hole that got the best and most to drink. In this jungle you had to pay a toll to get to the water hole and the only way to get it free was to sneak around at night and grab it. Water and whiskey and women. The guy who didn't give a damn got it. Joe always got it. He grew up having to fight for what he wanted, what he needed, and knew how. But now he faced something he didn't know how to fight. He always found a reason for what he did. He wondered what the hell could be the reason for his caring whether Ruthie slept with Ben or not?

He looked down at the street, muttered something about what's the use of being up above all the specks below when if you were one of the specks you'd be just as happy not knowing about anything more than an eight-hour day at work, three square meals and the same wife to lay in bed with every night, and he walked back toward his apartment.

The apartment was on the eighth floor of a building mainly occupied by offices and Joe would have preferred a place in a brownstone full of people, particularly women, of compatible attitudes and behavior, except for the roof outside his living-room window. That and the fact that almost all the offices closed at five and the elevator was the self-service kind and nobody was there to see or care who you brought up to your apartment or what you did there. When he first saw the apartment he was living in a rented room in an old building by the East River. They were tearing down his block to build a housing project. Since you can't get into a housing project unless you've saved no money and have a regular job earning a specified amount each week, he had to find a new place. He heard about this apartment from a friend, was reluctant to move into the printing and paper district where it was located, but grabbed it the moment he saw the setup. He was alone on the top floor, which had been used for storage but was converted to a large living room with a studio couch with an adjoining kitchen where he could cook his own meals and, of special importance, with a refrigerator where could store soda, ice cubes, and beer. He paid thirty bucks for one month's rent and signed a year's lease even if he had to go to work one week each month to pay the rent. Physical, automaton work, that is. Writing wasn't work. It was a racket. It was a racket because it was easy to do. It was a racket because only the big shots who controlled the writing game made any decent money out of it.

Joe stepped over the window sill, walked past the couch, stared dully at a chair with three days of socks, underwear and shirts on it, made a mental note to take it to a laundry within the next couple of days, picked up a bottle of bourbon from the top of a dresser at the side of the room, poured a half-glassful, started to the refrigerator to get some soda and ice, stopped, gulped down the bourbon, filled the glass half-full again, frowned at the emptying bourbon bottle, walked back to the window, stepped over the ledge and out onto the roof, his penthouse terrace, scraped a shoe inquisitively along the pebbled ground, sat on the curved sandstone cornice and laughed at the figures below. He lived in a castle and this was his castle tower.

But as he laughed, he frowned. While he intended to laugh at the people below, he realized that he was laughing at himself. He didn't want to because when he didn't take himself too seriously he felt he had no troubles. He didn't know exactly why he was laughing at himself and that made it a serious matter. His castle tower was his own Garden of Babylon, his Mount Everest where he could look down on an inferior and hostile world. He didn't know specifically why the people below were inferior, but he felt they had to be because if they weren't he would be like them and that meant he would be and have nothing. Even if it was a lie, he had to believe he had power. For him it was power over women. He knew that all the women he had lived with, all those he had spent one night with and wouldn't recognize again if he walked past them on the street, were part of his need. It wasn't an isolated need, it was part of his fight for survival. He fought for everything he could get. For everything he got. Some things came easy. So he took them. Women came easy. He counted the females on the street below and wondered how many of them he had had sex with. He wondered if he had made love to any of them. Maybe none. Having sex and making love were too entirely different things. He avoided making himself vulnerable.

He began to count in his mind the number of women he had slept with. It pleased him that so many anonymous faces became a jumble too big to count. He felt proud, elated at his accomplishments. But were they really accomplishments? He maintained that under the proper circumstances any woman will flop onto the nearest couch like she was made to do nothing else in her life. He wondered whether Ruthie was made for anything else. He knew she was and hoped she knew it.

He took a slug of bourbon, grinned as it began to trickle warmly down his throat, thought how nice it would be to be able to have bourbon any time one wanted, live in a real house with a real garden, a car in an attached garage and enough dough to go to a show any night in the week. Maybe it was Ruthie that made him think of that? He used to think about such things before, but never seriously. He would laugh at the poor bastards who lived like that. He was free. What the hell was the sense of having beautiful weekends in Central Park if you had to spend the rest of the week tied to a desk in some office? He wanted to laugh at the poor bastards locked in offices, but couldn't. His thoughts began to twist around like movie montages that became elongated and moved in and out of each other. In one frame he saw Ruthie lying in bed with Ben and for some strange reason he didn't hate Ben or Ruthie but hated himself and couldn't stand the picture and blacked it out. In another frame he saw Ruthie lying in bed with himself but he didn't feel exultation, accomplishment or pride. He kept this picture hazy in the background and created one of he and Ruthie sitting in a living room by a television set, then one of he and Ruthie in a car driving to the beach on a hot afternoon, then one of them playing in a yard with a couple of kids. These scenes disturbed him so he envisioned Ruthie in bed again, the hazy picture becoming clearer and clearer until it began to glow pleasantly. Was it because of another gulp of bourbon? Not fiery. Not white and not black. Just nice soft colors. Warm, comfortable, easy, relaxing. The word DULL in capital letters kept crossing the picture in his mind. He shook it off and the letters CENSORED replaced it, then disappeared.

He stared straight ahead and felt a strong wind and in his mind thought about a slowly moving ship with himself and Ruthie on it, the picture suddenly blown away by the shades of an apartment across the street being drawn down by a naked man, a naked woman behind him. Lucky sonofabitch, he thought: Three o'clock in the afternoon and he's going to knock off a piece. He tried to think of the ship again, but all he could see was himself lying in bed with a woman he had never seen before. He tried to change her into Ruthie, but couldn't. He gulped down the last of the bourbon. Damn it, he thought, that's the kind of thinking that could turn the entire world into a mass of flyspecks like those down there on the street.

Joe went back into the apartment. He stared at the pair of silk stockings draped over the top of the straight chair next to the bureau. He wondered what kind of a dead mind he had, thinking of everything and everybody but the woman he'd slept with for the past two years who walked out of his apartment only a half-hour earlier. He went to the refrigerator, got a couple of ice cubes from the bowl below the ice tray, poured some soda into a glass, drained the bourbon bottle of its last few neglected drops, gulped down the concoction, dropped the bottle into a paper-filled wastebasket and wondered what Julia was doing at that moment. Not because he really cared or wanted to, his mind insisted, but because it seemed to be some kind of duty to think of Julia at that moment.

He felt sorry for Julia. He almost felt sorry for himself. Julia was an enigma, if there ever had been such a thing as an enigma for Joe. He knew he had never really loved Julia, yet he had come closer to loving her than he had any other woman. He had slept with her longer than with any other woman. She must mean something to him, he thought. Not the one-night stand or the weekend when the husband was away on a business trip. She had almost become a part of him. But not really. Nothing was real to him except the jungle. As part of the jungle Julia was real. As a person unto herself she remained only a symbol. A symbol of something he needed. He had it and still wasn't satisfied. Like the bottle of bourbon, his for the taking, enjoying every bit of it, emptying it, and dropping it into a wastebasket. There was an analogy there, but Joe didn't see it. If it were any other woman, he would have been objective enough to see it, use it as the basis for a short story, with the bottle of liquor as the tag line. But he didn't see it.

He picked up the bourbon bottle from the wastebasket, put it on top of the dresser. He dug around the papers in the wastebasket, came up with the cap for the bottle. With much ceremony he screwed it on, smiled as he thought of the descriptive action, placed the bottle in the center of the dresser, reflecting squarely in the dresser-top mirror. He didn't know why he did this. Only a vague premonition of something he had to do. As if the Eumenides of Greek drama were after him and he had no choice but to follow an inevitable path, performing symbolically what would eventually happen in reality. He thought about that a moment. That seemed to make a little sense. Julia was kind of a symbol. He remembered that he had thought that before, pushed away thoughts of the Furies and the analogy. Analogies were bad, anyway. They only brought into focus other ideas that might, on some theoretical plane, have a connection or a parallel, albeit never perpendicular or intersecting with the main problem. His mind spun.

Joe never had time for anything but the main problem. Why bother with theory when the practical application was hard enough to deal with? On the bottle of bourbon was a picture of an old man. Old Grandad. He looked quite pleasant and unconcerned about life. What did he know about real life, about a New York where figuratively and sometimes literally every guy and his brother were ready to knife you in the back? Unless you knifed them first. He thought a moment and modified his conclusion. That was the code in elementary and high school, when he had to con every guy who came long into buying him something or giving him something so he could save up enough money to eventually go to college. Now it was a little different. But not much. It was more civilized to first take the knife away and then go after your enemy on even terms. To be a writer you have to go into character. To get into character you have to understand people. If you understand someone, you don't knife him. Not usually, anyway. You might want him to be thrown into a booby hatch or into solitary confinement or put a gun in his hand

and convince him to fight the enemies who are attacking you. Maybe Old Grandad had the right idea—was the right idea—after all. Joe searched the shelves above the refrigerator, found a forgotten bottle of bourbon, still half-full, looked at his thoughts as if they were written by a skywriter in big smoky letters right in front him, muttered "for Chrissakes, Templeton, what the hell is the matter with you?" and took an undiluted swig of brain poison.

When you get a little bit to drink, enough to put a cloud into your thinking but not enough to block it entirely, you're in a perfect rhythm for what appears to be profound thought. Why? Because your emotion begins to grow and your logic begins to wear thin. Any given person is usually too logical or too emotional. Rarely is there the median between the two that represents the truth and allows the person to know what he or she really wants to know and would be happiest knowing. Joe took another drink and consciously opened his eyes wide to take in what he felt was that median state. He put down the glass, went to the end table next to his bed, swooped up some papers sand magazines, threw onto the bed a pamphlet entitled "The Philosophy of Art of Karl Marx" that Jack Evans had given him to read, knew he would never read it but would tell Jack the next time he saw him that he had and that it was full of crap. He walked over to the low bookcase next to the dresser, took his typewriter from the top of it, cradled it under one arm, scooped up some paper from the shelf below, took it all to the end table, sat down on the bed. When your mind is numbed of its subjectivity you are free to concentrate on the typewriter and begin to write about things other than yourself. A higher pinpoint of direction. He put a sheet of paper in the typewriter and began to write.

Inspiration, that's what he needed. Hell. All he had to do was to sit down and do it. What will it be? Something easy and commercial or something hard and profound? At the moment he couldn't think deeply and profoundly. He felt he should be able to, but he couldn't. Maybe he didn't want to?

And he didn't feel drunk enough to be commercial. He decided he'd write about sex. You could always sell a good story about and with a lot of sex, he reasoned. Let's see now, a story about a guy who is sleeping with one woman but is in love with another woman. The first woman is in love with him, but he isn't in love with her. The second woman, who he loves, is in love with another guy. The problem the author will have to resolve is whether the second woman is sleeping with the other guy. If she isn't, then maybe everybody lives happily ever after. If she is, then everybody is immediately sent off to purgatory. Shit, he muttered, too trite for anyone to believe, and he tore the sheet out of the typewriter, crumpled it and sent it flying toward the wastebasket. Two points.

He knew what was bothering him now, bourbon or no bourbon. He glared at the bottle, snickered at the glass, laughed scornfully to himself, knowing that the liquor didn't do a damn bit of good. He stood up, walked quickly to the window, stepped out onto his castle tower, and looked at the people below. He told himself that they must be happy or at least think they were. Maybe not in the way he would like to be, but happier than he thought he should be. He went inside again, to the top drawer of the dresser, fished inside and came back with a bank book. The Farmers Trust Company of New York. An oxymoron of a name, he thought. Inside the bank book in the deposit column: four hundred dollars.

I can write, he told himself, looking at the proof. Even if only a lousy pulp novel. He had gotten that four hundred dollars for a two-installment short novel in Argosy magazine about a guy who lived on the east side of New York who wanted to marry a dame from the west side of 59th Street. The guy ended up marrying a dame from the east side of the east side and the dame married a guy from the west wide of the west side and everybody lived happily ever after where they belonged. specially Templeton, who reopened his bank account with four hundred smackers.

Withdrawn, fifty bucks. Rent money, food for a week, a concert, and some beers afterwards. Counting another fifty for the rest of the month, that left three hundred dollars. He speculated: Buy some clothes, a few presents for friends, live easily for a few weeks, and pay for a marriage license. He jerked away from that train of thought. Marriage license! If it were someone else thinking this, Joe would call him a crazy shithead. He felt afraid at the thought but couldn't or wouldn't admit what he was afraid of. Maybe he didn't know? He was thinking what he felt, not what he thought he should be thinking. He tried not to say it, but the word "Ruthie" kept building up in his throat. The thoughts pushed at him. He could live in that apartment with a wife, get a job, maybe with an advertising agency or with one of those new television production companies or in the public relations office of a department store. After a while he could make enough money to move to Long island, get a house, a car, have some kids. The three hundred would get him started. He found himself saying this out loud, looked in the mirror to see if was really himself talking. He watched his mouth move back and forth, saying swords that were alien to him. A Doppelganger talking. Not Joe Templeton. "You're a crazy bastard," he shouted at the mirror.

The life he was leading was the life he wanted to lead. He stayed in front of the mirror, talking, trying to convince himself. He reveled in his own eloquence. "Think of the poor suckers walking around down there. From eight to five. Every day except Sunday. No mornings, no afternoons of their own, and too tired at night to do anything but sleep. Dead, but they don't know it. A dead fish, a machine, an inanimate piece of ..." He was going to say shit, thought that word sounded too deliberate and ended with "... crap." He lectured himself. "Not you, Joe. Not somebody on a treadmill going around in a circle, not knowing where you're going, never getting anywhere, but happy because motion gives you the pretense of movement." He wasn't exactly sure what that meant.

Inside of Joe Templeton was a gnawing dissatisfaction. An unhappiness. The words flew at him, at first in a positive manner. "There is nothing really wrong with you. You just need security. You need someone to hang onto, to give your life more meaning." Then the words took a negative turn. "Unhappy, Joe? Here's another phone

number. And another. Call up Amy, Mable, Joanne, Susie, Kate."
Actions are louder than words. Julia stretched across your bed, he
told himself, your body naked on top of hers, your flesh etching into
hers, a helluva lot better than hearts and flowers. But he knew Julia
was not enough. She was plenty, but not enough. Ruthie was hearts
and flowers. She was the cozy little nest and the garden small by
the waterfall and the little home for two and the soft and sweet of
a nursery. And once it was in his consciousness his thought about
a nursery was not an unhappy one. He decided he needed security
and felt that Ruthie was it. Did he love her? He should, he thought.
But why? Maybe because she was different. Different from the open
minds and open mouths and open legs. Ruthie was the opposite of
slut and whore and lewd thoughts and indecent language of the life
Joe knew and led. He had to get away from it. He was caught in
a whirlpool of his own making and had to pull out before he was
drowned. Ruthie was the lifeboat on the vast sea and he grabbed
at her to stay afloat. He decided that it was Ruthie that he wanted.
Having done so, he now had to worry about her and Ben. If he was
going into a new life with Ruthie, it had to be as a clean slate. A
virginal Joe, a virginal Ruthie. It didn't occur to him that before he
jumped into a new life he had to do something about the old one.

Joe had to think now, make plans. Maybe continue to convince
himself. He sat on the edge of the bed, laid back on it, his feet
dangling to the floor. He shifted down, firmly planting them on the
floor. Solid foundation, yet floating in the clouds. He'd need a solid
foundation for Ruthie. He wanted it for her. He reached to the side
table, got a cigarette, lit it. Did Ruthie love him? She really doesn't,
he admitted. Did she admire him? That would be a good start, he
reasoned. By now she must be getting tired of chasing after Ben.
How long can a woman keep after a man, not getting the response
she wanted? He was sure there was no response. Ben wouldn't fuck
Lady Godiva if she rode into his bedroom on her white horse. Joe
laughed. Sure, she should be ready for me by now. But what if Ruthie
and Ben ...? Joe put the uncomfortable thought out of his mind. He

told himself instead that it wouldn't be hard for Ruthie to fall in love with him, to go away with him, settle down with him. He decided he would call her, take her to dinner, a show, and then right home. He'd play it safe. Dinner, show, home. Win, place, win.

Joe jumped up from the bed, ground his cigarette out in the sink. Why did Julia suddenly come into his mind? She wouldn't take his decision easily, maybe not at all. But couldn't he get rid of her like he did everyone else? Be a boor, tell he's tired of her, be cruel. Drop her in the wastebasket. Like the others, down the drain. After two years with her, it wouldn't be so easy. The jungle taught you to be unmerciful, but how much of a bastard could a guy be?

He didn't want to think anymore. It was beginning to hurt. He wanted to get away from the problem, from the confusion. He went to the telephone, flipped over a few pages in a notebook, picked up the phone, dialed a number, asked for Helen, muttered something about telling her to call Joe when she came in, then said never mind and put the phone down. Maybe if he did some writing he'd get the disturbing thoughts out of his system? He went to the typewriter, started to write, but all that came out was "Ruthie, Julia, Joe, what for, why" followed by a bunch of dots. He gave that up, picked up his latest copy of Writer's Digest, found a market for half-hour television scripts with a twist ending, went back to the typewriter, but now nothing at all would come out. Not even the little dots.

The circle tightened as it went round and round and if you stayed in the middle you were crushed and if you kept walking around the edge you fell off into the unknown. He had to jump. He got up and went to the dresser, picked up the bottle of bourbon, started to drop it in the wastebasket, glared at it, then smiled at it and purposefully, calmly, slowly began to drink it down.

CHAPTER 10
BEN

Ben, like Joe, lived in the Village. His apartment was less dramatic than Joe's. No penthouse, no terrace, no castle tower. But it was larger, more conventional. It was on Eldridge Street in a brownstone building. Enter through the front door, open the inner door with a key, walk down a hallway toward the back of the building, use another key to slide open the twin doors into a large living room. A small bedroom was off to one side of the living room and a kitchen and bathroom off to the other. The only item of luxury—and this is relative, depending upon what one considers a luxury—was a record player capable of accommodating the new LPs, the long-playing records, on top of a low bookcase in one corner of the room. Next to it was a pile of record albums. Below, in the bookcase, books neatly lined the shelves, pressing against each other from one end to the other. Perhaps the most appealing item in the apartment, consciously excluding the bed, was a large, deep-cushioned easy chair in the center of the living room, with a hassock for tired feet. At that moment Ben would have welcomed that easy chair. Ben was just finishing his almost-daily tour of publishing companies, mostly on Fifth Avenue, with a sore back from standing in crowded elevators, a sore buttocks from waiting on hard benches in outer offices, a sore disposition from constant refusals to let him meet with assistant editors, and sore feet from just too much walking.

Ben stepped out of the elevator at his last stop of the day, didn't even notice the long-haired blonde who brushed against and past him in her hurry to get home, and walked quickly out of the lobby and into the open. He needed some fresh air. He stopped outside, leaned against the side of the building, lit a cigarette. He felt a strange sensation on his back, turned around and saw he had been leaning against the publishing company sign carved in marble letters on a gold-plated surface, set majestically into the side of the 50-story building. He remembered the man who some months before had offered him a job with a small, now growing advertising company and told him that although the pay was small, the future was big and that someday that advertising concern expected to build its own 50-story building. He thought about the man, looked at the sign again, and moved away feeling he needed more fresh air.

Ben turned left, walked up Fifth Avenue. He saw the man on the corner selling hot chestnuts, the woman on the next corner selling small flower corsages. He looked at the faces of the people he passed going in the opposite direction, hurrying to do shopping, hurrying to an office, hurrying to deliver a message, hurrying home to a cold-water flat, hurrying home to a Fifth Avenue penthouse, hurrying to close a million-dollar deal. Sometimes he realized with embarrassment that he was staring at another person's face as intently as he was, the person staring back at him, some amused, some angry. One man looked back at him, smiled, and winked. He shook his head, smiled, and walked quickly past, looking straight ahead. But he couldn't help looking at faces again, deliberately trying to add each one to his memory as a future character in some novel he had not yet even thought of writing. In front of him was the Empire State Building. He didn't even look at it. Everyone else followed its outline toward the sky. He just looked at people. He was a writer. Writing was about people. If he was a writer, he asked himself, why wasn't he selling anything? Why couldn't he really write the way writers who publish million-selling books write. He continued to walk, trying not to stare at people, but he couldn't help doing so.

He walked up Fifth Avenue, toward Central Park. He'd stop looking at people and look at fishes in the lake. Fifth Avenue was a crazy avenue. Bookstores and record stores for the literati and music connoisseurs, and Tiffany's and Steuben glass and Bergdorf-Goodman and the Plaza for the filthy rich. And beggars in torn clothes, some blind and some lame, seeking a nickel or a dime for a cup of coffee or a beer or a place to flop when night comes. He muttered to himself, "a crazy pattern of patchwork lives," thinking he should remember the phrase to use in a future story, then dismissing it as said so many times before that it was now hackneyed, and he tried to put it out of his mind. He wanted to find the kinds of words that won Pulitzer Prizes.

A great thing, the Pulitzer Prize, Ben thought. Each year a bunch of elite people got together at Columbia University and decided who had contributed the most important work in their field to the artistic growth of America. These people certainly wouldn't appreciate phrases like "crazy pattern of patchwork lives." These judges were highly intelligent, educated people, weren't they, some wealthy, all of good social standing. That certainly made them the arbiters of taste, the arbiters of art in America, didn't it? That seemed to be an anachronism, Ben thought. There were millions of people in America with thousands of different tastes, experiences, understanding, thousands of judgments of what was art and what was schlock, what was happy and what was sad, what was good and what was bad. He wondered how many streetcleaners, union organizers, salesladies and bartenders, schoolteachers and students, priests and prostitutes there were on the Pulitzer Prize Committee, representing the broad spectrum of America. He knew the answer. How do you write for the people when you are judged by people who are not the people? He had no answer.

He passed the Empire State Building, still not looking up, his eyes following his footsteps in front of him, unconsciously stepping with alternate strides on the pavement cracks in the sidewalk. He tried to avoid getting back to his thoughts about the Pulitzer Prize. Yet, like a sailor who has sighted land from a ship drifting in the ocean, he was pleased with himself. This was what Jack Evans had told him, only in different words. He tried to take Jack Evans with several grains of salt. When someone believes too strongly in something, beware. Strength means force. Force can lead to violence. Violence might mean destruction. Ergo, belief is destruction. The words made him think of a man named Joe McCarthy. No, not the Yankees manager, he told himself.

He crossed 36th Street and berated himself for tangential thinking and tried to get back to what Jack Evans had said about people and art. Jack always seemed to be a step ahead of him in discussing serious issues. "They tell writers that the people can't judge," Jack had said. "That they don't have the education, don't have the time, don't have the money, don't have the understanding, don't have the inclination, don't have the appreciation. Which is true. And so was Franco true. And Hitler true. But that doesn't make it good. Or even acceptable. So they turn the arts over to people with Park Avenue Penthouses and toss in a few college professors with a sixty-buck-a-week income to give their deliberations an aura of legitimacy. Should we be satisfied with that? Because Mussolini fed the people from a socialist kitchen with a teaspoon, were they fed enough? We've got to write for the people, not the elite judges. We've got to publish books that ordinary people can enjoy, learn from, be stimulated by, and be persuaded by, enough to take action in their own best interests. Action that may be inimical to the elite who decide what books, what art, what music, what plays should get Pulitzer prizes."

How involved in the non-literary world should a writer get? He wasn't sure, but whenever he tried to discuss it with Jack, he found himself on the defensive. Maybe because Jack was always so quick to go on the offensive. He would insist that that was all well and good, but too many people can't put out a buck-twenty for a play or two-fifty for a book when they have to fight for enough dough to buy a new pair of shoes or go to a dentist or buy a quart of milk for hungry kids, and he would figuratively pat himself on the shoulder for being a liberal. And then Jack would tell him not to stop there, but if he really believed that the people deserved a fair share of the good things in life, then he would join organizations and take actions that would get him called a dirty political name in the New York Journal-American and The Chicago Tribune. Was Jack right? He didn't want to think about it further. There was something shivering cold about being forced to stop thinking, about forcing yourself to stop thinking.

Ben grew up with an independent mind. A mind that could think for itself, that told him not to be afraid of going beyond the boundaries of the obvious or the acceptable. He told the truth as he saw it, to himself and to the world. He knew what he wanted and wasn't afraid to say he wanted it. And yet, after a certain point, he felt uneasy. He felt afraid. He passed the public library, the lions guarding the front daring him to enter that world of passion and ideas. He wondered what all those successful writers thought as they wrote all those books. Was Voltaire afraid as he wrote plays satirizing the status quo? Was Marx afraid as he called for a new order of society? Was Paine afraid as he called for a revolution? They wrote to the people about the people, for the people. Ben knew he could do that. Why didn't he? What was he afraid of? Anyone who ever put their hand on a hot stove or got hit in the face with a policeman's club knew what it was to be afraid. Afraid, but because they knew what they were afraid of, also not afraid. Was Ben really afraid or was it simply valid emotion when facing something new, something not yet experienced?

Why couldn't he find an arrow pointing the way to a landing and then another arrow to another landing. Every time he tried to do something it was like walking in a circle and he ended up where he started. Great authors, really great authors, he told himself, don't go around in circles. Because when the world moved on they would have been left behind. An interesting thought. Maybe he could use it in a story someday? He crossed 47th Street, passed a men's clothing store, a record shop advertising records half-off for out of-towners, and stopped at a used-book shop with a long counter forming a circle in the center of the store with walls of book shelves surrounding the counter. He watched a woman enter, walk briskly around the counter past thousands of years of culture, and come out right where she entered. Is that what he was doing with his life? Sometimes a customer knew exactly what he or she wanted, chose it, and exited the circle with confident satisfaction.

Ben didn't know where he was going. Sometimes he thought he knew but wasn't sure. He was afraid. Of himself. Of pushing forward. Without a base from which to operate. He was uncertain. He tried to analyze who he was and began to see differences between his personal life and his artistic life.

Once he found a basis for a personal life, he could work on the artistic level. But to find a sound level for the one, he must find a sound level for the other. A person lives in the world around him. Is that where you start? Know your place in society? But to do that you've got to know yourself. Something that had earlier passed by his thinking passed by again. If he could just grasp it and hold it!

Was it women? At 54th Street he stopped and looked at the posters in front of the Ziegfeld theatre. Pretty girls in revealing costumes. Whenever one has a problem, just think about women. He thought about Ruthie and wondered. He thought about Julia and wondered.

Ben had slept with Ruthie and this had given him more self-confidence. It had given him a feeling of strength, of manhood, of a driving away of the fear of his own insecurity. Fear to Ben was something just below the surface. He understood physical fear but didn't understand the fear you don't know or can't see. He was afraid of himself, afraid that he didn't have the guts, the know-how, the what-it-takes to make the success he told himself he could make. Only he couldn't admit it because he couldn't see it. All he knew was that something was lacking. He needed to be sure of what he was. He needed to accomplish things. That these things would be only props to prove outwardly what inwardly was already there was immaterial. Not inconsequential, but of little relevance because it happened to a million Ben's the same way and sometimes they didn't find the truth till years later and sometimes they never found it. When Ben spoke to Joe about his insecurities Joe told him to get a girl and sleep with her. And he did. He got Ruthie. Ruthie was warm, understanding, intelligent, good, kind, sweet. As he walked along Fifth Avenue Ben picked out the faces of different women and tried to tell whether they were like Ruthie or not. Ruthie wanted the simple things of life. Nothing out on a limb overlooking a waterfall of diamonds, but the security of a man who was stronger than she, who she could admire and, in her own way, follow the dictates of society that, as a woman and wife, she would love, honor, and obey. Ben stopped in front of a bar on 56th Street and looked in the window, into a mirror, a green cloth across the bar window making it reflect like a highly polished surface. He saw a face that he decided was strong because Ruthie loved him, honored him, and depended on him. A man who had the ability to prove his strength with his writing. Before, he wrote because he wanted to. Now, he told himself, he would write because he had to, as well. Had he solved the puzzle? By sleeping with Ruthie, by taking from her what he wanted, by doing with her what he cared to, he felt strong. His body quivered as he thought about Ruthie in bed. When he would reach down and touch her naked breasts with the tips of his fingers and they would rise up to him, and when he would touch them again and her whole body would move in an arc, stretching toward his, this was a verification of his strength.

But what could he do with his mind, his brain, his pen? The whole world could reach out toward him. Ruthie was the proof.

He wrote profusely and well. Then why was he still dissatisfied? Shadows passing across a page, type-letters looking like grey outlines rather than solid black marks. What Ben didn't know was where his strength really lay. It lay in himself. He sought it in Ruthie. What he found from Ruthie produced long stories and short novels for True Romances and True Confessions and Argosy and even sometimes the Saturday Evening Post. Ben made a good living that way. A short story paid 300 dollars, a short novel with a big magazine five hundred to a thousand. The apartment on Eldridge Street soon had a closet with six suits and four pairs of shoes and dozens of ties.

As he walked up Fifth Avenue with a manuscript under his arm, a novel that took him three months and three hundred pages, he wondered if it was enough. He wondered if Ruthie was enough. He wondered when, if ever, he would write his Pulitzer Prize novel. The street darkened, a premonition of s chilling rain, and Ben wondered how warm or cool were the electric blankets and the bleached blondes in the Penthouse apartments stretching all around on top of him above 57th Street. A horse-drawn droshky passed him on the street. Horse-shit, he thought. I'm doing better than most writers. Why worry? He stopped walking, sat on a bench along the 59th street side of Central Park and began to run. He ran from himself and he ran from Ruthie. He ran toward Julia.

For Ruthie, Ben was strong. She was his sweetheart, could be his wife. For Julia, Ben would be weak. She should be his mistress. He mulled this over in his mind, thinking of it seriously, thinking of the conversations with Julia, of how he had said he loved her. How she hadn't encouraged him, and yet hadn't discouraged him. He got knots in his stomach when he thought of Julia making love with Joe. Sometimes, when the four of them were together, he wanted to speak up and tell them that they were all crazy. That they were sleeping with the wrong persons. He cracked his knuckles. When he found something, he didn't believe but wanted to believe, had to believe, he cracked his knuckles. There was an incongruity, and each finger twitched as he bent it back, squeezing the skin. The sound of a passing wheelchair made him open his eyes. He sat upright on the bench. A little old man, crippled, sat in the shopworn wheelchair, pushed by a younger man, both shabbily dressed. Both probably homeless, he concluded, looking for a place in the park to squat for the night. He felt sorry for them. Sorry and superior. He heard the significant words of an intellectual conversation and the old man and the younger man both laughed uproariously. They were making the most of where they were in the world. Ben thought of the word strength. It had a meaning here, something important that he knew he should grasp. He listened to the laughter fade as the wheelchair turned the corner. He got up and began to walk toward the lake to see the fishes. Suddenly he stopped. How long would a mistress be enough?

CHAPTER 11

RUTHIE

Ruthie was no longer the kind of girl who picks up the phone and you say wrong number. She had learned something. Like the girl named Fuchs in a midwestern college whose professor used the usual pronunciation, fewks, when he called on her for the first time in his freshmen class. She corrected him and gave him the pronunciation that made him blush every time he called the role during the year, fucks. The following year, her sophomore year, she got the same teacher and he started the session with a roll call. This time she corrected him again and told him not to use the pronunciation she had used the previous year but the one used in polite circles, fewks. "How come you used one pronunciation last year and a different one this year," he asked? Why, Professor," she answered, "don't you think I learned anything after a year of college?"

Ruth had learned a lot after one year of Ben. One year of Ben coupled with the last few months of Joe. One fading, the other growing stronger. If she thought about it, she wouldn't be quite sure from whom she had learned the most. With Ruthie things were still for the most part cut and dried. Either it was this way or it wasn't. It would have been difficult for her to take her relations with Ben and Joe, analyze them and see how much she had learned from each and from both. It had been a gradual process of maturing. From a girl who thought she should be interested in life. The unfortunate part was that she hadn't learned why.

The phone rang. Ruthie reached over the typewriter in the office where she worked and answered it. It was for Mr. Slovin. She said that Mr. Slovin was out, asked if there was a message, was told that there was none. She turned the carriage in her typewriter, picked up a piece of paper, looked at the heading in black print "S. Slovin, Contractor," put the sheet in the typewriter and began to type from a notepad a letter she had taken down. She wrote "Dear Sir," double spaced, without thinking, double spaced again before writing anything. She realized what she had done, laughed softly to herself, then playfully moved the carriage arm back and forth, double spacing down the length of the letter until the paper rolled right out of the carriage. She amused herself. Lately she was forced to amuse herself more and more. With little things. A year ago, working as a secretary in a contractor's office was part of the routine. A person had to eat. To eat, a person needed a paycheck at the end of each week. Working was the only way to get it. Certainly, it wasn't as happy as walking through Central Park on sunny afternoons or spending a rainy day in the New York Paramount. But those things weren't considered. Work was work. Even if you disliked it because it became routine you grew not to notice it enough to dislike it. At least, that was the benevolent interpretation. Whether it meant pulling and pushing plugs for eight hours at a telephone company or standing at a counter in a large department store and wrapping the same article the same way and seeing the same people and writing the same sales slips or walking into the same office every morning and taking the same dictation and writing "Dear Sir" and skipping two spaces on the paper, it was a living.

Sometimes you had neither enough money nor time for yourself. You'd get out of the office at five-thirty. By the time you got to the subway, pushed into the crowds and through the crowds, waited for the West End Express, got off at Flatbush Avenue in Brooklyn and walked home it was six-thirty. If you lived at home as Ruthie did your mother had cleaned the house and dinner was ready. Even so, by the time you ate, showered, and dressed, it was eight-thirty. If you had a date you went downtown. Downtown Brooklyn or downtown

New York. By the time you got into the movies it took another hour. Out by twelve. Unless you want to start getting lines and bags under your eyes, you need at least eight hours sleep a day. Ruthie settled for six and a half. No time for anything but going home. Seven o'clock in the morning is an early hour to get up. But a necessary one if you have to be at the office at eight-thirty. On Saturday night it was different. No work on Sunday and you could stay up as long as you wanted. One night a week of freedom. Unless the rest of the week you didn't catch up with washing, ironing, letter writing and the thousand and one things a girl has to do.

But at the end of the week there was the paycheck. Thirty-five dollars is hardly enough to live on. But everyone knows women don't have to have much to live on. They get everything paid for by men, don't they? Some don't. Fortunately, Ruthie had little expense. She contributed a few dollars toward the rent and a few dollars toward the food for her family. She probably didn't have to. Her father was not rich, but as the owner of a small business he made a good income. She did it because she had to feel independent. In some societies pride and independence are measured not by the individual but by money. Ruthie skimmed off the top of her paycheck and was independent. Until she walked along Fifth Avenue at lunch time and noticed rich furs and fine silks and sparkling jewelry. She wondered how many thirty-five dollars it would take to buy a Persian Lamb coat or a Silver Fox Muff. She looked at price tags that had three zeros on them. She tried to visualize a stack of pieces of paper, each numbered "35", and wondered how high they would reach. Most of the time she would laugh and forget about such childish thoughts. But sometimes, after looking in the shop windows, she would walk back to work and pass women in silver fox capes and dark glasses and slacks walking little dogs also wearing silver fox capes. And sometimes at night she would dream about it and see the pile of papers marked "35" with a beautiful coat resting on top of the pile, balancing precariously at the very tip and she would reach for it. The pile didn't look very big until she began to reach and then she found that no matter how high she reached it was always over her head. And little dogs with silver fox capes would stand around and bark derisively at her. But those were uncommon dreams, dreams that belonged to the past. A past of at least twelve months. Now they occurred only every once in a while. And they took different shapes, so it was hard to tell what they really meant. She tried to think about other things. Things that didn't seem out of her grasp. Things that didn't mean eight hours a day in an office and four hours a day of freedom. She thought about Ben and Joe and how they lived and what they did. The routine became dull, deadly dull. She looked for more and more ways to amuse herself.

She put the typing paper back in the carriage of the typewriter and began to write. She skipped the right spaces and wrote the right things and signed S. Slovin and folded the letter and typed an envelope and sealed the envelope and tossed it into a little wire basket on her desk marked "outgoing." She began to type another letter, looked at her watch, noted the time, went through the same procedure, and noted the time again. How long did it take her to type an average letter? Twenty minutes? Fifteen minutes if she concentrated. Thirty-two letters a day? She wondered whether the robot machine she had seen at the New York World's Fair a dozen years before could do any better. She looked at her watch: three o'clock. Another two hours. She wondered whether she should stop typing and start filing for a change of pace. She walked to the window, looked out, couldn't even see the street below, just the figures moving past windows in the building across the street. She looked up and saw that the sun was shining. The world looked so much better in the sunshine. Central Park, Riverside Drive, a roof on the eighth floor outside a Village apartment. She thought about Joe and how he must be enjoying the sun, sitting on top of his penthouse terrace, sipping from a tall glass filled with whiskey and lemon juice. She would like to be there with him. He knew what he wanted. He enjoyed himself for eight hours and then for eight hours more. And he got the better things in life. Music and art and theatre and literature. She knew a little about them now. She knew what they were and she enjoyed them. She wanted more of them. She knew that she could get it from Joe. Joe wasn't afraid of life. Joe would go out and fight. He was strong. She needed that kind of strength. She was a simple girl. A nice girl. A lonely girl. She saw a woman run past a window of an office directly across the street, saw an elderly man stop, reach his hands toward her, wave his hands furiously, then begin to run from the window in the direction the girl had gone. She looked at her watch, figured that Slovin would be back soon, and went back to her desk. She spread several dictated letters in front of her, leaned over them with a pen, pretended that she was busy. She was busy, inside, trying to figure out why she continued to think about Joe. She should have thought of Ben. It was Ben who she had fallen in love with. Sweet Ben. Intelligent Ben. Talented Ben. Kind Ben. Ben, the man who was the most perfect she had ever met. The man who she had been sleeping with for almost a year. The man she thought she was in love with.

She had learned a lot in that last year. She learned that love wasn't everything that it seemed to be at first. Ben was perfect because he was the most perfect one she had known. She saw herself as a little girl who wanted something. He offered it. Now that she had it, she wanted something more. She didn't know what it was. A mink coat or Central Park on a sunny afternoon? Perhaps it was both. A little bit of security with something added. It was no longer enough to go to the theatre at night and then call home and say that she was staying with a girlfriend, and go to Ben's apartment and make love with him. It wasn't enough to take the elevated train to Bronx Park zoo with Ben on a Sunday and laugh together and eat peanuts and throw a few to the elephants when the keepers weren't watching. It wasn't enough to go to Ben's apartment for dinner and pick up her napkin and find a gift of jewelry or move her chair and find a book or open the dish cupboard to set the table and find a record.

At first, sex dominated everything. She had thought to keep her virginity until marriage, but combined with Ben's caring, love-

making became more than sex. No guilt or regret. At first like
fireworks on the Fourth of July, sex began to hold less and less interest
for her. In many ways Ben was weak. He would want her to take
the initiative and make love to him. He would become moody and
get up and wander around the room and let her lie in bed waiting to
feed his body. Sometimes it happened. Sometimes she would go to
sleep and wake up in the morning and might just as well have gone
home to Brooklyn. Ben spoke to her of many things. Some things
she understood. Some things she didn't. He was vague. He wanted
something but didn't know what. A dream. A prize. He needed a
push, strength, someone to show him and lead the way. She couldn't.
She didn't have what he wanted. Though she loved him, she came
to know that her love wasn't enough for him. Now she questioned
whether he was enough for her.

Joe was lost, but in the shadows he saw some sunlight. He knew
how to fight for what he wanted. Joe was strong and needed just a
little help. Ben was weak and needed a lot of help. She remembered
the first time she had a serious conversation with Joe. At a restaurant
with a juke box. Julia and Ben were dancing. She told Joe that Ben
was going places and needed her, that she loved him and could help
him. Joe listened and could only respond that he needed someone
like her, too, to help him. She didn't think he actually meant it. She
remembered another conversation, not long afterward, when Julia
had to go to an out-of-town insurance convention with Walter. Joe
asked her to spend the nights with him while Julia was away. Not
just for sex, he said, but because he needed someone like her and he
knew that she wanted to be needed. She thought about it a moment
before she said no. She wanted to be needed but not depended upon
and that was the difference between Ben and Joe. Joe shrugged off
her answer as if it didn't make any difference to him one way or
the other. Reconsidering Joe's request flashed across her mind, then
stuck in her consciousness. She looked at her watch and saw it was
four o'clock and decided to do another letter. She didn't really want
to, but she didn't want to keep on thinking. She was coming to a

decision. One she didn't want to have to make. She looked out the window and it began to get dark. It clouded over quickly and there were a few flashes of lightning. Then some thunder. Then some rain. Windows were being shut in an unrhythmic pattern in the building across the street by large busts in yellow sweaters and thick arms in rolled up sleeves. It began to grow darker, as if the world was ending, and she wondered if that's what would happen if she stayed with Ben. She thought of the large busts in the yellow sweaters and looked at her own. She avoided a comparison. She thought of the arms in the rolled-up sleeves and saw Ben's, his hands on her breasts. The sky began to grow light again, the few drops of rain disappeared and in a few moments the sun began to shine. She felt warmer inside. A mixture of security and happiness at the same time. The sun meant strength and confidence and something ecstatic. She thought about Joe.

CHAPTER 12
JACK

There is one part of New York that most New Yorkers don't know about. It is the pulse that lies in the center of the city. It is the little circle in the middle of eight million people that keeps beating away and making New York, whatever else it may be, a city that keeps moving and moving and moving and always forward. The body is the dead weight, to hold back until it feels within it is the sting of life and movement. Before this inner feeling becomes large enough and strong enough to become sharp enough, there must be something else that keeps the body from drying up. This is the pulse. Jack Evans was part of this pulse.

It is a group of people who hold meetings, who march in protests, who distribute leaflets, who make speeches from street corners, who stop people to talk to them, who go to parties and tell their friends of ideas and happenings and unwanted facts. These are the people who dedicate themselves to the one-third of a nation they believe are still ill-housed, ill-fed and without medical care. These are the people who are called Commies and Reds and Bolsheviks and Nigger lovers and Black Jews and socialist sonsofbitches and make headlines in the New York Daily News and Journal-American.

Jack Evans was one of these people. He got out of the subway station at 51st Street and 7th Avenue, looked at the people around him, saw them as the body and pulse of New York. If anybody asked him to define them, he'd half-apologetically use terms like liberty and freedom and justice. He would talk about rat-infested apartments and babies with bloated stomachs and men walking the streets with torn soles on their shoes, looking for jobs And he'd talk about people with yachts and limousines and summer villas, people with plenty of plenty, as in the song from the musical, "Show Boast," keeping a lock on their door while they're out making more.

It was half-past eleven and Jack hurried. He was late. He walked up to Eighth Avenue, stepping in long, quick strides. He passed the small theater on 45th Street where an independent theater group, Peoples Drama, was presenting the play "They Shall Not Die," about the true-life false prosecution of the Scottsboro Boys, of Black men, for rape. He was concerned about the condition of some of the actors who had been beaten by a group of right-wingers who objected to the fact that white actors were in a play with Negro actors. In a time of blacklisting, segregation and rampant racism in America, the actors were labeled communists and it was open season on them. The police refused to protect the actors or to prosecute those who had done the beatings. Jack thought how the police had defined themselves: Only the club and gun counted. Brutalization and legal and illegal lynching of African-Americans were common in the South, Jack thought, but this was the North. Had Americans learned nothing from the prejudice and hate that led to the Holocaust and World War II? Who was next? These thoughts strengthened his commitment to his political actions and to this meeting to which he was now late.

Jack had tried to write what he believed. Material that reflected his politics. Was it worth it if no one published what he wrote and, therefore, no one read it? He was a good writer. He had a good imagination and had a good command of language. If he'd think up some nice simple plot, a love story, and describe in detail every sexual act, he would have a best seller and therefore contribute to the advancement of American culture and, not incidentally, to an obscene bank account.

He turned the corner of Eighth Avenue, muttered "sonofabitch," mentally told himself that he was being stupid to think of these possibilities because he knew he could never do anything but write what he believed in. Two blocks more and he saw the large neon letters that spelled CAPITOL HOTEL. He wondered if he had missed much of the meeting. Maybe if he toned down his ideas, suggested them rather than imposed them, told a few lies along with the truth, would he sell his manuscripts? He thought of Dr. Faustus and Mephistopheles and looked at the sign again and hurried on.

The Hotel Capitol, the place for so many meetings and luncheons and planning and action, was the center of his political life and a travesty of his personal life. He recalled the time he and Julia had been downtown and he had been drinking rather heavily. Julia had taken a glass of rum and coke and had turned her face up in a sour expression and been pleasant for the rest of the evening. He wanted to talk and he wanted to talk to Julia. He felt he was in love with her. A girl to pick up and sleep with and she turned out to be a girl who meant more to him than anything else. Almost anything else. And that night he wanted to talk to let her know what he felt. Find out what she felt. Come to an agreement. He might even ask her to marry him. She would probably accept. He had to find out what the consequences would be. Instead of going home, at nine o'clock they went to the Capitol Hotel. They rented a room for the night, went upstairs. He laughed as he thought how stupid he had been. How it seemed like throwing away a ten-dollar bill. He didn't even sleep with her. They talked. He talked about what he felt, what he believed. She talked about what she wanted, what she needed. He told her about his duty to the world. She told him about his duty to himself. She told him that if he ever would find a way to do what he wanted to for the world, he must first find a way to put himself on a sound, solid basis. And as they spoke he began to know what she meant. His mental grasping had found its priming factor in 1938 when the Lincoln Brigade went to fight in Spain. What was his relationship to the world and what was it to Julia? She told him that if he loved her and wanted to marry her, the first thing was to find an outlet for his writing, a sound basis that would enable him to make a living and support a family. She would help him. He would be happy with her. He would have to find a modicum of happiness with his ideas and writing. Inside of him the burning to do great things was so strong that it obscured practical considerations. He knew what she had meant by getting the most out of the world so he could do the most for it. It began to make sense. If you are to fight, you must have a base from which to fight. You must have enough armor and personal reserve so that you can venture out and then have some place to return, to recoup and rebuild and reevaluate. It didn't necessarily have to be a little suburban cottage with a back yard and a railroad timetable and kids running around the front lawn. But it could be a personal responsibility, to someone like Julia, to himself, to the necessities of competing in this society, accepting some things so that he could be in a position to do others. This was his rationalization. He knew now that this was what he could have done. But when he thought of it , it too often became a different scenario. It was a big house in the suburbs and a new car and jewelry and mink coat and a lot of money. It was Julia for Julia in the guise of helping Jack. Jack knew what she said and knew what she meant. He knew what she wanted and what he could give her. He knew what he should do and knew what he was going to do.

He walked into the hotel, past the front desk, over to the elevators, stepped into one, said six to the elevator operator and stepped to the rear. He would have to finish his reverie, have to talk it out of himself. That night he could have had Julia and had his ideal. There would have been a compromise. Julia was smart enough for that. She wanted the good things, and she would see that he would find enough happiness to give them to her. They had agreed. Julia thought she had found the love she wanted and the wherewithal to maintain that love. Jack thought he had found the security within himself and the base he needed to fight the world as he had to. He hadn't known how strong he would have to be. The elevator stopped at the third floor, a man asked if it was going down, the elevator operator said "up" and the door closed. He remembered

Julia getting undressed, getting in bed, waiting for him, waiting to form the physical union that had been theirs for so many months and for the talk, for the agreement of feelings and minds. Then suddenly remembered a scheduled political meeting. The liquor that had broken through the concrete shell of his thinking faded and the cloud turned into a bright sky. He kissed Julia and told her he would be back in two hours. He couldn't help it, he said. He didn't want to go, but they expected him. He would make it back as quickly as possible. It didn't mean he loved her any less or thought any less of her. If she wanted him to be happy, as she said she did, then these were the things she must do. An important meeting. A couple hours. Wait for me and it'll be a flash. Go to sleep and when you wake I'll be lying next to you. he elevator stopped. He got out and went to his meeting. As soon as it was over he rushed back to Julia, to the rented room, opened the door and found Julia gone. He had stood there angrily. Then he remembered having smiled, not happily, but smiling as if he were a demi-god looking down upon himself and watching his actions. If he were a philosopher he would have told himself that he had made his choice.

This evening he got off at the sixth floor, walked into the meeting room. Speeches were made, plans arranged, and prominent and non-so-prominent actors in New York City had banded together. He didn't know too many of the actors, but he knew enough. He mingled with them, talked with them after the meeting. Everyone was happy. Some decided to go to parties, others out for a bite to eat, others, unemployed and without enough money for carfare and not able to borrow any, would walk home and see if there was anything in the icebox and go to bed. But most of them were happy. Jack felt sad. That was not unusual because most of the time he wasn't happy. He was happy in what he was doing, but not happy with himself. Something was missing. He didn't want to think about Julia again, but he did, and wished that she were there and that he could take her to his apartment. And this time he would. Nothing would stop him.

As he was about to leave the hotel a tall blonde actress who had been at the meeting came up to him, kissed him gently, asked him where he had been keeping himself. Jane. An old girlfriend. They talked.

He asked what she was doing. He asked if she would like to go to his apartment for a drink. She smiled at him. He didn't know whether she felt sorry for him or not. He didn't care. She said she would go. He needed a woman tonight. Jane was a good woman to have. They started out the door when a man came up and stopped Jack. "Where the hell are you going? You know our writers group has another meeting tonight. Not a long meeting, but you'd better be there. They're expecting you."

Jane understood. She knew about such things. He told her to go to the apartment herself and wait for him. She knew where the key was, on top of the door ledge. Jane smiled and left. Jack walked off with his colleague. He stopped a moment and looked after Jane. He knew she wouldn't be at this apartment. He smiled as he admitted to himself that once again he made a choice.

You want to know something? If you stand on one side of the circle and look hard, you'll be able to see the other side. If you look real hard you'll be able to see yourself.

PART III

THE DECISION

CHAPTER 13
BLIND ALLEYS

When you've thought all you could think. When you've turned up every alley and crossed every intersection and waited for every traffic light. When you've leafed through the pages of a book and gotten to the last page, and even though you didn't understand it, whether you liked t or not it was finished and you had to close the cover and put it back on the shelf. Either you stopped thinking or you sat on the curb and got splashed in the face from a mud puddle or you remained in a void. Or you began to find new things to think about and you crossed against the traffic light and got a new book down from the shelf. When you reach a point where you can remain static no longer, you must make a decision.

Sometimes you know what you have to do. Sometimes you know you have to do something but don't know what it is. Sometimes you don't even know you have to do something, but something happens and you become part of it.

Julia, Walter, Joe, Ben, Ruthie, and Jack had reached the blind alley. They were all at a given point. Either they climbed over the wall and got away or started around the circle again. Each went their own way, different from the others, and each found themself going in the same direction as the others.

At Yale University some years ago psychologists experimented with blind mice. They found that if you put six blind animals surrounded by four walls the animals will go in all directions trying to get away from one another. But invariably, no matter how far they went and how hard they tried, their paths always crossed and they always became part of each other again.

In houses in Shaker Heights, in Beverly Hills, in Ladue, in New Rochelle, people were trying to be more than people. They were trying to be names in a social register and on six- figure bank accounts.

"Hurry up, Julia, Mack Ellis and his wife will be here in a few minutes."

"All right, I'm hurrying."

"I've been calling upstairs to you for an hour. And you keep hurrying, but don't come down."

"I'm not hurrying and I'm not coming down until I'm damned good and ready. Because you got a promotion at the office and can tell a bunch of girls sitting at typewriters what to do, don't think I'm going to bow down at your feet and say "Yes, sir, Mr. Mitchell.."

"I didn't mean it that way, Julia. I'm sorry. I know you're doing your best. Except that ..."

Julia silently mouthed her reply: "And for all I care, Mack Ellis and his wife can drop dead."

Sometimes, no matter how sure you are of yourself, you know you are wrong. You can be too selfish and it begins to hurt a part of your pride. One can pat oneself on the shoulder when they can feel they are being magnanimous, even if they don't believe in what they are doing. Julia knew she was wrong.

"I'm all ready, Walter. I'll be down in a second. See if Helen has the dinner ready and the highball glasses out."

As a hostess you have certain obligations. You can either serve dinner and keep quiet. Or you can turn on the television set and everybody keeps quiet. Or you can pull out a deck of cards and everybody argues. Or you can sit and talk with your lady guest about silks and laces while the men solve the problems of the world—at least of their own little world.

"I'll tell you, Walter, these god-damned communists have got to be stopped," Mack pontificated. "Why, before you know it they'll take over this country and all of us will be sent out to the salt mines in South Dakota someplace. Not that I mind South Dakota, but with my thyroid condition I'm kind of allergic to salt. That's pretty good, huh?"

"Maybe not so funny, Mack. Look what they've already done. You don't agree with them anyplace in Europe and right away they give you a trial and throw you in jail."

"Yeah, and they preach democracy. Probably not even a fair trial."

"Of course not."

"But we're getting the right idea here, Walter. Read the papers. We're getting rid of them Reds. Anybody suspected of being a Red gets fired right from their job. No trial to drag on for years and years. Nip this thing in the bud. We're beginning to wise up in protecting democracy."

"Yes sir, get rid of all those commies, I say."

"Sometimes I think the Ku Klux Klan's got the right idea."

They both thought: Women don't understand those things. They really are the weaker sex.

"They're not married, Julia. And they got a hotel room together. Of course, I'm not one to harp on morals. I live and let live, but his father was a foreigner, born in Italy, I believe, and you know how those foreigners are."

"Maybe they're in love, Mitzi?"

"But such goings on, in public?"

"You think it should be in private. Run away from it?"

"I don't think such things should go on at all, Julia."

"Haven't you ever slept with Mack, Mitzi?"

"What an awful thing to say. Of course, I have. We're married."

"Maybe they're in love?"

"Well, Julia, I don't see …"

"Forget it, Mitzi. Shall we turn on the television?"

When minds move in a certain direction, nothing can change them—except the red headlines of a newspaper or the rancid voice of a radio commentator or the unquestioned pronouncements of a great industrialist. The stagnating agreements of similar minds.

"Great little thing, that television, Walter. Great little thing. I've been telling Mitzi that we ought to get one. She'd rather have a baby. But I think we ought to get a car and a television set instead. You don't have to change diapers on a television set. Pretty good one, huh?"

"One good thing about television. It takes all these actors off the streets. Gives them some work. Gives them a few bucks in their pockets and they stop bothering us normal people to pay taxes to support them. One thing, Mack. These actors and writers and painters. Most of them are communists, you know."

"That's because we let them do what they want, Walter. Look at Hollywood. Perverted, all of them. Every one of them a Red. And after they made all their money in this country, too."

"We ought to have stricter control over them. Make them behave like normal people."

Julia couldn't let that pass. "Who decides what normal people behave like?"

"Since you ask, Julia, the answer is simple. People like us. We're normal people. We believe in God, democracy and moral behavior."

"If that's so, Walter, then everybody who doesn't act like you isn't normal."

Mack's turn. "Right again, Mrs. Mitchell. Julia, you should be on a quiz program."

"If I were, Mack, I'd follow that question with the statement that only about 10% of the world population acts like … like we do. That would make who abnormal?"

"Smart little wife you got there, Walter. You see, Julia, we don't have to think about that. Because we know we're normal, wholesome, fine upstanding people."

"How do we know that?"

"Just look at the others. They're different, ain't they? That's pretty good, huh?"

The young leaders of tomorrow spend their hours developing their minds. They are the wholesome, normal people. They are the people who believe in democracy. They are tolerant, wise, courteous, intelligent, growing. Aren't they?

"Well, we'd better be getting home, folks. Thanks an awful lot for your hospitality. Nothing like it. Real friendly like. The only thing that's missing is the hula girls in grass skirts. You get yourself a grass skirt next time, Julia."

"Why don't you stay awhile, Mack? Another hand of bridge?"

"Like to, Walt, but the little woman gets scared at night driving home, so we'll leave now."

"Yes, it's frightening. Where we live in the Bronx, some colored families started moving in and I hate to take any chances."

"Yeah, you know how they are, Walt."

"Yeah, I know."

Julia again. "I know a lot of Negroes and I've never had anything to be frightened about more than I would have from anyone else."

"You maybe just met the cream off the top, Julia. But we know better, Walt and I, don't we? When you come down to it, a nigger's a nigger."

"And it's our duty to protect our women-folk, Mack."

"Right, Walt."

"Good night."

"Good night."

"Let's get together for golf soon, Mack."

"We'll do some talking without the women to ask questions and disturb our great minds. That's a good one, huh? Good night."

When the walls of a room begin to move in on you, you can take a drink and forget about it and walk into another room. When the walls of that next room begin to close in, you can leave that room and go into another room. When the walls of that room begin to come closer, you wonder whether it's the walls, the rooms, the house, or something else. If the something else is part of the house, then drinking and walking won't help. Maybe nothing will help?

"C'mon to bed, Julia."

"Not now, Walter. I want to walk around a little. Maybe I'll sit up and read."

"The Ellises are nice people, aren't they?"

"Yes, nice people."

"Mack's got some good contacts, Julia. Good ones."

"Yes, I suppose so."

"What's wrong, Julia?"

"Go to sleep, Walter."

"Come to sleep with me."

"All right, I'll come to sleep with you."

In the middle of a bed the walls are further away. There's nothing to relate yourself to but yourself and the bed and that which can make you forget about the walls. You stretch and move your body out far and open, as if there were nothing covering you, as if you were free. You feel hands touching your bare skin, moving back and forth, up and down your body. You keep your eyes closed and you think of a bed in an apartment on Eighth Street. You begin to feel an automatic reaction. You begin to ache inside, and something inside your stomach begins to move and contract. Your body begins to arch upward and move as if there were a magnet that was tuned to your frequency and whenever the magnet came near you, you moved because you had to. You feel a body come over yours and part of it brush against you and touch you and melt into you. You forget about the walls and feel far away, in a world that belongs only to you. Free and relaxed. You begin to pound inside and your body wants to move and you dig your fingernails into the form on top of you and think of a long thin body with black hair and a mustache and strong arms and sweet words and you open your eyes and see a big fat face, breathing heavily into yours and large paws digging at you and a fat belly lolling on top of yours and big lips splashing as they move across yours. Suddenly the walls become large and heavy and ugly and twisted and begin to move in on you, ready to smother you and crush you.

"Julia, Julia, what's the matter? What happened?"

"I'm sorry, Walter. I'm sorry. I can't stand it."

"But why then, why then? Another minute, Julia. Another few minutes. What's the matter?"

"The walls. You wouldn't understand. I'm sorry, Walter."

"What the hell! A wife is supposed to. What have I got a wife for? A wife is supposed to."

"All right. I know. I'm sorry."

"What the hell did you marry me for? We've got a license. You're supposed to sleep with me."

"Is that all, Walter?"

"No, there's more you're supposed to do. But this, anyway."

"Do you want a divorce, Walter? I'll get a divorce."

"No, I'm sorry, Julia. I didn't mean it. I love you. You know I love you."

"You don't show it."

"But sometimes, sometimes can't you sleep with me the way I want?"

"You really want it?"

"Yes, of course. I ask you, don't I? I always ask you."

"Yes, Walter. You always ask me."

"What are you getting dressed for? Where are you going?"

"For a ride, Walter. I feel like going for a ride. You go to sleep. Don't wait up for me. If my ride isn't satisfactory, maybe I'll let you ask me again."

At New Haven the experimenting mouse bumped into one wall, turned away, and thought it was free. But it went around in circles and didn't know how close the other wall was.

To drive to New Rochelle from Eighth Street you see a lot of things and think of a lot more. To drive to Eighth Street from New Rochelle you see the same things. The car is the same, the route is the same. Perhaps the time is changed, but the difference is only between light and dark. If you drive back and forth for a period of two years, the same way, for the same purpose, even the thinking remains the same. But while other things, relatively, can remain static for a long time, thinking cannot. As Julia drove out of New Rochelle, through the Bronx, onto the East River Drive, hers didn't.

There was no more time. The time had run out. All that remained at New Rochelle were four walls that kept closing in. Four walls. Wall Street. Insurance. Mack Ellises. And on top of them and on top of her, Walter Mitchell.

This was Joe Templeton's day. Everything was his. I belong to you, Joe. I'll live with you, sleep with you, go away with you, be your wife, be your whore, be whatever you want me to be. I don't want to live with Walter anymore. I can't live with Walter anymore. Shall I drive a brand-new Cadillac off the Tri-Borough bridge into fifty feet of water, or will you live with me? Will you let me live with you? This day belonged to Joe Templeton. Julia belonged to Joe Templeton.

When you're far away from a thing you're not afraid of it. You can almost be objective. When you set out to do something, and the something is on the other side of the world you find the courage to fight a windmill with a lance. But when you turn the wheel of your car up a street and the thing and the doing is no further away than pressing a button in an elevator and going up eight flights, then you begin to be afraid. Sometimes you're afraid that what you want to do, you will not have enough nerve to do. Sometimes you're afraid that something will stop you on the way and that you won't get where you're going. If you're a strong minded individual and have the strength and the guts then neither of these will bother you. Sometimes what you have to do involves somebody else. You're not afraid of them, either. As long as you know and understand what you want, how can you be afraid? But what happens if they don't understand?

"Baby, come in, come in. What the hell, it's four o'clock in the morning."

"I had to see you, Joe. Give me something to drink."

"Drink, Julia? You drink?"

"No, I guess not. I'm just confused. I'm not confused. I'm perfectly straight."

"A fight with Walter?"

"No, with myself. I finally decided something."

"You're going to leave Walter?"

"That's right, Joe. That's right. You've been right all the time. I finally decided I'm going to leave Walter."

"Good, it's about time."

"You understand, Joe?"

"Waddya think, I'm stupid? Of course, I understand."

"And it's all right."

"For a year I've been telling you it's all right. It may be a little rough, but at least you'll be out on your own."

"Not that way, Joe."

"Look, Julia baby. Plenty of people are out on their own. They don't have Cadillacs or furs or houses in New Rochelle. But they have nice jobs and a steady income and they live happily and raise families and have fun and most of the time do what they want."

"You never talked like this before, Joe."

"I never felt like this before. Sit down, Julia. Over here. On the bed. I've been doing a lot of serious thinking."

"What is it, Joe?"

"It's about us that I want to talk to you."

"What do you mean by out on my own?"

"What I said, Julia. You'll get yourself a job, associate with people you want to, and you won't have a blubbering whale climbing over you in bed."

"For Chrissakes, Joe, cut this shit. What's this all about? Who will I have crawling over me in bed?"

"Look, baby, don't get excited. I'm trying to talk to you calmly."

"I came here to talk to you, and you're talking to me. Am I going crazy? I came here to walk in the door and pull my clothes off and say Joe, here I am, and lie down in the bed and wait for you to get in me and the next thing I know I'm sitting here and you're talking shit to me. Am I crazy or what?"

"Will you let me talk to you?"

"Alright, talk to me. Goddamn it, talk to me. Give me a drink. Give me a drink, Joe. If you won't lay with me in bed, give me a drink."

"All right, Julia, here's a drink. What shall I say? I'm sorry? I didn't want anything like this. But I got something to say first and maybe I better say mine before you say yours."

"Good drink. I should drink more often. Maybe I will? It burns down the inside of me and I don't mind the rest of me tearing so much."

"Let's go for a walk, Julia."

"Let's have another drink. Why wait? At least the windmill's still turning. As long as it still turns you've got a chance. It's when it stops turning that there's no more air and you lay down and die."

"What the hell's all that mean?"

"Nothing."

"You want to take that walk?"

"One question, Joe?"

"What's that?"

"Would you sleep with me now if I asked you?"

"You're drunk, baby. One shot and you're drunk."

"Will you sleep with me, Joe? Will you fuck me, Joe?"

"We got things to talk about."

"You fucking bastard son-of-a-bitch."

"Julia, what the hell is this?"

"Throw me in the gutter, Joe. I'm used up. Pull off the prophylactic and put it in the garbage and throw me in after it."

"Shuttup, goddamn it. All right, Julia, you want to talk, I'll tell you. Lie down or sit down or stand up, I don't give a damn. But listen. Because I'm going to tell you. And I'll tell you once and that'll be all. That'll be the end."

"Joe."

"Yeah?"

"Can we take that walk first? Can we go for a little walk first?"

A little time can feel like a million years. It can change a million things and make a different life. It can begin life and end life. If it's the right kind of life, it can be worth a million years. When you walk past little shops with darkened windows and underneath yellow street lights that are more dirty than bright, and up and down curbs and past trees and by people walking or people running or people propped in doorways or lying in gutters you can think how wonderful it is to be the only one alive out of all those inanimate things. Or you can think how terrible it is that tomorrow those things shall be alive and you shall be dead. If you are with someone, you can talk and try to say something. Or you can know that talking will do you no good and you just continue to walk and watch your footsteps move in an automaton pattern in front of you and hope that the footsteps never stop and that the clock in the garage window will stop at the number five and never move again and that you will keep walking and walking because when you stop walking there will be nothing left.

Or you cannot think about anything but the passing of a million years and trying to hold a dirty street indelibly in your mind at five o'clock in the morning because as you stop in front of a building and get ready to step onto an elevator you know that that moment in time will have to do for the million years that you will never have.

"Feel better now, Julia?"

"Yes, I feel better."

Even if it's numb it's better than hurting.

"I understand how you feel, Julia, and I'm sorry. Now try to understand a little how I feel."

The elevator shoots up and your stomach stays down and you feel your insides beginning to drop to the bottom of the elevator shaft. Only the elevator hasn't started yet.

"I can't understand anything except that I love you, Joe."

"I've known that. And I told you not to."

"Tell me to stop breathing."

"Here's the floor. Let's go inside."

You walk inside the Elysian Fields and you want to stretch out naked on the floor and want Joe to get on top of you and like the Elysian Fields want it never to end. But instead you walk in quietly and don't look at the bed and you sit in a chair. You try and think of the many times you walked into the apartment and what happened when you got there, and you think of what is happening now and you know nothing that happened before will ever happen again and you wonder why the elevator doesn't stop.

"Joe, I'll get down on my knees. Take me away with you. Keep me here with you. Kill me and kill yourself. But let me be with you."

"I told you before I was a sonofabitch. I told you I couldn't be serious about a woman. I told you not to love me."

"You never loved me, even one bit?"

"I loved you more than I ever loved anybody and I didn't love you at all. Does that make sense?"

"With you, Joe, anything makes sense."

"Let's finish it, Julia."

"There's no use talking, is there?'

"What the hell, Julia. Make me cry. Kick me where it hurts the most and I'll shut up and not say a word. You're a wonderful kid. You should have gold and jewels and the stars. Me, Joe Templeton, talking like a stupe. But I mean it. I wish I could give it to you. I wish I could marry you, sleep with you, go away with you, or anything to make you happy. But I can't. I'm me, and I come first. If I loved you, maybe I wouldn't, but I don't, so put an 'x' mark at the bottom of the page and call me a bastard and finish it."

"I came here to give you myself, Joe, at your terms."

"Kick me again."

"I'm all right now. I'm just telling you. Don't you want to talk? Okay, you've said everything, so you want me to get the hell out of here."

"I wish you could stay."

"Joe, I want you. I'd die for you."

"Maybe you'd better go. I'm throwing you out like garbage. Get the hell out. I'm a bastard. I'm the lowest scum that ever lived. Get the hell out."

"You are hurting, aren't you? I can hurt you a little."

"You can't hurt me a bit. I'm hurting myself. By letting you stay here. I don't want no more. I'll throw you out."

"Go ahead."

"What do you want, Julia? For Chrissakes. You know. I know. What the hell do you want?"

"Are you going to marry Ruthie?"

"I need Ruthie. I need something stable. I need somebody who's not…"

"Not what, Joe?"

"Nothing."

"Who's not a whore. Who doesn't sleep with Joe Templeton. Who's not one of a dozen or dozens who've spread their legs for Joe Templeton because he's Joe Templeton. Because I'm one of those tight skirts and rounded pelvises you look at from your little castle tower out there and laugh at."

"All right, you said it."

"And if I wouldn't have slept with you, you'd marry me?"

"I'm not in love with you, Julia."

"But you are in love with Ruthie."

"Yes, I'm in love with Ruthie. I told you. Everything is past. I've got to start new. I'm going around in circles. I'm slowly walking around myself and covering myself up. If I don't stop, I'll die. I don't want to die. I'm going to start now. A new life. A new me. A virgin for a wife. A family. Fresh and clean. That's what I need.

"Who the hell are you fooling?"

"I said that's what I need. I'm fooling nobody but you. Anybody but you would have sense enough to forget it. You got your lays for the last couple years. You had a fat husband and couldn't stand him. So I slept with you. So you were happy. So get the hell away now and leave me alone."

Even a woman on her knees will rise up and scratch. You begin to fill up inside with hate and self-pity and love and you don't know which is which and then the right spark will tear you open and you have to do something. You scratch.

"You bastard!"

"What the hell did you slap me for?"

"You're not kidding me, Joe. This is the easy way out. For you. But you can't take it and tell me I was just another whore for your bed. Tell me anything, but don't tell me I was just another woman."

"Okay, Julia. You're right. I'm sorry, again. But it's over. It's all over."

"Give me something, Joe. Give me a promise. Give me anything. Tell me you'll be back. Let me come and sleep with you. God. How low can a person get? How much can I give? I'm even begging you to let me sleep with you."

"It's over, Julia. The old Joe Templeton is gone. Maybe it's the stupidest thing in the world, but this Joe Templeton thinks he's a good, normal, family loving man, and if I stop to let myself think otherwise I...I'm fighting to live, Julia. And this is the only way I know to do it."

"Never, Joe?"

"I'd like to say otherwise, but I can't so I'll say never."

"Give me a baby, Joe."

"What the hell are you saying?"

"If I can't have you, I want something of yours. Give me a baby?"

"Go home, Julia."

"I love you that much. Give me a baby. Fuck me. Right here. Right now. If I can't have you, let me have your child."

"Get out. I can't take any more of this shit."

"How much can I take, Joe? All of you. I can take all of you. Give it to me now, Joe. Give me a baby, damn it, give me a baby; don't push me out. A baby, you bastard, a baby, you son of a bitch, I love you and I want your baby."

"I'll take you down to the car. We'll talk about it when you're not so drunk. I'll see you again."

"No, you won't see me again. If not now, it'll never be."

"Get in the elevator. You're going home."

"Please, Joe, please."

"Forget about me."

"All right, Joe, I'll go. But I'm going to have you, Joe. I'm going to have your baby."

No matter how high the Tri-Borough Bridge and no matter how welcome the waters of the East River, the circle remains strong and once you are on it it's almost impossible to get off, one way or the other.

CHAPTER 14
TRANSITION

For Joe it had always been easier to let go of the past than to go into the future. It was no trick to put one step behind, but to put that next step out in front was difficult. This was the way Joe measured his progress. If you can move ahead easily with no worry and no inhibitions then you're getting someplace. Throw the last one off into the moat to float with the rest of the pinpoints below. That was easy. Bring the new one up through the twisting corridors and into the magic tower, that wasn't so easy. But this time it was different. This time it was easier to face the future than to forget the past. What had been amorphous became concrete, a place specific, a happening, an indelible. It ran its course. It could be placed in a corner by itself with brackets around it. A wall shut it off from the present. It was morning when Julia finally left. Six o'clock. The future was sleeping in Brooklyn. Even with a stomach that twirled as if a top was spinning around inside, it was easy. It's funny sometimes how you stand up high on a precipice and when you look back everything is a single blank cloud. And you have only one way to move and that's forward. It doesn't matter that you may go around in a circle and on the other side of the past there may not be a wall. All that matters is that something is behind and the step forward becomes easy. Easier than anything had ever been.

"Hello, Ruthie."

"Hello."

"This is Joe, Ruthie."

"At six o'clock in the morning?"

"Can you come right over here?"

"Is something wrong?"

"I'll explain later. I need you over here right away."

"No girl for tonight, Joe?"

"I'm serious, Ruthie. I'm more serious than I've ever been."

"I'm sorry, Joe. I thought it was a gag."

"No gag. On the level. And no girl, either."

"You're not feeling well."

"I'm feeling perfect, Ruthie."

"Impotent?"

"Never less impotent in my life."

"I'm sorry, Joe; you picked the wrong time of the month."

"For Chrissakes, Ruthie, I'm trying to be serious. Will you listen to me a minute? I want to talk to you. Seriously. Can you come over here right away? Can you? I've got to talk to you."

"About what?"

"Not over the phone."

"I'm supposed to be at work at nine, Joe."

"The hell with work. You've got a lifetime ahead. Forget about work. Don't you know what I'm talking about, Ruthie?"

"Yes, I do, Joe. Was she there?"

"Yeah."

"All finished?"

"Yeah!"

"Do you want to talk about it?"

"There's nothing to talk about. It's a dead issue."

"Are you sure?"

"If I wasn't sure, I wouldn't be calling you now."

"Then tell me over the phone, Joe."

"Will you come over, Ruthie? Please."

"Tell me!"

"I love you. I want to marry you."

"I'm coming right over."

And the top begins to spin faster and you wonder what you've done. And you begin to think that there still is time left. You can bolt the door. You can pack your things and leave. You can call again and say you've made a mistake. You can pick out one of the dots from the moat and bring it to the tower. You can drink and be ugly. You can do a thousand things to change again what you've just changed. But you don't. Because you've taken one of the steps away from the wall, and you're afraid that if you step at all backward the wall you built will come tumbling down on top of you.

The morning wasn't yet awake. The sky was still grey when Ruthie arrived.

"Before anything else, Joe, you've got to tell me about Julia. What's going to happen to Julia?"

"I don't know. Maybe I don't care. Maybe I do care. There's nothing more between Julia and me. There never will be."

"How do you know you love me?"

"Because I need you. Because I'm dead right now. And I'll only live again if you live with me. Maybe I never told you because I was never sure. But now I'm sure."

"You know how I feel about you."

"I think I know. But I want you so much I don't care. If you don't love me now, Ruthie, you will."

"I do love you now, Joe. But what's going to happen? We've talked, we've been together. But never about us. This is new. This is sudden. This is something we haven't planned for. What do we do? Just get up and get married?"

"Maybe I should have waited, Ruthie? Maybe I should have taken you out for the next couple months and let it come out slowly? But what the hell. What for? I wouldn't get to know you any better. I know who you are. Good, clean, kind, soft, pure, real, alive, and any and all of thousands of beautiful things. I love you now. I know it. What should I wait for? You say you love me?"

"Yes, Joe. Because I need you, too. Because you've got the kind of strength I want. If I wasn't sure before, seeing you this way, I am now. You need me for always."

"I do."

"Joe?"

"Yeah?"

"What do you want to do?"

"I want to marry you right now."

"And then what? I mean, what happens? Do we live in this apartment and be bothered every night by some blonde trying to push me out of bed, or every week by the grocer trying to collect a food bill we can't pay, or by the landlord every month?"

"No. All that is gone. We're going to start out fresh and clean. Virginal."

"And I fit in?"

"You don't fit in anything. You are everything. You're the whole works. It's you and me. Everything is new. That's what I want."

"I'd stay with you here, Joe."

"I don't want to, Ruthie. I want us to go away."

"I'm putting you through an inquisition, Joe. But these things I've got to know."

"Ask me anything. I've got the answers."

"You've always had the answers, Joe."

"No, not always. There's been something missing. You. Now, with you, I always will have the answers."

"I'll marry you, Joe."

When you talk to a woman and whether you mean it or not, when you have to come to an agreement of love or warmth or understanding or sex, it's always the cue for a kiss or an embrace, or in some cases of going to the nearest bed and pulling back the covers, or in other situations using the couch you're sitting on. When you talk of marriage it becomes different. If you really mean it, it becomes different. Sex is no less useful or less important. But it is less necessary. If you need someone for themselves, then even though your body may ache to make love or just to have sex, you are content to just hold back and just be soft and warm and close. If the rush was to get in bed, the reason for marrying, pick out some big-bosomed broad from the nearest whore house.

"What are we going to do, Joe?"

"Let's get away from New York."

"Where?"

"You're not worried about Ben, are you?"

"No. I was in love with Ben."

"I know you were."

"But I'm not anymore. I haven't been for a long time."

"I'll keep my mouth shut. I won't ask you anything about Ben anymore."

"You can ask me anything, Joe. I know what you think and how you think. I don't have anything to hide."

"I know, Ruthie. I don't have to ask you anything."

"That sounds like it has a double meaning, Joe."

"Forget it. Ruthie, how would you like to go to Chicago?"

"Why Chicago?"

"I can get a job with an ad firm there. One of my friends has a brother who has a contact there. They want a young writer, married, serious, who's willing to make ninety-five bucks a week. We could live on that."

"Very nicely."

"We could buy a house, Ruthie. We could raise a family."

"This doesn't sound like Joe Templeton."

"It doesn't, but it is. I've got to get my feet on the ground."

"Going commercial, Joe? What happened to your ideals?"

"I've got them. But I can't live on them. I'm going places and, with you, I'll get there. You're almost thirty years old, I told myself, and what have you got? Start something new before you get down deep so far you'll get buried. Get out and live a normal life. We'll do the things we want. Art, theatre, music. Central Park in the afternoon or whatever the name of the park in Chicago is. So I'll work five days a week. But it'll be better than okay. Are you with me?"

"Of course, I'm with you, Joe. I'll always be with you."

"Next week."

"Next week?"

"Let's get a license tomorrow. We'll be married next week. Let's get away from here as soon as possible."

"I've got things to do, Joe. I can't get married just like that."

"How long, Ruthie?"

"All right, Joe. Make it two weeks. Nothing fancy. Two weeks."

"As soon as possible, Ruthie."

"As soon as possible. I've got to see Ben."

"To say goodbye?"

"To say goodbye!"

"Come here, Ruthie. Come real close. We're going to be very happy together."

"Yes, Joe. We're going to be very happy together."

The grey gradually melts away and the sky becomes lighter and lighter and lighter, and you begin to move forward. But sometimes it can become too light and it blinds you. Or it becomes light in one place only and ahead it is still grey and muddled. If you don't know where you're going, but see a light in front of you, sometimes you can get there anyway. If you don't know why you're going and the path you're going to take, the light doesn't remain very long and you can't see more than a couple steps in front of you.

The rain pours down outside the window of Ben's apartment and you want to leave, but it continues to rain and you stay. Both Ben and Ruthie knew that it was best for her to go. But it was hard to say it because it meant they had been wrong for the past year. They knew that was not the truth, but sometimes the truth is better as a lie.

"We've wasted this past year, haven't we, Ruthie?"

"I don't think so."

"It's all coming to an end. The rain will stop and you'll walk out of here and it'll be all over."

"I'll think about you, Ben."

"Don't bother. I don't know if I'm worth it."

"You are, Ben. You've got it inside of you to do what you want. I haven't been able to help you. Maybe if I'm not here, you'll find you'll have no one to depend on and you'll have to do it yourself."

"You're probably right. But I don't want you to go."

"Do you want me to sleep with you, Ben?"

"You know I won't ask you to."

"I know."

"But you would if I wanted you to?"

"Yes."

"That's strange logic. But it kind of figures. With us, anyway. Does Joe know about us, Ruthie?"

"Not everything."

"I'll never say anything."

"What are you going to do, Ben?"

"Do you think you'll be happy with Joe?"

"I will be."

"You don't love me anymore, Ruthie?"

"No. Sometimes I don't think I ever did. I think it was only because it was something new."

"I never really loved you either, Ruthie."

"I know, Ben. But I want to thank you, anyway."

"For what?"

"For letting me think you did. It helped me grow up."

"Shall I say thanks or I'm sorry?"

"Neither. Especially, don't feel sorry. And don't be bitter."

"Maybe I should have been in love with you, Ruthie? I should have married you."

"Not me. You've got too much to do. You don't need me. You can do it yourself. Joe needs me. That's where I belong."

"The rain's beginning to stop."

"I know. I can hear it."

"I can feel it."

"I feel kind of sad, Ben."

"I do, too. Shall we say goodbye?"

"You don't feel really bad, do you?"

"A little. Not really bad."

"Me neither. Maybe we'll see each other again, Ben. Let's say so long."

"I feel better, Ruthie. I feel much clearer inside."

"I know Ben. I was never for you."

"Let me kiss you goodbye."

"Not goodbye, Ben. So long."

"Yes, Ruthie. So long."

Ben looked after her as she left. He looked at his bookcase and tried to pick out a particular title. He thought of a passage he had read in one of his books. About a guy who thought he might have been in love and he let the girl pass out of his life. He worried about it for years afterwards, wondering whether he had made a mistake. Years later he saw her. She didn't see him. He listened to her talk. Dull. He watched her walk. Dispirited. He saw her face. Vacant. He turned away, didn't even say hello, and went to the nearest bar, half ready to cry and half ready to laugh. Ben wondered whether some day he would see Ruthie and head for the nearest bar. He was alone now and because he was alone he was a different Ben. This was neither one year ago nor ten years from now. This was today. He went to the phone, dialed long distance, and asked for a New Rochelle number.

CHAPTER 15
CONFRONTATION

If Ruthie and Ben were happy inside and Joe was happy outside, Julia was neither. Julia cried and swore and would have destroyed the earth if it would have saved her. She was slowly sinking into a whirlpool at the bottom of which slime kept blowing up into shapes that looked like Walter and she clutched at the edges of the water trying to pull herself up. She felt like the boxer who kept losing the fight, but kept getting up to come back for more, feeling that there was always the chance.

This was on the outside and she didn't understand it. She only felt it. What was on the inside was a product of the outside and Julia couldn't see that one had any effect upon the other. She only knew it was there. The feeling had to be changed. Joe couldn't be. Could Ruthie?

"I've been waiting for you, Ruthie. I used to wait by this elevator for it to take me up, but now I wait for it to take somebody else down."

"I expected you, Julia. I thought you would come to speak to me."

"Why did you do it, Ruthie? He belonged to me. What the hell right have you to do it?"

"I haven't done anything, Julia. He asked me. He loves me."

"He should love me. Nobody else. Why the hell are you taking my man away from me? Why?"

"Please, Julia, not here. Let's go someplace else. I'll talk to you, but people are watching here."

At first you want to crush something, to tear something, because that will bring an end to it and maybe it will clean out what's festering inside. But sometimes it only makes matters worse. So you walk down the street, holding it all in and wondering when the rage is going to go down. The sidewalks are grey and you watch them because they move along at the same dull rate of speed as you, moving calmly, insensitively beneath your feet. Slowness and dullness outside and a pounding inside. As you walk, the sidewalk seems to become more alive and the inside of you begins to become grey. Your feet take wider, softer steps and the pounding inside begins to get slower. You feel like the boxer who has lost the first round and has caught his breath and is ready to come out for the second. And even as he does he wonders why because he knows inside that when it's all over he's going to lose.

"Let's go in here and have cocktails Julia, and we can talk. Oh, I forgot, you don't drink."

"Let's have a cocktail."

And you wonder whether the boxer will win any of the rounds or just get beaten and beaten and beaten until he melts into the canvas.

"You had to do it, didn't you Ruthie?"

"You've known it for a long time."

"Maybe I have, but it isn't right. It isn't fair. You know how much he means to me."

"I'm going to marry him, Julia. He means a lot to me, too, you know."

"When will you marry him?"

"Wednesday."

"So what do I do? Kill myself? Join a nunnery? Tear my insides open and try to take Joe out of them and put them back together again and pretend that they're whole?"

"What can I say, Julia? I've always liked you. I still do. But this is my life and Joe's life. What can I say?"

"I don't know. I don't know what you should say. All I know is that you murdered my soul."

"If I tell you I'm sorry, would that do any good? Tell you to forget him? I know you can't, no more than I could. Tell you I'm glad I'm not you and sound like I'm laughing when inside I'm crying because it hurts me, too? I know what I've done. If it'll make you feel any better, go ahead and call me a bitch."

The bell rings and the round is over and you get up all bloody and not only your body and your insides but your pride is hurt because the person you want to fight is trying not to hurt you and you wonder if you are only hurting yourself.

"I'll have another drink, Ruthie."

"I'm not making it any easier for you, am I, Julia?"

"It'll never be easy."

"I'm afraid of you, Julia."

"Why? Do you think I'll take him back from you?"

"No, but I think you're going to try. And I'm afraid for Joe. I'm afraid you can hurt him."

"Hurt you, you mean."

"Alright, hurt me. I'm part of Joe now, so you hurt me. It doesn't make any difference."

"Little Ruthie thinks she's in love with Joe Templeton. Listen to me, Ruthie, in two months he'll have drained every ounce out of you and throw you away with the rest of us."

"He's in love with me, Julia."

"Love? What the hell do you know about his love? He slept with me for two years. He laid on top of me and under me and alongside of me and inside of me and you talk about his love. It's me he knows love with. It's me that has seen him strong like an elephant and weak like a mouse. It's me that's touched him and fondled him and petted him and kissed him and spread my legs for him. What the hell do you know about his love?"

"I should slap your face, Julia. I should call you a bitch and throw this glass in your face and get up and walk out of here. But I won't. Now I feel sorry for you. For a long time I envied you, but now I can look down on you and think how fine I am because I don't lean over and spit on you. No, don't say anything, Julia. You've said all you had to. You talk about love. You think you know. But you don't. You know passion and sex. That's only part of love. Joe and I have found the real thing. Maybe you don't understand what I'm saying. Think of it in relation to your husband and then to Joe."

"Shut up, Ruthie!"

"No, I won't. I have just a few more words to say, and I'll say them. Our love is a real love. Not the kind you find in a whore house. That's your kind. He needs me and I need him. Not for a night or a weekend or enough time to throw ourselves onto a bed and have an orgasm. He needs me for his life. It's nothing without me. And mine is nothing without him. And sex is only secondary. We have a real love. That's why you are no more and that's why I am. Now I'll leave."

"Then let me say something. I know what I've said. But only because Joe means more to me than my pride or my life. And I'll do anything to get him back. Why don't you go back to Ben? Leave Joe and take Ben. You'll be happy. Let me beg you on my knees. Give me a chance to live."

"You've had too much to drink, Julia. I don't love Ben. He's the one who would throw me away. He only needs me like Joe needs you. But in the long run he's strong. He can do it without me. Joe can't. Ben and Joe are very much alike on the outside. But on the inside there's a great difference. And I'm in love with Joe."

"He thinks you're a virgin? He doesn't know about Ben?"

"No, he doesn't."

"What if I tell him, Ruthie? That'll hurt, wouldn't it?"

"Yes, it would. But he wouldn't believe you."

"Then I'll have Ben tell him. Ben will tell him and he'll believe it."

"Ben won't tell him, either."

"Ben loves me. He never loved you, Ruthie, but he loves Julia. He'll do anything I say."

"You're desperate, aren't you Julia?"

"Ben will do what I say."

"You're hurt now, Julia. Don't hurt yourself more."

"I'll go to see Ben. I'll get Joe through Ben. Don't leave, Ruthie. I'm warning you."

"You don't frighten me, Julia. I pity you, but you don't frighten me. Goodbye."

"I'll get Joe through Ben. Ruthie... Ruthie! ... No, waiter, nothing's wrong. I'm fine. Bring me another martini, please."

And the crowd is gone and the ring is empty and you're alone and hurt and bleeding. Outside and inside. And you try to remember what's happened and all you know is that you have been hurt and you drink liquor to try and forget. And you forget almost everything. Everything except that someone or something has hurt you and that someday there will be another fight and that next time you will win.

.

CHAPTER 16
JOE'S BABY

"Ben, I didn't know you'd be home. I came, but I didn't know you'd be home."

"Come in, Julia. I've been home for the last couple of days. I haven't stopped writing."

"I didn't know, Ben. But I came over anyway. What are you writing, Ben?"

"You don't look well. Come here, Julia, sit down. What's wrong?"

"Nothing's wrong, Ben. I came to you and didn't know. What are you writing? The same as usual, Ben, the same as usual?"

"This one is good. A novel. What I want to write. About two people who know where they're going and two people who don't know where they're going. And I'm not afraid of them."

"But I'm afraid, aren't I, Ben? I'm afraid?"

"Are you sick? You've been drinking."

"Tell him, Ben, tell him. Go tell Joe, tell Joe, Ben."

"Here, lie down on the bed, Julia. ."

"Tell him, tell him, tell him. Get me a drink."

"No more drinking, Julia. What happened?"

"Joe's leaving. With Ruthie. Joe's going away. Joe's dying. No more Joe. Tell him, Ben."

"Tell him what?"

"Tell him you slept with Ruthie. Tell him and then he'll come back to me."

"Don't be a fool."

"He'll believe you."

"No. First of all, it won't make any difference. And second, what they're doing is best for both of them."

"You love her, you want her back."

"No, I don't, Julia. I never really did. Now lie down and relax. Try and sleep. You'll feel better."

Even the boxer gets a minute between rounds. He gets instructions from his manager. He knows what to do when the bell rings again. But when the fight is over and he doesn't know it and he keeps on fighting because if he stops there's nothing more to live for and there's no manager and instructions and nothing to do but lie back and try to think and, not being able to think, just keep on fighting.

"Ben?"

"Tell me about it, Julia. What happened?"

"I'm sorry."

"There's nothing to be sorry about."

"About just now."

"It's all right, Julia. You've had a couple drinks too many. You're all right."

"I'm sorry."

"It's okay."

"Ben?"

"Yes."

"You know how much Joe means to me."

"I can't do anything, Julia."

"You can tell him about you and Ruthie."

"No, I can't."

"Even for me? Don't I mean anything to you?"

"Don't ask me that, Julia."

"Ben. I need you now."

"I know, but I won't get in the way of Ruthie and Joe."

"I had too many martinis. I'm sober now, Ben. A little, anyway. What did I do?"

"When?"

"When I came in. Never mind. I know what I did. What are you writing, Ben?"

"Something good, Julia. Something with guts."

"You're sure?"

"I've never been surer in my life. I can feel it."

"When did this happen?"

"It didn't happen yet. But it's going to. I knew it when Ruthie said goodbye. And I didn't hurt. I was me, by myself, and I didn't need anyone."

"You're sure?"

"Yes."

"Are you? I got your message at home, Ben."

"I needed you then, Julia."

"And you don't need me now?"

"I thought you needed me now, Julia."

"Five minutes ago."

"Not now?"

"You've loved me, Ben?"

"I thought so for a long time."

When the outside becomes raw then you can't feel the inside anymore. But you've got to feel the inside so you hope and wait for the outside to heal. But it just doesn't happen.

"You're very much like Joe. Do you know that, Ben?"

"Joe and I have been friends for a long time."

"You even look alike. A little, anyway. In some ways you even think alike."

"Does it bother you? Do you want to leave, Julia?"

"Joe is gone, Ben. Do you still love me?"

"I don't suppose I could suddenly say I don't love you anymore."

"You know how I feel about you, Ben."

"What is this, Julia?"

"What?"

"What are you doing. Am I going to become Joe for you?"

"You've always wanted to sleep with me?"

"Yes."

"And you need me, don't you? You need to make love to me."

"What the hell do you want?"

"You, Ben. Don't you want me?"

"Yes."

"Are you hard up, Ben."

"Don't make me angry."

"Are you hard up, Ben?"

"Lie down and I'll show you."

"That's what Joe would do. He'd get angry and throw me on the bed. Are you going to throw me on the bed?"

"No, Julia."

"Be Joe, Ben."

"I'm not Joe."

When your eyes are closed and your body is bare to the world you can think about many things. You can be a beautiful princess being carried away on a cloud by a handsome prince. You can be a queen lying on a plush bed and choosing the strongest, most manly knights of the kingdom to come and lie in bed with you. You can be a virgin angel floating in the clouds. You can be a woman in love making herself open and free to the man she loves. Or you can be in an apartment on Eighth Street, waiting for a guy named Joe to get in bed with you.

"You need me, don't you, Ben"

"I'm not going away."

"I know you're going away, Joe. "

"I'm not Joe."

"I mean Ben. I'm sorry."

The desire becomes the will and the will becomes the desire. It becomes Joe.

"My God, Julia, do you know what we're doing."

"Yes, give me what I need."

"Hold me tight inside of you, Julia."

And everything inside of you rises from your toes to the top of your head and it pours out like a volcano of hot fire.

"I feel it. Inside of me. I feel it. Joe's baby. Now I have Joe's baby."

CHAPTER 17
APARTMENTS

If you were to look at an apartment on Eighth Street, a flat on Barrow Street, a home in New Rochelle, it would seem as though everything that had been life had disappeared into a passive substance that appeared to be death, but was not quite as final as death.

What was before: love, sex, life, frustration, hope, fear, belief, lies, everything that goes into what is reality, was gone. When a castle tower falls down, the invading forces burn what is inside, rape, pillage, or all three. In any case, what was before is no longer, and if there was light before there was darkness afterward. In the rooftop apartment on Eighth Street in the Village that had been Joe's castle a far different world was born. It featured a long table to which, every day, in freezing weather and in 90-degree-and-above temperatures, women from 50 to 80 years old came to work from eight in the morning to five in the evening sewing pieces of fur together for twenty-five dollars a week. They never wore the piece of fur they worked on, nor rarely found time to go any place where they saw anyone else wearing the fur. All they knew was that they needed twenty-five dollars a week to support themselves, to support a fatherless child, to support a drunken husband, to support an ill mother or father, to support anybody or everybody and they never wore anything in their life but a cloth coat from a Brooklyn department store that cost too much of their entire week's salary. The gate to Joe's castle tower was shut tightly in the winter and opened wide in the summer. From twelve to one it would become littered with wax paper and banana peels and once a month a janitor would come up and clean the trash that had piled up along with the leavings of low-flying birds. No longer were there small articles to pick up in the morning, after a night of wine and women, that had to be carried quickly into the bathroom and flushed down the toilet. The castle was empty. Only an occasional splotch of sun came through into the room and splashed around the table where women fitfully handled a needle and thread that grew heavier by the minute. The sun formed a perfect circle around them, and no matter how hard they sewed and stitched they never seemed to be able to move even one inch from the pinpoint on the circle.

In Ben's Barrow Street apartment there had been books and an open typewriter and knowledge and creation and hope. They were still there, but not the creation that took humanity a step forward and made life better between seven in the morning and eleven in the evening if you worked on a night shift or between eleven at night and seven in the morning if you worked regular day hours. Or made it any easier to pile up coins, goods, contacts, trade, assets and other requirements that grew into mansions, vaults, bank accounts that accumulated in the pockets of the few who could sit at home and clip coupons or sit in an office and contemplate monthly reports that signified wealth. Even that which was sacred wasn't. Custom, fear, ignorance, false shame, false pride, a man laying on top of a woman, sometimes creating feeling and passion and sometimes dining on a dinner plate to be used and washed and put away until the next day. Love was intercourse. Intercourse was simple. Simple meant love without love.

Children are the pivot of civilization. They make people work to get bread to put into their mouths. They keep people working. They stop people from doing work other than the work that they are doing. They avoid radicalism, new ideas, independence, self-thought. They are the stabilizing forces of an economy. They grow up and have children into whose mouths they have to put bread.

There is no bread other than that which they get from nine or ten hours a day, less or more, bread that comes in a little envelope and without the envelope there is no civilization.

The apartment at Barrow Street held the future of society, playing on the rug, sleeping on the bed, crawling on the floor, banging at the door. But the creation was a static one. It held society in a pivotal vise..

In New Rochelle, a house became a home. A husband found a wife. A bed that had been half empty became full. Not completely full, not always full, not really full. But it became a bed where a husband could sleep on a woman and get up in the morning with pride and righteousness because she had signed a paper that said she was his wife. Love is decided by a white gown and flowers and twenty dollars to a magistrate or clergyman who in his lifetime may know or may not ever know what love is and could be. Where there is formality all else disappears, especially in New Rochelle. A wife returns to a home and lights begin to burn in the evening. A husband begins to bring over friends and friends become clients and clients become money and the husbands begin to bring over more friends and newer friends and richer friends and money becomes more money and a wife becomes the little woman, the cook, the hostess, the entertainer, the sweetness and light, the door opener, the soft smooth pillow for relaxation, the deed to a slave and a tool.

The Cadillac becomes sparkling and shiny. It doesn't use as much oil and the tires remain grooved and clean. The Bronx Parkway and the East River Drive have less traffic. The motorists speed along a little bit faster.

What was darkness becomes light. A husband has a wife. The electric and gas companies add a few dollars to the monthly bill. An elevator on Eighth Street gets less use in the evenings. The gas station owner suffers. A woman tries to forget and in trying to forget loses herself and succeeds in becoming a good wife, hostess and door opener.

Sometimes darkness becomes light. Sometimes light becomes darkness. Sometimes darkness just remains. Sometimes people keep their lives on the inside, sometimes on the outside. Sometimes people lose themselves in each other. On Eighth Street, on Barrow Street, in New Rochelle there was darkness and light, light and darkness and, mostly, nothingness.

PART IV

THE INTERPRETATION

CHAPTER 18
NEW CIRCLES

A circle can be large or small. It can stretch from New Rochelle to 8th Street to Barrow Street. Or it can touch New Rochelle, go south into Tennessee, move north into Chicago. It always comes back to New York.

In Chicago it was something new. It was walking, not running. It was peace and contentment and security and a release from the fighting for something that wasn't there. It's never there if you don't know what you're fighting for.

Joe Templeton was happy in Chicago. A job with an advertising firm isn't so bad when you know it means eighty dollars a week whether it rains or shines or even if you don't have enough money to pay for first class return postage on manuscripts. So you write about contented cows and stainless steel machinery and personalized homes and blended paints and special lift bras. You don't think, you don't worry, you don't write. You copy words on paper, have a strong drink at lunch time, think of something funny to say and copy it down on a piece of paper for another all-star ad. You're home at six and you're free for more than twelve hours. Nothing to write at night, nothing to worry about at four o'clock in the morning because there's no more money for another drink or another taxi ride or another woman. This was free and clear and honest and calm and peaceful. It's nice to get lost sometimes. It makes it so much easier.

"Templeton."

"Yes, sir."

"I like you. I like your work."

"Thanks."

"These ads you've written the past couple weeks. Good stuff. Got a quality that'll hit hard. Dramatic. Ever write dramatic stuff? Dramatic. Know what I mean?"

"Yes, sir. I used to write plays and radio and television scripts."

"Good boy. Knew you had it in you. If we get any new television ads, I'll let you write them."

"Yes, sir."

"Well, just wanted to tell you how much I liked your work. That's all, Abrams."

"Templeton."

"Oh, yes, Templeton. Well, that's all."

"Yes, sir. And thanks."

Sometimes it's not so nice to get lost. Particularly if you once were a person, whole and alive. But even getting a little bit lost, a man stops covering himself up. He has something to live for, he has something to work for, he has something to go home for.

Even in the trolley and on the elevated station there's a difference. There's the difference of a flat on Eighth Street and a wondering who was living there now and passing a dirty window in a tenement house and thinking how much better a small home in the suburbs of Chicago was no matter how many roof-tops there might be in tenement houses. What the hell good is a rooftop without anyone there? The castle disappears into a lot of hot air. Knocking yourself out in New York for a check one month and a free meal mooched the next, and nothing at the end of it except a shot of whiskey if a buddy had an extra buck. What the hell happens to rainbows in New York?

A guy sits down next to you in the trolley and you wonder what happens to him when it's six o'clock and when it's eleven at night and when it's two in the morning. Where does he wind up? In a flophouse, in a whore house if he's got a couple bucks, in the gutter with holes in his shoes, or in a bar with a ten-cent glass of beer in his hand.

What the hell has he got? What does he look forward to? You pass over big streets and big buildings and you wonder what happens to those thousands of kids walking around with manuscripts under their arms, designs in their briefcases, if they have a briefcase, a play in their hand, a new tube of paint in their pocketbook, ,and then you think back just a little way and you know what happens to those kids and you feel good because you know what has happened to you and it isn't the same as to those kids.

You get off the trolley and you walk a few blocks and the air feels good and you take a deep breath and you feel good because you put your hand in your pocket and you know you have enough money to pay for that gulp of fresh air. You think what a guy by the name of Jack Evans would say to that and you immediately stop thinking of a guy by the name of Jack Evans because that was a point on a circle and that was a different world.

You open a front door and you smell something cooking and you feel like a man and you feel like you've been successful and have accomplished something you can hold in your hand, and you know that the best thing about everything is that you've got something to come home for.

"This is good, Ruthie, I'm happy. Are you happy?"

"Of course, darling. Of course, I'm happy."

"You don't miss New York?"

"We've got more than New York, Joe. We've got a little house. We've got a car. We've got movies and theatre and concerts and night clubs. We don't have them twenty-four hours a day, but we've got ourselves twenty-four hours a day and that's what matters."

"Fifteen hours a day. I still work. The Writing Craft Better Ad Agency, you know."

"Even fifteen hours. It's as good as twenty-four."

"C'mere darling."

"Joe."

"C'mere. That's better. You know, I think you're right. Sometimes it does seem as good as twenty-four."

"Joe."

A man who is going around in circles finally stops and goes in the other direction. The scenery is new. He is happy. The woman who kept looking for something in a shop window and out of the tenth floor of an office building stops looking and holds onto a star. The star shines brightly and she is happy.

"Joe, darling."

"What, Ruthie?"

"Do you love me?"

"Oh, hush. I married you for your polo ponies. You didn't know I was an expert polo player, did you?"

"Stop kidding."

"I'm serious. A ten-goal man I was rated as."

"Joe."

"Yeah, baby?"

"Will you get mad if I ask you something?"

"I shouldn't get mad, should I?"

"No."

"Then ask it."

"Do you miss Julia?"

"Do I . . . no, of course, not. What made you ask that?"

"Do you miss New York?"

"I've never been happier, baby. You know that."

"Sometimes you seem kind of listless, kind of disappointed. I was just wondering."

"You know me, don't you? We've been married a year now. You've known me longer than that. You know that if I was dissatisfied I'd do something about it, don't you?"

"Yes, I do. But I also know that if you thought it would hurt me, you'd keep quiet."

"Are you happy, Ruthie?"

"I couldn't be happier. You're what I've always wanted. You've given me love and security and life and a home and entertainment and the arts and all those things that never seemed to go together before I knew you. But they do now, and it's all your fault."

"Then you are happy?"

"Of course, Joe. Of course, I am."

"Then what's all the fuss about?"

"No fuss. No fuss at all. I was just worried about you."

"Well, Ruthie baby, don't worry about me. I'm happy, baby. Happy as I ever could be."

A man who is going around in circles finally stops and walks in a different direction. Even if he keeps going in another circle the scenery is new. For a long time the scenery remains new.

When a guy is disillusioned, sick, tired, lost, he runs away. That's the guy Ben saw when he looked at himself. Sometimes it's easy to run away. Sometimes you start to run and then realize that everything isn't as bad as it seems and don't run. Sometimes when you think you're no longer lost and seem to have found yourself, a girl comes along by the name of Julia and suddenly you begin to need again and that need is fulfilled for a moment and then the fulfillment goes away and you wonder what there is for you and where and whether you'll ever be strong enough to find it.

So you start walking to the Brooklyn Bridge and from the Brooklyn Bridge you see hundreds of specks below and you wonder how many handfuls of specks would go into two billion and you know that you're going in the wrong direction. Hey, bud, which way is away from the Brooklyn Bridge? No, I don't know where I'm going, but I know this isn't it. You begin to feel better. You tell yourself that you know where you're going, but you don't know in which direction to start. And then you wonder who you're kidding and think about the Brooklyn Bridge again and figure maybe that's the best way after all. Where does the circle stop? Where do you stop in the circle? Is it in Ruthie? Is it in Julia? Is it in a guy named Ben Stevens? And the last is the easiest of all to say and the hardest to understand. How many guys are Aristotles?

So you go away. You go away because you keep looking, and if you can't find it here it may be someplace else. But keep moving. If you stop, you think. If you think, you look. If you look, you find what you can't find, so keep running.

"No, Jack, I can't stay. I've got to get away from New York."

"It's not a woman, is it, Ben?"

"Look, Jack Evans, what the hell do you want? I ask for a favor, and you want my life story."

"I know your life story, Ben. And I didn't mean Julia. I know enough to leave you alone on that. I mean, you don't need a woman to sleep with now?"

"Do you have to ask?"

"No. I just wanted to make sure. Okay, I'll call some of my friends at the Highlander Folk School in Tennessee. You'll get to know people. You'll see how they live, how they breathe, how they think, how they work, how they starve, how they die. And you'll also probably be called a communist."

"The hell with names. I want to write about people. Can I do it?"

"You can do it like you've never done it before. In Tennessee you've got every sonofabitch of an industrialist breaking the back of every poor white and colored bastard who can't fight back. If they want to vote, they throw them in jail. If they speak up their family gets a cross burned on the front steps and a daughter gets gang raped. And every so often they pick up some poor Negro and put him in jail for allegedly molesting a white woman and he gets the electric chair or a lynching and everybody is happy for a few months or a few years. Like this guy Willie McGee. In 1950, not the 1800s, damn it, with the hypocrisy of Supreme Court decisions and Truman's rhetoric on civil rights, Willie McGee gets crucified by the state for a crime he didn't commit. Never mind, Ben, you'll see enough of that shit when you're down there."

"How will I fit in at Highlander, Jack?

"One of the things they've been doing is making films. Documentaries, educational outreach. Pamphlets. Flyers. Lectures."

"I'll have a chance to write?"

"I think so. You get only room and board and a few bucks a

week. But you'll see people, you'll write for people. And you'll have enough time to write your novel or whatever else you want to write."

"Why aren't you there, Jack?"

"Because I'm needed up here. Maybe no one person is really needed in New York. Maybe nobody at all. Maybe we should all go to Tennessee and Mississippi and Georgia and South Dakota? But when New York starts firing school teachers because they want to join a union and won't support the same kind of politics as the mayor and the school board, and when people are fired from jobs because somebody sends an anonymous postcard from a vacant lot accusing them of being a commie or red or fellow traveler and the politicians and employers let it happen . . . you see what I mean."

"I'm beginning to understand you, Jack."

"You've always understood me, Ben."

"I think I have. If I haven't, Tennessee ought to help me."

"Good luck, Ben."

"Thanks, Jack. I'll need it."

You board a train at Pennsylvania station and hum the song about the Chattanooga Choo-Choo and wonder whether you're making a mistake. You look at the people in the station and every man looks like a guy named Ben Stevens and every woman looks like somebody named Julia and you get on the train quickly and hope this really is something new, something that will let you know which way to go, how to go. As you leave the station every track seems to go around in a circle and every railroad tie looks like every other railroad tie and they begin to go around and around and you wonder if you'll ever get off them.

When you hurt, you hurt all over. You want only to hurt inside because that belongs to you, but you hurt outside as well. Time is a great healer. It heals what is outside. Inside there always remains something that doesn't belong there and also something that's missing. For Julia everything was wrong. There was no place to go, no man to run to. Joe was gone. Ben could have become Joe after a while, after the feeling began to become something she could put her hands on and look at and hold and understand. But Ben was gone, too. There was nothing else. The life that could be shared belonged to no one. What had been Julia's was now non-existent. There was no more Julia. Now it was just Mrs. Walter Mitchell. How much can you forget and still not forget everything?

You try to replace Eighth Street with a house in New Rochelle, and you try to open a bottle of milk and make believe it's not a bottle with a picture of an old man on the label and you try to drive to the corner grocery and make believe that turning the corner is not turning the corner or Avenue C in the Village, and you try to sit down and talk about insurance with people named Max and Mitzi and make believe it's not talking about a new show or sex or the living world with people named Ruthie and Ben. Even Ruthie and Ben become things that are happy to think about next to Max and Mitzi, and you don't, want to think of Ruthie and Ben because that comes right back to a guy named Joe, and you learn to tune in the right television programs and plan the right things for dinner and say the right things to business men with bald heads and vests, who have too much money to know what to do with it and so put it into insurance.

"Julia, I love you. I love you even more than when we were first married. Does that make you happy?"

"Yes, Walter. Of course, it does. I'm your wife."

"For the last couple of months; ever since you quit that club in New York, you've been like I've always wanted you. And the way you treat those clients. Boy, you should've been an insurance salesman yourself, you know that Julia?"

"I'm glad you're satisfied, Walter."

"Am I? Why, you're the best wife of any of the guys down at the office. At least you help me sell more insurance than any of the others."

"That's wonderful."

"And you know what else, Julia?"

"What?"

"You're getting a new mink for your birthday. Five grand. Five thousand dollars I'm going to pay for it. How's that?"

"Walter, you really try to do everything you can for me, don't you."

"Of course I do. I told you, I love you."

"I know. And I appreciate it, Walter. I want you to know that."

"Don't thank me. All that's expected. You're my wife, you know. What would the guys at the office think if I didn't get you mink coats. I'm a junior executive now."

You wear mink coats and diamond necklaces and emerald rings and the sparkle almost blinds you and you think how lucky you are and how nice and secure and comfortable your home and life is and you wonder why the hell you ever stayed with it so long. Then you think of things you don't want to think about and you go driving in a new Cadillac and look in store windows and pick out a new evening dress and the newest hat styled from Paris. You wonder how long you can keep on buying new hats, but what else is there in life?

"What's wrong, Julia? I've been watching you lately. Aren't you feeling well."

"I'm all right, Walter. Maybe it's the weather."

"But a month ago you were all full of pep and did so much around the house. Planned dinners and made parties and even went out with me to my clients for dinner. Something's wrong."

"I'm just a little tired."

"Do you miss that group in Manhattan."

"No, why should I miss them? Damn it, why should I miss them?"

"Don't get excited; I just asked."

"Don't ask me again, Walter. Never ask me again about the Village."

"Okay, I'm sorry. Maybe you need fresh air, exercise. You do seem to be gaining a little weight, you know."

"I don't need exercise. Leave me alone, for God's sake, will you Walter? I've tried my best around here. Just leave me alone."

"It's for your own good, Julia. That's the only reason I'm saying. Why don't you come down to the Country Club gym? Play some racketball. That's a terrific game, racketball."

You want to scream and tell him to go away, but you wonder what the use of that would be. Then you feel your stomach and you think of Joe. And you think of a night in the Barrow Street Apartment. And you think of Ben and Ben becoming Joe and life coming from Joe through Ben into you and Ben disappears and only Joe remains. You've kept part of him with you. Inside your body.

"Walter, I'm going to have a baby."

"A baby!"

"I thought you wanted a baby."

"I do. I'm…I don't know what to say, Julia, this is wonderful. A baby!"

"You've wanted a baby for years, haven't you?"

"Yes, now we'll have one. My baby. Julia, you don't know how happy it makes me. My baby!"

"You wanted a baby and I brought you a baby."

"I've got to call up the boys. Tell them I'm going to have a baby. I've waited a long time, Julia. It's wonderful. I'm going to call Mack right now. Right this minute. Imagine; a baby. I'm going to have a baby."

Walter disappears and you go into the living room and open a cabinet and take out a bottle of liquor and pour one drink and another drink and another drink and you wonder do you just keep going around and around and around in a circle and does it ever stop.

CHAPTER 19
DIRECTIONS

Two years can be a long time or a short time. Two years can disappear in the normal course of life and one day you wake up and say "Isn't that funny, I don't know where the last two years have gone." As if they never were. If you took out two years from your life and began where you had left off there might be no difference whatsoever.

Two years can also be a long time and an important time. Two years can change an entire life. It can take you further around on the circle. It can take you off one merry-go-round and put you on another. It can give you a new road and a new understanding. Or it can bring you full circle and start you again from the same place..

Joe didn't know which applied to him. If he thought about it he'd say his entire life was changed because he knew it had to be changed. You couldn't live for two years in a new city with a new conception of work, play, love, of everything that goes into living and not say that there was a change. Chicago is a big city, although not nearly New York. It gave him what he thought he must have always wanted or at least what he thought he should have always wanted. The mortgage on his house was being paid regularly, the car had no lien, there was a television set in the living room, dinner downtown twice a week, an occasional show or concert, sometimes a night club on a Saturday, an easy job with one-hundred dollars a week for merely sitting in an office and writing eight hours a day. This was good, he supposed, and yet something was missing. Maybe it was too good? Maybe he should have been a bum on The Bowery with a perpetual quart of gin and a dame in a cheap whore house until he got too old and too broke? He kept looking for something more, something different. He kept telling himself that he was happy, but he still kept looking. He didn't know what he expected to find. He didn't know if he should find anything. He didn't even know why he looked except that after two years he had to and so he did.

"Hey, Harry, how about some relaxation tonight? I know a little men's club over on the south side. Plenty of liquor and plenty of women."

"I'm a married man, Joe. What the hell do I want with a club like that?"

"So am I married. That doesn't mean you can't have fun."

"Not that kind, Joe. Besides, you can't tell who might find out. And then where will you be?"

"If that's the reason, it's a helluva lousy one."

"How long have you been married?"

"Two years, Harry."

"Well, when you're married as long as I am you'll see it a different way. You know what happens to fifteen bucks out of my paycheck each week?"

"You booze up and lay in the gutter from Friday to Monday."

"I'm giving you some advice, Joe. I take this fifteen and it all goes to pay the rent on a little apartment out on Moreland Avenue. See what I mean?"

"So why the hell don't you get a divorce?"

"Divorce, Joe? Don't be silly. I'm a happily married man. I love my wife."

What makes a happily married man? A paycheck each week? A membership card in the Parents-Teachers Association? A certificate signed by a priest-pastor-rabbi or clerk-of-the-court? Joe looked around the office, wondered who would go to a club on the south side and who would support a twenty-one-year-old blonde in a northside apartment? He mentally set up two boxes, put each man into a box as he sized them up. When finished, he looked at another box and it grew into a house with a front porch and a woman in pajamas, a woman with an apron, a woman in an evening dress. He wondered how many men fit exclusively into that box. He wondered whether those boxes had to be divided or if there were gates between them and if men were supposed to go from one to the other. He wondered where he belonged. He wondered whether he belonged anywhere. He took off his coat and rolled up his sleeves and blamed his mood on the hot weather. Only the weather was no hotter than usual, so he rolled his sleeves down again and sat and thought some more. He would think about being happy and a picture of his house kept running through his head and he kept walking out of an upstairs window onto a rooftop that wasn't there.

Even in his office.

"You look like you're far away, handsome? What are you dreaming about?"

"Beautiful girls, Susie. I always dream about beautiful girls."

"A place for me there, Mr. Templeton?"

"Sure is, Miss Swift. Right up there, front of the stage."

"I dream about you, too."

"Yeah?"

"And in my dreams you're always the only one out there in the audience."

"Go back to your ad art, Susie, before the Sta-Put Brassiere company winds up flat-chested for the month."

"If they did, I'd take over and fill up their requirements. Don't you think I could, Joe?"

"By all means, Susie. If anybody here could do it, you could."

"And without a brassiere."

"I've got very good eyesight."

"I know you have, Joe. I've noticed."

"Your sweaters are too tight."

"No. Just right. You've noticed how I've moved my desk. Facing you now, Joe."

"Sweetheart, two years ago you'd be spending your nights just where you'd like to be spending them. But right now I'm a married man."

"So are a dozen other guys who work around here. Did you ever watch them look at me? Sure you did. Did you ever hear them ask? Probably not, because they're afraid of anybody finding out. They don't get to first base."

"You know, Susie, with the heat from outside and with you standing so close to me, it's getting mighty damned hot in here."

"It could be hotter."

"Christ, babe, I'm married."

"All right, so was I."

"I am now. I'm in love with my wife. I'm happily married."

"I'm only trying to help you, Joe. I've noticed how you've been looking lately. Maybe you need someone to talk to? Real confidential like."

"I'm all right. It's the weather. Too hot."

"I've got a place that's real cool. On Roosevelt Avenue. Not a new house, but it's an apartment on the eighth floor with a roof out from my bedroom window. Like a balcony. I call it my castle tower."

"Oh, shit!"

"Don't be so surprised. It's really nice. Real cool at night. Wonderful sleeping. You know my phone number, Joe. Some night when you're feeling hot."

Joe felt hot. He had felt hot for months. Blame it on the weather. Where do you find the answer to what's inside of you? Maybe it isn't in Chicago? Maybe it isn't in a wife and a home? This was new; this was virginal. This was something that had never been done, never been touched. And how do you find out whether that's what the inside wants? You think about these things and the clock says five o'clock and you stop thinking and put on your jacket and cover your typewriter and lock your desk and go home. Even the trolley begins to look different. The guys with the bottles in their pocket seem freer. The apartments with the dirty windows become exciting. The people hurrying back and forth are living adventurous lives. Even the streetcar conversations begin to mean something more.

"Now, Hank, I wouldn't take her out on a bet. You get under her dress and then she wants to go home."

"Technique, Jerry; that's what does it. Four different ones I had last week. And all blondes. Only there ain't no difference. You turn out the light and the blondes are the same as the brunettes."

"I'm after a new one, Hank. I don't know yet if she does or not. Some of the guys have taken her out and tried and haven't gotten anyplace. But she might. And boy, that body."

"If she does, it sure is worth it. Wish I had one."

"If you're that hard up, Jerry, come up to my apartment. I got one chick that you'd really go for."

Your station is called. You get off the trolley and you realize that you're smiling. You wonder what you're smiling about and you think about a rooftop that becomes a castle tower and you wonder what Hank's bedroom looks like and you suddenly remember that you know what it looks like and you think about all that for a couple of blocks, and you're home and there's no more smile. What the hell does a guy do, you wonder?

"Joe, I think you ought to stop drinking so much."

"Aw, Ruthie, lay off, will you. I'm not drinking so much. Just a shot now and then."

"I don't care, Joe. Except that it's no good for you. You know it makes you angry and cranky."

"Maybe because you're angry and cranky first. Now leave me alone."

"What's happened to you, Joe? These last couple weeks. What's the matter?"

"Nothing."

"You're not happy. You're not like you've been. Are you sorry?"

"Sorry about what?"

"Sorry that you married me. Do you miss Julia?"

"Shut up. I asked you not to mention Julia."

"Joe, I've got to know. If you can't be happy, then I want to do something about it."

"Nothing's wrong."

"You've said that."

"Then why the hell don't you leave me alone, Ruthie?"

"All right, Joe."

"I'll be all right. Just not feeling well. I'll be all right."

You know what's wrong, but you're afraid to say it. So you keep on drinking and you wish you had enough courage to do something, but you know it takes more courage not to do something, so you get crankier and angrier and you can't help yourself.

"Joe, please talk to me. Tell me what's wrong. I want us both to be happy. But if you're not, if you're going to keep on this way, then I can't take it either."

"What do you want, a divorce?"

"Is that what you want, Joe?"

"No, I don't want anything. Just let me work it out in my own way, will you?"

"Is it other women?"

"Have I been out with other women, Ruthie?"

"What do you want, Joe? I've given you everything I can. For two whole years now. What more can I do for you?'

"Nothing. Not a damned thing. I'll be all right. Just stop nagging me."

"You want to get another woman?"

"Shuttup."

"All right, then leave me. But don't keep going on like this."

"Ruthie, please. Leave me alone. I married you because I needed you. I need something now. Maybe it's you, maybe it isn't. But I've got to find it in my own way."

"How long are you going to be looking for an answer, Joe?"

"If you don't let me find it …"

"All right. Whatever way is best for you. I've got to find one myself."

"What's your trouble?"

"Joe, I know what it is. Let's have a baby."

"No baby!"

"Maybe that's the answer? I'll give us something to bring us together again."

"No baby!"

"Then what, Joe? What?"

"God damn it, leave me alone, will you? Leave me find it. Let me look for it myself. Let me live my life myself."

"All right, Joe; all right. Maybe that's best."

"I'm sorry, Ruthie. I'm sorry I talked like that, but...oh, hell... give me time, will you?"

"Okay, Joe. I'll give you time. All the time you want. If you need me Joe, I'm still here. I'm going out for a walk now. I need the fresh air."

"I'm sorry, Ruthie. But I can't help it."

You begin to wonder if you can't help living, either. You wonder if there was a fate that put up a little chart with the name Joe Templeton on top of it and then decided that all during the life of the chart this would happen and that would happen and that Joe Templeton would have no say. That Joe Templeton was like a horse on a merry-go-round, up and down and round and round and always the same path and in the same circle. And you begin to be smothered and the circle begins to grow tighter again and once more you've got to run. And if your name is Joe Templeton the easiest way to run is to run backwards. So you go over to the phone and dial a number.

"Susie? Hello, babe. This is Joe Templeton. Yeah, it's plenty hot. Sure, I know how to get there. And...uh...babe...that window still opens out onto your castle tower, doesn't it?"

A king looks down from his castle and surveys his people. He confers with his ministers and meditates upon his kingdom. Then he retires to his bed at night and sleeps peacefully and, for the purposes of history, politics, journalists and fairy tales, he knows all about his people.

Joe had been a king on the balcony of an eight-story brick building. Ben had been a king sitting in the corner of a room surrounded by shelves of books and albums of records. The king lives and dies and except for once in every great while is sheltered from truth and reality and in his lifetime knows no more than on the day he was born and on the day after he had died.

But you cannot escape reality in an apartment on the east side of New York City. Not and be happy and walk the streets without visiting an analyst every other week. Joe tried to find the answer in a new city and a new life and in a new castle. But it made no difference whether the king has learned anything or not. A king does not have to face reality.

Ben tried to find the answer in the question: Which way to the insides of the minds of two billion people? Which way to the inside of myself? On the sharecropper farms? In the driftwood huts? In the dirty, loused, lightless flats you find too much of in Tennessee? The inside sticks out into the open and only a blind man or a man who does not want to see walks away and shrugs his shoulders and says too bad and forgets about it. Ben Stevens did want to see.

A man becomes complicated to himself. He cannot see himself clearly. In a big city like New York, when things keep happening, only the difficulties become visible and pretty soon the skeleton of the man himself disappears. In Tennessee you can see a man naked as truth. There is no lie to live on brown bread and scraps of meat under a leaky roof, if a roof at all, and wear torn shoes and frayed pants and a ragged shirt and be able to put all your worldly possessions in your pockets, both of which have large holes in them. There is no lie in this kind of man. He is simple and naked and this was the man that Ben saw. Seeing him, he could begin to think about himself and judge himself. What would be his problems in a torn shirt and ragged pants and an empty stomach? Not a new book or a phonograph record or a musical comedy or a woman to sleep with or somebody named Julia. Where the hell do you find a garbage can to fill your belly and a gutter with a lit cigarette to fill your soul? You see them and then you visit them and then you talk to them and then you live with them and then you become one of them and then, eventually, you really begin to know who they are. Hey, Mac, how can two billion people jump off the Brooklyn Bridge?

"Ben Stevens?"

"Yes, and you're Howard Nelson?"

"Right. Glad to meet you, Ben. Glad to meet anybody from New York who's willing to give up the comforts of civilization to come down here. Jack Evans said a lot of good things about you."

"Thanks, Howard. I'm still kind of uncertain about this whole business. It's new to me."

"It's new to all of us, Ben. It's always new because once you've done one thing, there's always something else that comes up, and we've got to start all over again. Did Jack tell you much about our organization?"

"Pretty much."

"Then you know it isn't too easy a time. You'll see a lot of things that'll tear your heart out. You'll fight to make it good and sometimes you'll succeed. But the minute you turn away it'll go bad again and you'll find yourself up against the same problem with different faces. In New York things work fast. They're slow here."

"I want to get to know these people. And I want to write."

"You'll do both. If nothing else, you'll get that. To write the kind of educational films and radio shows we're trying to produce you've got to know these people. And the writing has got to be good. We're fighting every industry, every business man, every white-collar worker down here who wants to keep the Negro in his place and keep the poor whites where they have to fight the Negro for the few cents that the big landowners toss their way. They're professionals at hate and murder and every other dirty trick you sometimes read about in books but don't believe because it's all seems too ugly to be true. With the rich and powerful and the bigots against us, a lot of people are afraid."

"I'm not, Howard."

"Good."

"I'm here, Howard, because I've got two billion people in back of me."

At first you walk through the farms and watch the little Black bodies, almost naked, running from house to field and field to house and picking cotton and shoveling manure and plowing land and you want to know what they think and what they feel and you go to talk to them."

"Mr. Wilson."

"Yes, sir."

"I'd like to talk to you."

"Yes, sir."

"My name is Stevens. I'm from those people with the moving pictures down the road. The Highlander School."

"Yes, sir. We like 'em fine, sir."

"Tell me about yourself. About living on the farm, working the farm."

"We like it fine, sir."

"How about the hard work, the poor pay?"

"We eat pretty near regular, sir, and we got a roof over our heads."

"Don't call me sir, will you? I'm a friend of yours. I'm not from down here. I'm from New York. Don't call me sir."

"Yes, sir!"

And you wonder what's wrong and why you can't get close, until you walk down the street of a city and see the Black men and women and children step to the side or into the gutter because a white skin passes, and you watch the landlord's agent come to collect the rents and the Wilsons and the Smiths and the Davenports see their last few pennies disappear into the pockets of the white men who allow them the crumbs to live another day and harvest another acre, the white hand pocketing the money and wiping itself against a trouser leg. The next time the money changed hands it would no longer be contaminated.

And you begin to stop often and talk often and pretty soon you begin to be talked to and welcomed and known.

"Mist' Ben. Glad to see you."

"Hi, Jimmy. How are you today?"

"Miseries again."

"Brought you a pack of cigarettes. Extra-long kind. That ought to ease it a little."

"It helps, Mist' Ben. It helps. Only you shouldn't spend your money like that."

"I'll smoke one too. How's that?"

"Fine. Have a seat. Would you like to eat somethin' with us? Ain't ate supper yet."

"Not tonight, Jimmy. Some other time."

"Okay, Mist' Ben. But sit down and talk to us a while."

A figure on a census report becomes a figure in a book of photographs which in turn becomes the man in the street who turns out to be a next-door neighbor who becomes a friend. And you begin to know a friend.

"Ben, you shouldn't come around like this to help us pick cotton. We got enough help."

"I need the exercise, Charlie. How's the crop coming?"

"Not so good. They ask us for more than last year, but I'm getting old now and one of the kids got that rickets or whatever it's called and little Betsie, she ain't never walking yet."

"Well, then you need an extra hand. Let's fill a couple more bushels here and then go and eat. I brought you some food today. Mind if I stay and eat with you?"

"Sure, Ben, sure, you're welcome any time. Any time at all."

You get to know the person and you get to know the group and you even get to know the statistics. The Black girl is taken into the white automobile and nine months later a baby is born. There is no outcry. Perhaps someday the girl will marry and raise a family and the child will grow up and no word will be said because no word can be said. The husband belongs to the wife and the wife belongs to the husband. And if they're Black they both belong to the white man. A man with Black skin talks to a woman with white skin and he has no more job and his family has no more food and if he should protest being called a dirty nigger or a black coon or a slimy nigra bastard he is thrown in jail for disturbing the peace, for assault, for manslaughter, for attempted robbery, for rape. The sights and sounds of the South: chain gangs, beatings, bare backs and forced perversion, tar and feathers, rape, starvation, ropes and trees and electric chairs against a background of laughing white faces. Justice for the Negro. Stay in your place, or there will be no place for you to stay in. Be a good nigra, be one of our nigras and you'll live another day.

"What's the matter, Irmalee? Something happen?"

"I'm out of a job, Mist' Stevens."

"My name is Ben. Tell me about it."

"It's James, Ben. My husband James. I tell him not to try and vote, but he does it anyway, and they beat him up. 'The man I work for, he says his wife hears about it and they don't want no bad nigger working for them, so I'm out of a job."

"Where's James?"

"He's hiding. But I think he's okay. They say they won't do nothin' to nobody if we don't try and vote."

"Anybody going to?"

"Guess not. Nobody wants to be beat up. And they take your job away."

"I'll go and talk to them, Irmalee. See, if we do go and vote, then there'll be enough of us to take away the guns from the men who beat us up and we'll be able to vote just like anybody else all the time, and maybe even have a colored man as a judge or a congressman."

"I'm afraid of talk like that, Ben. A lot of us are. But you come and talk to them anyway. I hope you can do something."

"We can all do something if we stick together. And don't worry about your job. We'll fix you up with something down at the center."

"Thank you, Ben. We got a lot of us willing and able to stand up for It folks liker you, Black and white, comin' down from the north, that gives us s big help."

You begin to reach part of the two billion and you feel good. You think you've found the answer. You think you know the solution. But then there is no job, and thousands have no food. The film center runs short of money and the truck gets stopped and the films are taken out and burned. And the more you try and reach the people the more the others try to stop you. And the people shiver, figuratively and literally, and you wonder what the hell you're fighting for and why you don't go back to New York and write a book about your adventures among the happy, contented Black people of Tennessee and make a fortune for being a good white liberal humanitarian. It's easy to look around you and see people doing the same thing you're doing and still feel that you stand alone.

"Look, Ben, what kind of crap are you giving me? My people down here can't do what you and I are doing. You know that. If they open their mouths they'll find a noose around their necks."

"I know that, Mitch. But when?"

"Not now, not yet. But it's coming. We're working together. It takes time for a movement to grow.

"You're an exception."

"No, I'm not. There are more and more like me."

"Willing to gr their heads cracked."

"I got a lucky break, Ben, when I got out of the army and was able to go to college. My skin is still as black as any of them out there picking cotton. if I don't say yes, ma'am and yes, sir to any white person who looks at me, I'll land in jail whether I have a college degree or not or whether I speak better English and know more about law than the judge does himself. You're on the outside. I'm in the sardine can with the rest of them.. You're on the outside trying to help us open that sardine can and we appreciate it. We're getting stronger and we're coming out."

"I guess I'm too impatient, Mitch."

"So am I, Ben. I'm making speeches, I'm talking to people, I'm showing them your films, I'm trying to get them jobs. I'm doing what I can. I can't take a sign in my hand and walk up and down in front of the city hall. You know how long I'd last that way."

"You're right, Mitch. I just get a little discouraged."

"I do, too, Ben."

"And I guess you should."

"But look what we've got to look forward to. It'll come, Ben, marching shoulder to shoulder through Tennessee, through the entire South. But right now, tonight, Ben, I got a meeting setup with bunch of people working at the mill. Join us and bring one of your films."

"Mitch."

"Yeah?"

"Give me your hand, Mitch. Next time I talk like I did just let me have a few of the knuckles."

You go into town and see a show and hear a concert and take a book out of the library and someplace you meet a soft, sweet southern girl and you begin to ache inside for a woman and you wonder whether a bed in New York wouldn't have solved your personal problems after all.

"Come on up, Ben. Just because you're from New York you don't have to be afraid of southern girls. We won't eat you alive."

"Sure your folks won't be home?"

"They'll be out all night. They always are. This is my bedroom."

"You've got a nice figure, baby."

"Baby?"

"I had a friend who used to say that. Baby. Just like that."

"It's okay with me. My figure's better this way though, isn't it. See, they're not false."

"No, they're not."

"Well, its your turn to start, Ben."

"My turn?"

"With your clothes. That's so we come out even. It saves a lot of time. Don't you think?"

"You're a cute kid."

"Thanks, Ben. Ben, you still haven't told me what you do."

"Is this a time to ask me?"

"I always ask. I mean, I'm interested."

"I work for the film center."

"Film center?"

"Outside of town."

"With the niggers? That nigger place?"

"There are some Negroes working with us."

"Now, look. I thought you were okay, but I don't want nobody who's around those niggers getting inside of me. I've had plenty of northerners, but they weren't no nigger-lovers. I'm a clean girl, I am."

"Yes, I can see you are, babe. Have you ever been on Eighth Street in New York?"

"What're you getting dressed for? I didn't really mean it. C'mon, Ben. I was only kidding. Ben, I'm standing here naked. I'm ready for you, for God's sake, don't get dressed now."

"I asked you. Have you ever been on Eighth Street in New York?"

"No, I've never been north at all. What do you want to know for?"

"Because, babe, there's a wonderful apartment there where a year ago you and I might have had a lot of fun if a guy by the name of Joe had had a bottle of whiskey in stock. But I'm afraid at this point you're just a little too late. Get yourself a nice fat traveling salesman. They've got a lot of energy. Good night, babe."

Ben breathed fresh air outside and wondered whether he had gone crazy or should enter a monastery. What the hell is the matter with me, walking out of a woman's bedroom when I should be glad to stay there for weeks and weeks? A little too late. He said his thoughts out loud. He was seeing himself. He had tried to know and understand the feelings of Black people, subject not only to nature but to the beliefs and whims of most of the people in their environment, and he had tried to see beyond the screen that covered up his own feelings. He was beginning to know what he wanted, what he should want, what he would want. There was no circle. There were no high walls on either side. Everything was free and clear around him. Only people. Two billion of them, clamped down under a giant gold piece. But now he was both on the outside looking in and on the inside looking out. There was no need for a southern whore or sweet belle to make Ben feel strong or give Ben confidence. All he needed was Ben. All he ever needed was Ben. Now he was beginning to know it.

"I'm going over to that plant, Howard. I want to get on that picket line in that strike."

"They'll tab you, Ben. You won't be able to show your face around town."

"Those people are fighting for a living wage. If we don't get enough of them out to picket, they'll get those goons and cops to bring in tear gas and clubs and guns."

"You could get hurt, Ben."

"If all of us stay under our beds, Howard, then they'll be nobody to stop them and pretty soon they'll come after us under the beds. I'm going to fight while there's someone fighting with me."

"I agree with you, Ben. I'm just warning you. It's a rough job. They'll beat you up, label you, throw you in jail, call you a communist. You know what it means to be labeled a communist today. No job. No freedom. Maybe jail. Maybe worse. It's open season on communists. They beat up a bunch of people in New York. Remember, at Peekskill? At the Paul Robeson concert. Called them commies and the governor whitewashed the whole thing."

"So what shall I do, Howard? Get a pair of track shoes? Or a bed pan?"

"What you want. I can't tell you. But I've been here a long time. You've been here a year. I've watched you and I know what's happening to you. You're finding yourself. You're finding a lot of truths you never knew before. You can run into it blindly and pat yourself on the shoulder and call yourself a liberal. But that won't last long. The going will get tough and the only pat you'll get is a policeman's club alongside your head. Did you know the police in New York beat up people they think are communists and the mayor there doesn't even give them as much as a reprimand?"

"No."

"You see, you lived in New York for years and didn't know. But it's happened, time and time again. You're starting to fight, Ben. Think it over."

"Thanks, Howard, I will think about it."

In the South you're called a communist for speaking to Negroes or helping whites striking against unjust working conditions. In the North you're called a communist for advocating peace in the world and fighting for your brothers in the South. Ben wondered what a communist was. Did he have horns? Did he carry a bomb in his pocket? Did it mean because you believed in life, in people, you were a communist, a Republican, a Democrat, a Negro, a white man, a Chinese, a ... Ben stopped. I'm going in circles again. What the hell difference does it make what they call me. Let them call me whatever the hell they want. as long as I know who I am myself.

As Ben watched and worked and knew and fought, he learned what he wanted to learn. Here were the people. Eleven million whose skins were a different color. Millions more who didn't have a bank account. Others whose names were too long, others who went to the wrong church, who talked with a different accent, who worked at a different job, who came from a different country. Two billion of them, all different and all people. He knew which way from the Brooklyn Bridge. He knew which way into two billion souls. He just had to look into his own gut and he knew what to do.

He worked on the farms, in the huts, in the tenements with the people, among the people, lived with them, talked with them, knew them. He knew them almost like he knew himself. This was real now. He thought about Steinbeck and "The Grapes of Wrath." A handful of Okies. A handful of people. He wondered why Steinbeck didn't write about these people down here? Why Steinbeck? Why not Stevens? Ben began to write. And the words went straight, row after row, page after page, chapter after chapter. Ben Stevens wrote and as he wrote he knew that the circles were finished. His writing meant something. His writing was going somewhere. He was going somewhere.

CHAPTER 20
ALTERNATIVES

When it's sunny and bright in New Rochelle on Sunday it's as nice as it is anyplace. There are flowers and back yards and lawn chairs and children and cool drinks and shade trees and portable radios and people sitting and enjoying something they feel they should enjoy by being out in the sun. Julia sat in a lawn chair and looked at her swollen belly and wondered how it would feel when it happened. Walter sat in a lawn chair next to her and looked at her swollen belly and didn't think of anything except that it was going to happen and the sooner the better.

"It's wonderful, Julia. We've been married four years and finally we're going to have a baby. I've already ordered cigars. Hope it's a boy."

"It'll be a boy."

"Good. Glad you want a boy, too. Nothing like it. We'll make him an All-American quarterback. A big shot. Might even become a bank president someday. Or in the stock exchange. We'll make him a big man."

"Suppose he doesn't want to become a bank president, Walter. Suppose he just wants to be an ordinary young man who wants to enjoy life?"

"Can't enjoy it without money. Nothing like money. We'll worry about that later. Nelson will find his own way."

"Nelson?"

"Of course, Julia. We've got to name him something, and we

may as well give him a tradition to follow. Nelson is a great name in financial circles."

"Not my son. That's funny, Walter. If you probably weren't serious, I'd laugh. Nelson!"

"It's a good name. One of the finest names in the country. It's associated with greatness, with money, with talent, with culture. What more could a boy want in a name?"

"I've already decided to call him Joe."

"Joe!"

"Joseph. Joe. It's a good name. A clean name. I won't call him anything but Joe."

"It's my baby, too, you know."

"No, Walter. This one is my baby. You can name the next one, if there is a next one. But this one can never have a better name than Joe."

The brightness and the sun disappear and a hospital bed becomes cold and no matter how much progress medical science makes, it still tears to have a child. If you are able to think when you open up and a child comes out, you think how much easier it is for a man to go in, and you wonder if you ever want a man to go in again and is it worth it. The child comes out and it looks like any other child. But you look at its face and you know that the right name for it is Joe. You hold it tight and you whisper Joe, and you look for a husband and a father to hold you tight and you want to say I love you, Joe, and you look up and see a fat dark suit with sweaty hands and a round dripping face and a pocketful of fountain pens and cigars. You close your eyes and wish everything could have stopped when you opened up the first time to let Joe come in. When no one else would ever have ever been able to. You close your eyes and go to sleep and wake up and close your eyes again and wake up and it doesn't matter as much anymore that you had a husband named Walter because you have a son named Joe.

"Joe is six months old now, Julia. You ought to be all right. Let's have another. Maybe it'll be a girl?"

"I had a bad time, Walter. Not yet. Please. Not yet."

"There's been nothing since the baby was born. You don't even know I exist."

"Please, Walter. In another couple months. Then we'll have another. Another couple months. Let me sleep now."

You toss in bed at night and your stomach tightens into little knots, and you feel a heavy, fat hand or a sweaty leg move across your body and you want to throw up and run and run. But you can't run because in the next room there's a little boy who you can't run from. And besides, there's no place to run.

"Happy Birthday to you, Happy Birthday to you, Happy Birthday dear Joseph, Happy Birthday to you."

"Can't wait till he's another couple years old, Julia. First thing I'll do is get him a set of golf clubs and take him out on the course with me. Won't that be something! My own son out playing golf with me. Won't that be something! I can see the other fellows faces. You know, Julia, probably more business deals are made on the golf course than any other place. I will certainly have to teach him how to play golf."

You lose yourself in your child and after a while you don't even mind the Ellises. You bathe and play with and fondle and dress and kiss and teach and you know that the most wonderful thing that ever happened to you was to have Joe's baby.

Julia wasn't drunk or crazy when she slept with Ben that night. She knew what she was doing. And she knew that the baby was Ben's. But Ben never knew and she never told anyone, and she wanted to believe that she had held onto something of Joe's so she kept telling herself it was Joe's baby. And though she knew that it wasn't, whenever she thought about it she believed that it was. She lost track of the Village. Entire track. She had thought about her friends. Once she had met someone whose name she couldn't remember at Horn and Hardart's when she was shopping on 57th Street, and they told her that Ben was down south someplace. At first, it mattered. Ben was something important because he was a link with something important. But she remembered not having reacted with more than a "is that so?" and then Ben disappeared. Once, when she had talked Walter into taking her to a play she saw Jack Evans in the crowd during intermission and wanted to ask him about Joe, but she was afraid to with Walter there and she put out her cigarette quickly and they went back to their seats so that Jack wouldn't see her. She called him up the next day and asked about Joe. Jack asked her to meet him for lunch sometime, she said she would, but never bothered to go. He had told her that Joe and Ruthie were still in Chicago and, as far as he knew, very happy, and that was as close as she wanted to get to the past. So Julia buried herself even deeper into New Rochelle with her little son and tried to be happy. If she never thought of two years ago, then there was nothing to hurt. When she did think of it, it hurt even more. Because the further away it went, the harder it was to bring back. Sometimes even the baby didn't help. Sometimes she would sit softly and sing to him and call him Joe and wonder what Joe would be like, living with her in the house instead of Walter, being the father of her baby, and then she would try to forget, but she couldn't. It was good that Walter was an insurance salesman and entertained clients. That meant that there was an ample supply of whiskey and bourbon around the house. Particularly the kind with the picture of the old man on the label on the bottle. She would hold it up in front of a mirror and ask herself what the old man was thinking, sitting there so peacefully, and what he saw, but she would try to forget and instead of pouring the liquor into a glass for someone else she would drink it herself. A person can forget for only so long. Running away from reality sometimes makes it that much stronger. Like the deer running in a circle from the forest fire. The faster he runs the deeper becomes the circle and the hotter it gets.

"You've been drinking too much, Julia."

"You give it to your clients. I can have some, too."

"It's not the money or the liquor. It just isn't good for you."

"Let me decide."

"Maybe you're sick? Do you want to take Joey and go on a vacation?"

"Yeah, to Chicago."

"Why Chicago, Julia?"

"Why not?"

"You can go to Chicago if you want."

"Go away. Leave me alone."

"What's the matter with you, Julia?"

"Nothing. I just had a little bit too much to drink."

"What's with Chicago?"

"Nothing. Nothing, Walter. I'm not well. I'll be all right. I'm just nervous. Working too hard with the baby. I'll be all right."

And everything gets cool again, and there is more of Joey and less of liquor. And it seems that the whole thing is a bad dream and if you can be left alone for a while everything will become calm and peaceful and happy.

"Just leave me alone for a while, Walter. Everything will be all right."

"Then why do you even come to bed with me? Why did you come to bed with me tonight? If I can't even lay on top of a wife and touch her with my hands what's the sense of it?"

"The sense of what?"

"The sense of being married, Julia. I shouldn't have to beg you. I know you're not passionate like I am. But sometimes, Julia, sometimes you should give in to me."

"All right, Walter. Here, I'll take off my pajamas. I'll open my legs. I'll lift my breasts. Get on top of me and go inside of me and jump up and down on me and then get off and go to sleep."

"What the hell do you think I am, Julia? A cow, a sheep, a horse?"

"Do you want to or don't you, Walter? Let me have some peace, will you? Let me live my life."

"Why don't you divorce me?"

"You really want me to?"

"Give me a wife. Give me a woman in bed."

"I have no choice now, do I, Walter? I have a child. All right. Come on, my husband. Crawl over me. I love it and I love you."

"That's better. How about another baby, Julia?"

"Take my body, take it and let me be. Be happy with me. I'm full, I'm beautiful, I'm firm. Be happy with that. I don't want another baby."

It becomes tight inside and tight outside and to sleep with Walter you might as well live in a whore house and be done with pretending. And the bed gets smaller and smaller and Walter gets bigger and bigger and, just like it used to be, the walls begin to move in and begin to crush you. Unless you run there'll be nothing left of you. You get out of bed and get dressed and tell Walter that you need some fresh air and get in the car and drive to the Bronx and onto the East River Drive and without thinking you are two years younger and nothing has changed. After the fresh air and the old scenery, it becomes new again and something has changed, but instead of going forward you go backward. You become five years younger. Julia turned the Cadillac onto 72nd Street and parked in front of a brownstone house.

"I don't love you anymore, Julia."

"I didn't expect you to, Jack."

"Then why did you come here? You're used to having people in love with you."

"You don't have to sleep with me, Jack. That's funny. Telling Jack Evans he doesn't have to sleep with me. I remember when…"

"So do I, Julia. That's all over."

"I guess a lot of things are over."

"Why did you come here?"

"Christ, Jack, I can't stand it anymore. Two years. Two whole years like that. Even if it's just to talk to you."

"You can always talk to me, Julia. You have a child?"

"How did you know?"

"I heard. Mind if I pour myself a drink?"

"No. And one for me, too, please."

"For you? You never drank."

"I've become sociable, Jack."

"You used to know different ways of being sociable."

"Let's not discuss that, Jack."

"Okay. Here."

"Thanks."

"Walter again, Julia?"

"It's the whole thing, Jack. When Joe came…"

"Joe was there?"

"That's my boy's name."

"It figures."

"When Joe was born I got lost in him. Every once in a while when it would hurt, I'd get lost again."

"That's why you never kept our lunch date."

"That's right; but it's hurt too much lately. I had to get out. You're the only one I can talk to now."

"I'm always here."

"How's Joe?"

"I'm glad I'm good for something."

"I thought you understood me, Jack."

"I do, Julia. I'm trying to break the ice."

"It's broken. How's Joe?"

"I got a letter from Ruthie a couple weeks ago. She doesn't sound happy."

"Joe's coming back?"

"He got a raise. He's still there."

"Oh."

"That's all I know about him. No children. They were happy for a long time. Even Joe wrote for a while and he never writes. But now every so often I hear from Ruthie. Do you really care, Julia?"

"Shall I go there, Jack?"

"Don't be silly."

"I can make him come back."

"Maybe."

"I've got ways, Jack. He'll have to."

"The baby?"

"Yes."

"Forget about him. I know you can't, as much as you've tried to. Do you really believe Joe has changed?"

"He'll never change, Jack. I know that."

"So you got even with Walter."

"No. I got even with myself. For letting Joe go."

"He doesn't know?"

"Nobody does. Just you."

"You've had a rough time, Julia."

"Thanks for the sympathy."

"Once I would have felt sorry for myself and envied you, Julia. Now I feel sorry for you."

"That doesn't help."

"Sorry. I'm thinking out loud. I was lost. I'm not anymore. Now you're lost."

"You'll always be lost, Jack, in all your radical politics."

"I may end up in jail, but I won't be lost."

"You're not afraid of women anymore?"

"I never was. I found out I was afraid of myself. I looked in the mirror and I found out I wasn't a genius. I was just a little guy with some writing talent who believed in something. And that's what I'm doing. I know what I want to do and whether it's right or wrong it makes me happy."

"Maybe I ought to join the Communist Party, too?"

"It's not the Party, Julia. It's me. I got straightened out personally. I do what I feel when I feel it. And I understand the others as well as myself. That's important."

"I'm still trying to understand myself."

"I know. Do you have to go back tonight, Julia?"

"Not if I don't want to."

"You know where the bathroom is. And the bed is still the same."

"Thanks, Jack. I didn't want to say anything. It's been a long time."

"I loved you once, Julia."

"I think I loved you."

"If it was now, Julia, I probably would marry you. Things like marriage and politics do go together, believe it or not."

"I know. After the last two years I might even marry you."

"Thanks."

"I'm sorry."

"Come on, Julia, the night's getting late and we're wasting time. Let's see how quick we can go back five years."

"Five years ago, Jack. More, wasn't it?"

"A long time.

"Come over, Jack."

"Like this."

"Yes. And more."

"Still the same?"

"I had almost forgotten how good you were, Jack. It kind of makes up for a lot of things."

"It does for me, too."

"I ache for you, Jack. Come inside."

"I've been waiting for this, Julia."

"So have I. Slow, warm, calm, easy. I feel at home. I feel like I belong."

"You do, Julia, you do."

"That's good, Jack. That was good."

"Sorry. I guess I'm out of shape."

"No, Jack. It was good. Thank you. It was something I needed."

"Then why stop, Julia. We can begin again."

The theaters and restaurants in New York become alive again. Not very often. Once a week. Or perhaps a weekend. It's better than running away. The fire gets too hot. When you get closer to the trouble you can see it much clearer. Sometimes it doesn't hurt as much.

"You're looking much better, Julia."

"Thanks, Walter."

"Going to New York tonight?"

"I think so. Why?"

"Nothing. I don't mind as much now. You're acting so much better. Like when you stopped going a couple of years ago. Probably you needed a rest then from all those gossipy women."

"Probably."

"And now it's become a little too quiet, I guess."

"I guess so, Walter."

"And Julia, never mind a babysitter this evening. I'll be home myself all night. I'll take care of Joey myself."

"All right, Walter. I may stay over at one of the girls, so don't worry about me."

"All right. But don't plan anything for this weekend. I expect to have the Ellises over. We haven't seen them for too long now."

Even the Ellises become bearable when there is something else to give you relief. Jack was the something else. The baby, Joey, became a child. As a child it became Walter's son. Sometimes Julia wondered if it should have been named Nelson, after all. But then she thought about Joe and knew that someday he would come back and then she would need Joey again. For a while.

"Nothing from Ruthie, Jack?"

"It's been a couple months now. Not a word."

"Maybe something's wrong?"

"Don't get up any hopes, Julia."

"I'm not."

"Do you mind reading a book this evening, Julia?"

"Another meeting?"

"Important one."

"I remember you walking out on me for a meeting. We were at the Marlowe."

"It's different now. Then I felt guilty. Now I don't. Maybe because it's happened so often?"

"So often? You've had more women than I thought."

"Sure. I'm an incorrigible playboy. I just decided to place myself and women and everything else in a showcase. I can see life much clearer. Part of me says I should feel that I'd rather be making love to you here, another part knows I've got to be at the meeting."

"A guy could become a celibate that way, Jack."

"Probably. Will you wait?"

"Do I have a choice?"

"My celibacy is disappearing."

Walter becomes calm, Jack is calm, everything is soft and smooth and life begins to breathe with regular breaths instead of in spasms that run hot and cold. Sometimes. Other times there is Joe again. Sometimes there is the wondering of what will happen when there is no more Jack Evans, when there is no more beauty on and in Julia Mitchell. In that case does one find a loaded pistol? Or before that happens does a guy named Joe come back?

"Ben just got back in town, Julia."

"Ben. That's nice."

"Not interested?"

"I am, Jack. He's successful now, isn't he?"

"He wrote a good book. A very good book. About the South. He's been published and it's selling like hotcakes."

"Good. I'm glad."

"What happened between you and Ben?"

"Nothing."

"Don't you want to see him?"

"All right."

"He's coming here."

"Then I guess I'll have to see him."

"I saw him today and told him you visited me every once in a while. He asked about you and I said you'd had a baby. He's coming up here tonight and said he'd like to talk to you. You're sure nothing happened between you?"

"No. I mean I'm sure."

"Julia, I got a letter today."

"From Ruthie?"

"From Joe. He's split up with Ruthie and is coming back to New York. He wants to stay with me here for a while."

If you wait long enough there are no more intersections or valleys or walls or traffic lights or crossroads. You can think forever and not find the answer. Sometimes you don't have to think at all but just wait and the decision is made for you in an apartment on 72nd Street.

PART V

THE RE-STATEMENT

CHAPTER 21
GOING

Jack Evans walked out of the brownstone into the rain and wondered if the rain was an anesthesia or a stimulant. It was slow and warm and heavy and he listened to the sound of the drops as they hit the roofs and the sidewalk and the pieces of paper lying in the street. A pounding that made him think of a bed, a bed that made him think of comfort, comfort that made him think of peace and contentment. Nothing to do but live a life and sleep in a bed. It made him think again of Julia. He looked at the rain and felt it hit his face, now sharp and cold. It woke him up and he wondered where else the rain fell and upon how many people and who these people were and what they thought and what they needed and he realized, because he felt he ought to realize, that he was one of these people. If the rain fell on them it should fall on him. Bed was warm and heavy and slow. Now the rain was cold, sharp, and alive. It was also wet. He thought about contented cows mooing in the rain and not being able to close their eyes and sleep standing up.

What kind of a problem is a problem that isn't a problem? Jack knew he had gone over it all before. He cursed himself and praised himself and rationalized to himself and went out and paid five bucks to bring a dame from 45th Street up to his apartment because he was alone and afraid and he could have had a woman to sleep with, a good, honest, clean woman, but gave up his chance because he thought something else was more important. He thought about a guy getting killed and he wondered did it make any difference.

This he went over a thousand times. This he answered a thousand times by going to a thousand different meetings where people talked and made placards and wrote addresses on postcards and sent out leaflets and contributed money. And he was only happy doing what he was doing. Only you can't look in the mirror and say, "Jack Evans, you're happy, you're happy, you're happy!" This is what he told Julia and he believed it as he told it to her. But how else could he say it? Why couldn't he be like Julia with only sex and an illegitimate child and Cadillacs and love for a guy that didn't deserve it? She had to find something in her life. Everyone had to. Yet he knew the finding was more than just talking. He had to feel it. The brain is supposed to be above all else, but give the body a good zoftig blonde and see how many guys leave their wives and kids or spend the dough they saved for next month's rent and food. Intellect? Moo! Like a cow. Be a hero and get your head bashed in. Freud and Darwin. And Einstein. Who's right? Maybe it's the individual? Oh, hell.

He walked to the subway. He put his dime in the slot, heard a train go by, and stopped by the entrance to light a cigarette and hoped a cop didn't see him and he waited for the next train. A guy and a gal stood by him.

"It's raining, sweetheart. There won't be many in the class tonight."

"Old professor Munroe will sure be sore."

"They won't miss us at City College night classes, anyway, Marcia."

"No. We can always say we had to work late, Milt."

"Yeah. But suppose there's a test? It's bad enough going six years at night for a degree without flunking courses on the way."

"There might be a test. But I don't care, Milt."

"We, the educated leaders of the country. I've got three bucks, Marcia."

"I know where to go for three bucks, Milt. Remember last week?"

"Yeah, let's go."

"You know what, Milt?"

"What?"

"This is much better than developing our brains."

The guy and gal invested twenty cents, gave up an hour of lecture, and went out into the rain.

Jack wondered what his own trouble was. There was Julia. Waiting for him. Ben might come later, but for a while there was Julia. There was more to Julia than any other woman. He had loved her once. That makes a difference. You always wonder with a woman you once loved who you don't love anymore what might have been. Sometimes, when you're really happy, then you don't give a damn. But when you still pay five bucks for a one-night-stand then you think about it. Jack laughed and told himself that he was thinking about nothing. That this was passé. Why the hell did Julia have to show up? He had the matter long since settled. Always, when things seem to be straight and you know where you're going, a symbol turns up and you go around in a circle. Get the hell out of the circle.

A train sounded close and Jack was about to put out his cigarette and then it sounded not close enough so he figured it was going uptown and he took another drag.

"Hey, mister, could you give me a dime to get to Brooklyn? Honest, I had the dough, but I lost it."

"Yeah. Here."

"Thanks, mister. Thanks. If I get to Brooklyn I can get a place to sack for the night. Thanks."

"Yeah, bud, okay."

When a guy with a dirty work shirt and a worn overcoat and torn pants and high laced shoes asks for a dime in the middle of the summer, then you know he needs it. Pat yourself on the back for doing your good deed for the day, Evans. Sucker. Give out a dime to every poor bastard you see and what the hell will you wear for shoes? Oh, hell. Once. How many more like that? How many others without a dime to get to some shack in Red Hook or down by the Navy Yard in Brooklyn? Or to Pigalle or the railroad station in Munich or Stepney Green or any other god-damned place.

The train came and the cigarette went out onto the wet floor and Jack rushed down the stairs and onto the subway train. He sat down and looked at the people around him. He could have gone home to Julia. Or to Mabel or to the little wife or to mother or to anyplace and settled down and supposedly been happy, really happy. Instead, he was going to meet with a bunch of other people, some who lived with the wife, with the kids, with the husband, with mother, with a toilet out in the yard, with a terrace at the penthouse, without even the five bucks to get some of the basic needs of life. It had nothing to do with what he was doing or the way he should live. He was just one individual out of billions, So why the fuss, why the bother?

He saw the train doors open and the train wait for a local to arrive at the adjoining platform. He could have gotten off and in five minutes he could be lying in bed with the symbol of happiness and ease his conscience of the pros and cons of being happy. He laughed. It was ridiculous. Maybe the rain does that to a guy? Maybe when you've made an important decision you have to think about it every so often to see whether there is a need to change it or amend it? The doors closed and he settled back in his seat and looked at the ad placards overhead lining the edge of the ceiling of the subway car. He knew the minute he left that there wasn't a chance in a thousand that he would go back.

CHAPTER 22
FRESH AIR

Ben walked up the steps of the brownstone house and wondered how many years it was since he had been there. He found himself instinctively stepping over a large crack in one of the steps and knew it hadn't been too long. But as he looked down at his feet and saw the new shoes and adjusted his new clothes and looked at the new Chevy parked by the curb right in front of the Cadillac, he realized that it was a long time. With Picasso space and time are one. With Stevens time and happening follow no pattern. Two years could be a thousand years. He opened the front door and was afraid. You wanted to come, you wanted to know, so go ahead. He walked up the steps, down the hall and stopped again. Go inside before you turn around and walk away and never know. He opened the door.

"Hello, Julia."

Get the hell away while you can or you may never get away.

"Hello, Julia."

"Come in Ben. I've been waiting for you."

"Jack told me you were here. He said he'd tell you I was coming."

"I've been waiting two years to see you again."

You've written your book; you'll write more books. Make that your life. If it's got to come, take it, and make this something else.

"That's what I was afraid of, Julia. I was afraid you didn't have to be afraid."

"I don't know what you're talking about, Ben. Come over here.

Sit down. I'll pour you a drink. You're looking prosperous."

"You did start drinking after all, Julia."

"Only once in a while. You're looking well."

"You're just as beautiful."

"Thank you."

"We sound like strangers, like we'd never known each other. Is it that late? Has that much happened?"

"Not to me."

"Maybe to me, Julia? The introductions are over. What about the baby?"

"Jack told you?"

"Yeah. I didn't know. I guess I should have known."

"You think it's your baby, Ben? It isn't."

"That night before Joe left. I thought that was it. I didn't think about it till Jack mentioned you had a baby and all day I've been reliving that in my mind.."

"Miss it?"

"I don't love you, Julia."

"That doesn't answer my question."

"You've heard about the silver platter?"

"Okay, Ben. I just wanted to know."

"I found out I didn't need you, Julia. I thought for a long time I did, but I didn't. I guess I never did love you."

"I think I knew you didn't."

"If you're feeling sorry for me in my success and freedom, don't. I'm not going to fall apart and I'm not dependent on anything but myself anymore. Is it my baby?"

"I said it isn't."

"If it is, I'm ready to marry you. I can give you the comforts you want now."

"Conscience bothering you, Ben?"

"Not now. But it will. Unless I can be sure. It's not Walter's baby, is it?"

"Don't beat your head against a wall. You're too nice a guy to do that. It's Joe's. Who the hell else's baby could I ever have in this world besides Joe's?"

"When?"

"The night before he decided to leave with Ruthie. Count it on your fingers. I'll show you the birth certificate. Almost to the day."

"Can I have another drink?"

"The strong man is relieved."

"Shut up."

"I know, Ben. You want to do the right thing by me and now you're just a little disappointed because you haven't proven your manhood and your superiority over me."

"You think you still have me on the end of a leash, Julia?"

"Things don't change that quickly. You, Jack . . . ."

"But not Joe."

"No, not the one I want."

"Don't kid yourself, Julia. You've fooled yourself enough."

"I'm not, Ben?"

"Yeah?"

"What if I told you that the baby was yours? Remember when I screamed that it was Joe's baby? But it was you inside of me."

"Then at least Joe would be relieved. Maybe I wouldn't be, but there'd be only one of us left on the end of your chain."

"How would Joe know?"

"Okay, let's stop playing games, Julia. I don't know if that baby is mine. I don't know if it's Joe's. I don't know if it's the postman's who has the New Rochelle route."

"You bastard."

"Maybe I am a bastard, but if I am it makes me a smart, selfish one. I've found something new. I've found I can live. All that came before was rotten. It was like wallowing in a garbage can. If you asked me to sleep with you now I'd feel sorry for you and pour you another drink and put you to bed. I don't want any part of it. But I found out that if I can't be honest with myself, I can't be honest with anything. If you say it's my baby, we'll get a blood test and if they say it is then I'll marry you and support you. Otherwise, I'm going to break clean. My conscience is going to be lily white. One way or the other."

"You've figured it all out?"

"I've figured it all out."

"What about Joe?"

"I don't know. Jack told me he left Ruthie. That Joe couldn't take Ruthie and that Ruthie couldn't take Joe. So he found himself another castle with some woman who worked in his office, spent his money on her, couldn't go back to Ruthie, and is coming back to New York. That's not a pretty picture. Maybe he wants you again? Maybe he doesn't? Maybe he wants the apartment on Eighth Street and every coed he can find in Washington Square who wants to learn more about life?"

"And if it's his baby?"

"Joe was a good guy once. We were pals, buddies. You changed Joe a lot. Maybe you didn't change him that much. I don't know. If that kid belongs to him, he might take you and it."

"And if he doesn't want to?"

"You don't know what to do, Julia?"

"Ben Stevens, you're a bastard."

"I told you I was. But I'm still an honest one. Shall I leave?"

"Get the hell out."

"Okay."

"You couldn't be the father, Ben. Not of my child. Didn't you know that?"

"You're right, Julia. Now I could be. But I wouldn't be. Two years ago I would have been. But I couldn't. Maybe that doesn't make sense?"

"It's Joe's. It couldn't be anybody's but Joe's. It even looks like Joe. Just like him."

"I'm sorry, Julia. I don't want to make you cry. I'm going now. I don't want to sound corny, but there was no goodbye last time. Let's make it this time. If there is anything I can ever do, in any way, I will."

"I know you will."

"Goodbye, Julia."

"Ben!"

"What?"

"Can't you stay a little while longer?"

"It's better this way."

"Then just stand there. Let me look at you. For a minute. Please?"

"Julia, I'd like to tell you what to do. I'd like to tell you how to be happy. But I can't. I don't know how. I've been too close to you. I've been as close to being in love with you. I can't talk to you. I wish I could."

"You don't have to. I know what I want."

"That's the trouble. Goodbye, Julia."

"Ben, will you kiss me before you go?"

"I should have thought of that myself."

"Like old times. Only it isn't old times anymore."

"No, it isn't."

"Where are you going, Ben?"

"Up."

"I know that. Now?"

"To Nirvana. Goodbye, Julia."

The door closed and the hallway and the steps and the front door suddenly melted into Picasso's space and time and the crack on the front steps was stepped on. At the foot of the steps Ben stopped and breathed the air. He thought he should breathe fresh air. He had walked back into the circle and had walked out again and outside felt light and free. Inside he felt just a little heaviness. He took another deep breath. The heaviness was still there. It would go away.

CHAPTER 23
TIME TO GET OFF

The plane circled over New York City. Ben looked out of the window into the miles of concrete and stone and wanted to yell out to whatever was below. Hey, Ben, where did they bury you? Where under all that stone and concrete did they put the kid who had big ideas and didn't know where to find them? Maybe he jumped off that bridge below? Because he isn't here anymore? This isn't Ben Stevens. This is a guy with big ideas who knows where to find them and knows where he's going. This is a guy who can believe and write what he believes because it's strong, and because it's strong enough he buys a new suit and a pair of new shoes and a plane ticket to Chicago. This is Ben Stevens. Not Ben Stevens, but Ben Stevens.

Throw out a rotten apple and let it bury itself into the ground. Deep into the ground, where it can smell and breathe the earth and the air and the elements that made it. And if it grows straight it becomes an apple tree and it isn't rotten anymore, but something fresh and clean and giving,z producing life.

How many men and women are buried under that pile of concrete and steel? How many men and women who had dreams and even confidence got lost walking through a maze of ideas and confusions and ended up back in the same place? Every so often they'd pass through the green of a park and feel that here indeed was truth and beauty. They'd stop and drink and continue, feeling refreshed, but always in the same direction, around and around and around.

"Round trip ticket, sir?"

"No, just one way. To Chicago."

"You save money on a round trip flight in case you're coming back. And you can get a seat reserved now. Save you a lot of trouble."

"Do many people get round trip tickets?"

"Those that are coming back. Going round trip is always cheaper and easier."

The city of New York flew out from under the plane and Ben stared into the buildings as they got fewer and smaller and thought about how much easier it would be to come back to New York. Going round trip is cheaper and easier. Once you sell a book and the publisher decides that he can make enough money by plugging it, it immediately becomes a good book. A great book without advertising in the New York Review of Books or The New York Times Sunday books section can sell as little as a few thousand copies and the author will get his five hundred dollars and next time he writes one the publisher will look twice before he considers putting it in the presses, no matter how good it reads. A lousy book can get a big investment of advertising and if there is sufficient appeal to popular motives and mania then it becomes a best seller. After that anything the author writes is a best seller. But black isn't always black. There are exceptions. Ben's book was an exception. It was a good book, it was plugged as a good book and it sold as a good book. And because people read it, more people bought it. The people responded. Not like they respond to a Senator who gives out jobs or a cereal that gives out free diamond rings or a television program that gives out free autographed pictures or a quiz show that promotes a culture of stupidity. Ben was drawing fat royalty checks. In New York he could have what he had never had before, what he always thought was the second part of what a successful author wanted. The first part was a way to get to the two billion. He felt he spoke for part of them to all of them and they understood. A third part was the cocktail parties and autograph appearances and campus lectures and celebrity publicity. Everyone wanted to meet Ben Stevens because Ben Stevens was the success that they were never able to achieve, but still hoped to reach someday. There were more agents and producers and editors and advertising managers than Ben ever knew existed. It was fun, it was joyful, it was a bromide and a hangover and a celibacy of the mind.

He could go back to Tennessee or Oklahoma or Mexico or Korea or Indo-China or Greece and get to more of the two billion. Not that he couldn't write in New York. Not that there weren't people. Not that he didn't know about Hester Street and Third Avenue and Marcy Avenue and the twelfth floor of the Waldorf and Greenwich, Connecticut, and all the rest of the living and the lives of the people. New York was big. New York was the end point. When everything else was exhausted, then came New York. Because New York was more than everything else. Its 309 square miles was the center of the world. You couldn't write about New York until you knew it. All aboard for points east and west.

"You want a round trip ticket, sir?"

"Just one way, thanks. It may be a long time before I'll be back."

As the plane flew away from New York and toward Pennsylvania and Ohio and Indiana and Illinois Ben knew that part of the past was left behind. He was half free. When he came back from Tennessee, he brought back a new life, but before he could begin that one, he had to settle the old one.

The taxi passed through a miniature New York. This was the first time he had been in Chicago. It was New York on a smaller scale. On the outside. Just as Chattanooga had been New York on an even smaller scale. But when you go down into the guts of other cities, they are no more New York than the sharecroppers' farms in Tennessee.

He hadn't thought about Joe much. Joe wasn't the kind of friend you think about much. He's either there or not there. A little or a lot. What the hell happens to a guy when you don't know him anymore? Inside you know him and outside he's a stranger. Like a city you leave for ten years and come back and find a new skyscraper. Everyone changes. Ruthie was different. She was something he had known and would always know, no matter what happened. Ruthie was the kind of girl who wouldn't change. She might try to, but inside there was a simplicity that remained. Like the letters r u t h i e. Small and simple.

"Coming home after a vacation, huh, bud?"

"No. Just paying a visit."

"Well, same thing. I been driving these cabs for fifteen years. I can tell that look in a guy's eye."

"A wife of a friend of mine."

"That's an old angle, too. Nice section they live in. Must be doing pretty good?"

"Not bad."

"An old friend?"

"Yeah."

"Well, look, bud, if you don't want me to talk, I won't, you just looked like a nice guy so I was making conversation. A cabbie don't have to make conversation, you know."

I know. I'm just thinking."

"Yeah. Me too. What if the guy ain't home for a couple days, huh?"

Sometimes a cabbie makes the right kind of conversation. Sometimes he says the obvious and because it is, you don't want to think about it. Maybe he got it right? This was about Ruthie. Once he had called her his Ruthie. Maybe she needed him? Maybe she didn't? But this was a cord he was still tied to.

"Here it is, bud. Two-forty."

"Long ride. Keep the change."

"Thanks, bud. And good luck."

What do you say to a girl who gave you her virginity, herself, and who walked out on you because you gave her nothing in return? How are you? How have you been? You're looking well. This wasn't Julia. To Julia you either say "hi," or "go to hell." This was Ruthie. Maybe you just forget everything and as soon as the door is opened take her in your arms and give her a big kiss and let her know everything is all right. And let yourself know that everything is all right.

"I knew somehow that you would come, Ben. After I read your book, I knew you'd be in New York and hear about what happened and I knew you'd come."

"Whose fault was it?"

"Nobody's fault. Joe had to live like Joe. Not like he thought Joe ought to live or like I wanted him to."

"I walked in expecting to find you in tears, but you seem to be very calm and collected. It's all right, isn't it Ruthie?"

"Yes, it is. I was in tears when you came in, but only because I was glad to see you. I'm not afraid, Ben. Joe is over and it doesn't hurt. At least not very much. It'll go away."

"Those things always do, don't they?"

"It did with you, didn't it, Ben? Why did you come?"

"To see you."

"But you don't love me anymore, do you, Ben?"

"No, I don't."

"I didn't think so. Feeling sorry for me? You don't have to."

"I'm not. I thought I might, but I don't have to."

"I got what I wanted from Joe. I learned about life from you and I tried it out with Joe. And now I'm all grown up. I can face life. And I'm not afraid of it because I know where I'm going."

"Do you?"

"Yes. I tried to get what I thought I wanted out of life and I found out it wasn't what I wanted after all. Now I know what I want. That's what you used to say. You knew where you were going but didn't know how to get there. I do now."

"How?"

"We'll talk about that tomorrow. It's late. This isn't New York and we don't stay up till morning here. At least I don't. Do you want to go to bed, Ben?"

"That isn't why I came."

"And that isn't what I meant. I was a simple girl once. I got the experience I wanted. Now I'm a simple girl again. There are two bedrooms upstairs."

"You know, Ruthie, I could fall in love with you again."

"Don't. I intend to remain a simple girl for a while yet."

Ben Stevens goes to bed and wonders whether a person has to have her life torn apart before she finds out how to live. His mind is clear and the cord isn't a cord but a pink ribbon held by a little girl with pigtails and a soft voice. The circle is almost complete.

Ruthie Templeton lies in bed and thinks about a man named Ben who did what she knew he could do. She wonders whether she should have stayed with him and tells herself that if she would have, Ben would never have found his answer. There's something that tears a woman apart, like the tearing when she first gives her body and soul to a man, when it is taken and not held gently and securely like a woman wants to be held. A woman like Ruthie. But after the tears the pain goes away and the body and soul belong to herself again. This time it knows what tore it before and knows when not to be hurt. Joe was the search for the self. Joe was the trek across the desert for adventure. Joe was the climbing of the mountain. Joe was the way. But the bluebird was there all the time. It was with Ruthie herself. Now she knew it. Now she could find happiness in herself. Maybe she wasn't such a simple girl as she thought? Without looking any longer for the bluebird of happiness, like in the song. Otherwise, she might have dreamt more about Ben. Instead, she shut her eyes. When your mind is active when you go to bed it's hard to fall asleep. She tried to mix her thoughts into a crazy pattern so that her eyes would get tired and her brain would get muddled and she could sleep. She thought about what had happened and knew that just talking about it out loud with Ben had made her more sure of herself. There was no need for confusion. She knew where she was going. Suddenly it was easy to get to sleep.

"Are you coming back to New York, Ruthie?"

"No, Ben. I'll stay in Chicago."

"Afraid?"

"I don't think so. I've never been on my own here. But I have in New York."

"That makes sense."

"Everything does after a while."

"Does it, Ruthie?"

"Right now it does to me, Ben."

"Will you get a job?"

"I'm well provided for. I can sell the house. The mortgage is almost half paid off and that's worth a few thousand dollars."

"Is that wise, Ruthie?"

"I haven't been happy here these last months. I'd rather live in an apartment, anyway. We did have a car. But that went on a bleached bimbo."

"I heard."

"I'm not bitter, Ben."

"You're a terrific girl."

"You know, Ben, in the time we lived together you did everything for me. But you never once said that."

"I was going around in a circle, too. Maybe I'm just beginning to see it?"

"Let's not make any new circles. How about a show tonight?"

"Fine. You know what, Ruthie? You're terrific!"

Have you ever thought you were in love and not been? Have you ever been in love and thought you weren't.? It's easy when it's that simple. Then you either are happy or unhappy. It's black-and-white. But Ben didn't know whether one or the other was true. And if it was, he didn't know whether he wanted to do anything about it or not.

"I might be in love with you again, Ruthie."

"I thought we talked about that."

"We still are talking about it. If I were in love with you, would you marry me?"

"No."

"You're not afraid of me?"

"No."

"Or of my career? We're both not needy, like before. I'm set now. I know where I'm going. If I marry it will be because I need a companion, a partner. Not a crutch."

"I know that. I don't want to think about it yet. I need to be on my own, be myself."

"I shouldn't have talked about it. You go, girl!"

"Thanks, pal."

"You're welcome, pal."

It started with a girl in Tennessee and moved to Julia in an apartment in New York and then to Ruthie in Chicago. Ben stayed two weeks and found out that maybe Freud was wrong and sex did place third after all. When it doesn't become something that you have to latch onto because there is nothing else, then it finds a place. Ben was happy. He laughed when he thought about it. He was really happy. And partly so because Ruthie was, too.

"I guess this is goodbye, Ruthie."

"Not goodbye. Just so long."

"You read too many novels."

"Maybe you write too many? No, not too many. I hope you write enough. I know you will."

"My offer still goes"

"Your conscience is clear. My answer still goes."

"You'll be okay here?"

"If I ever need any help, I will call you."

"That's a promise?"

"So long, Ben."

"So long, Ruthie. Maybe someday?"

"Yes, Ben. Maybe someday."

The plane stands above the earth and below a line stretches from New York to Tennessee to Chicago and back again. The circle is completed and two people find their way out of it.

CHAPTER 23
STARTING AGAIN

You can go through your life being a bastard. You can lead women astray, you can kick little children, you can chase away hungry dogs or cats, you can vote Republican, you can vote Democratic, you can live in a penthouse and eat caviar with the money you made putting other people out of business, you can live in a slum section and collect relief funds from the city and spend the money on booze on Friday, a ball game on Saturday, and pay off on a television set. You can do any number of things that any number of people would call you a bastard for doing. But unless you feel there's no justification, unless you feel that you were doing wrong, you would either laugh or ignore them or tell them to go to hell. And then go on doing what you were doing. Free and easy and it doesn't hurt.

But Joe Templeton did hurt. He hated himself. He hated his own guts. He hated his nerve. He hated where he was, what he had done. He walked across Central Park West and wondered why a car didn't hit him and then he wouldn't know anything and he'd be through with the whole fucking business of life. Why do you keep going around in a circle and keep stepping on people and keep sinking lower and lower until you're too far in to get out? How the hell do you get out? Maybe a car will hit you? There's a subway station that can get you to the Empire State building or the Brooklyn Bridge. But that takes guts. Joe Templeton knows he doesn't have guts. He doesn't have nerve. He doesn't have anything but a confused, perverted desire that doesn't know where it's going but always ends up in the gutter. You get a woman who will let you keep your castle and you give it up. You get a woman who gives you another kind of castle and you throw it away on a dishwater blonde who offered you no more than the dishwater blondes who played one-night stands at Eighth Street and then went away without so much as a plugged nickel. You keep running away and find that you're back where you started. So you decide not to run anymore. Back to New York and the Village. You only thought you wanted to run away. Here's an apartment, here's a bed, and here's Julia. You should've stayed right here. You've stopped running. Now everything will be all right, won't it? What the hell, Joe Templeton, who are you kidding? Yourself, a girl in Chicago, a girl in New York? Are you coming back or are you still running? Are you here or are you just stopping by because you were here before? Where do you stop? It goes round and round and round and it comes out here. That's simple, like the music in the song. But what comes out is that you're still a bastard.

"There's no answer, Julia. If there were, I wouldn't have come here. We tried it before."

"But don't you see, Joe? You did come back. Because I asked you to. Because you wanted to be with me. You've tried everything and nothing is left but this, nothing but me."

"How do you know? How does anybody know? What do you want me to do? Sleep with you?"

"Anything you want."

"Maybe I'll get tired of the color of your hair? Maybe I'll want a redhead?"

"You're just talking. You don't mean that."

"I don't know what I mean. Maybe I don't mean anything? Maybe I'll get drunk some night and come home and lay down next to you and pull some whore in after me? What then?"

"You're talking ridiculous, Joe."

"I am ridiculous, Julia, I am the most ridiculous person who ever lived. I don't want to do those things, but I'll keep looking for something and the first thing you know they'll happen."

"Joe, you've looked. You haven't found it."

"So?"

"So stop looking. Take what you've got. It's here. It's me. I want to marry you."

"And starve to death."

"Or love to death. I ran away, too. I looked, too. But we had it in the first place. Now we can have it again. Don't you understand, Joe?"

"Yeah. It sounds nice. But it doesn't work. Don't you know what happened in Chicago, Julia?"

"I know."

"It'll happen again. And again. I'm a bastard, Julia. I'm a no good rotten sonofabitch and I know it. If you want to sleep with me, that would be fine. But that's all. If you live with me I'll do the same thing to you. I'd like to stop running away, stop going around in circles. But I won't."

"Chicago was wrong for you. You were searching for something, and it was wrong. Now it's right."

"What the hell's the use of talking, Julia! I had two days to think about it on the train from Chicago. It's no good."

"Not even try?"

"What for?"

"Joe, I have a baby."

"Jack told me."

"He's named Joe."

"That's nice."

"For Chrissake, Joe, you still don't understand?"

"Why the hell didn't you tell me?"

"I wanted to keep it. For you. For us."

"What the hell is the matter with you? You could've gotten an abortion. Who else knows?"

"Walter doesn't."

"Who does?"

"Jack and Ben."

"What did they say?"

"Nothing."

"Why the hell did you do it, Julia?"

"I wanted some part of you, Joe. I loved you."

"Now you want me to marry you."

"Yes."

"You got a weapon. What if I say no?"

"You can't say no. You can cut my throat, you can take my heart out, but you can't tell me no. Joe, I've got to have you."

"What about the baby?"

"I want to be with you right now."

"I don't have any money, Julia."

"I have some."

"What about the kid?"

"Not yet. We'll take him later. First you and me. Then I'll get a divorce. Then we'll get married. Make it yes, Joe. For godssake, make it yes. Take me anywhere you want me. I'll strip naked and kneel at your feet and let you lay on me and step on me if you want to. But take me!"

Maybe that's it, Joe thought. Maybe I've got to be selfish, hard and tough? Maybe I've run enough and came back to start again where I left off? Someplace in this god-damned world there's got to be an answer. Leave her alone and find it yourself? Try to find it with her? Which is the Fountain of Youth and which is the Valley of Death? Is there a road that starts out and goes straight instead or in a circle? And what happens when you come to a crossroads? Left or right or up or down? Where do you stop?

"You know what will happen, Julia."

"It won't. You know it won't."

"It will."

"I'll give you whatever you want."

"Last week I slept with a dirty blonde and a bleached blonde and a bitch of a blonde. Do you want me to sleep with you tonight?"

"Not tonight, but right now."

"Julia, you really love me?"

"I'm just tearing myself apart because I'm trying to be dramatic."

"I don't love you enough, Julia."

"You will."

"Could I?"

"This is the answer, Joe."

"Maybe it is? Can you stay here tonight?"

"Yes."

"Jack can go out to a hotel. Tomorrow you go up to New Rochelle and get your things and whatever money you can get ahold of."

"Yes, Joe. Yes."

"I'll get a furnished place. I'll even look for a job. This is what I should have done two years ago."

"We'll find it now, Joe."

"Come here, Julia."

"I'm on the bed, Joe. You come here. This is the beginning. Let's start at the beginning. Let's not waste even a minute."

"You know, Julia, I feel good. I think maybe you're right. I think maybe this is the answer."

The drive to New Rochelle was different. It was quick now. For two years it had been slow. For two years it had been without feeling, dull, false, insecure. But now it was real again. There was Joe. There was no more Walter. When the lights were out and there were only sheets and a pillow, it was the same Joe. But in the light of day something was different. Something was gone. The bravado. The false confidence. Joe faced his fears now. Maybe the change didn't matter? Maybe he'd be the same undependable egocentric Joe? But when Julia thought about fat, pawing Walter, it didn't matter. The Cadillac, the suitcases, the clothes, the jewelry, she told Walter, all for a two-week trip to visit Ruthie, an old friend in Chicago who needed help. The same streets, the same boulevards, the same avenues. Even the apartment, although it wasn't the one on Eighth

Street, looked the same. A bedroom window that led out onto the roof made it complete. But it was different. This time it was for keeps. You try not to wonder whether it was Walter you were going from or Joe you were going to. If you think about it, it goes round and round. But if you don't think about it, it stops and there's nothing but the residue of uncompleted satisfaction. It's easier just not to think.

"Joe, are you going to get a job?"

"Let me get settled. It's only a week. I've been looking."

"Our money won't hold out much longer."

"Okay. Okay."

"Joe, what's the matter with you? I thought this was going to be it. I thought this was going to be all right."

"What the hell do you want me to do? I told you! Have a drink and forget about it."

"No."

"I thought you learned to drink."

"I don't want you to forget about it. You're not even trying."

"Then let me take a drink. Why the hell don't you go back to Walter?"

"Anything but go back to Walter."

"Even me."

"I didn't mean that. I love you, Joe. But please try and help. Try and make this work."

"I told you I'm a sonofabitch."

"We could be happy."

"How many times a night do you want it?"

"Please, Joe."

"That's all I'm good for. I told you last week. I'm telling you this week."

"I'm sorry, Joe. Let's forget it."

"Give me the bottle."

"You're drinking too much."

"If you're jealous, then take some too."

"I don't want the lousy stuff."

"Here, Julia. It'll make you feel better."

"All right, pour me a glass. Maybe if I drink enough I won't be able to think about anything."

For a few days a two-room furnished apartment with old furniture and greasy windows and a roof splashed with garbage can be interesting. It can be Bohemian. You can stand it for a weekend. Even a week. But you can't spend a week in bed. You have to get up sometimes. When you realize it isn't going to go away you take another drink. But after a while even booze doesn't stop you from thinking. When you're kicked in the face you can't turn away and not feel the pain. If you have someone to turn to, it doesn't hurt as much. If there's a guy named Joe who knows and has confidence and a joke for every hurt, then the hurt is less. But if you don't have anyone to depend on, if there's no Joe with strong open arms, but a Joe with a bottle of whiskey and a dazed look and a crooked walk and no smile, then it hurts even more. You watch a guy named Joe climb into bed and become a machine and go out in the daytime and wander back at night and you have no love, no warmth, no affection, and you become a machine yourself and try and forget about feeling and even living. You watch Joe walk out on a roof and look over the side and ask yourself when it's going to end.

"Joe, it's a month now. I called Walter and told him I'm staying another few weeks. When will we get the baby? It's your baby, Joe, it's our baby."

"Okay, okay. Don't you think I know it's my baby? What the hell do you want me to do about it? I didn't want it. You did."

"Because I loved you."

"Then take the damn thing and leave me alone."

"What's happening here? What's happened to us?"

"I don't know. Nothing's happened. You wanted this. You're getting this."

"Not this. I wanted love, Joe. Love me."

"Maybe tomorrow? Maybe yesterday? Maybe a hundred years from now? In the meantime I make you suffer and I can't help it.

Why don't you leave?"

"I have no place to go."

"Back to your husband."

"I'm sorry, Joe. I don't want to nag you. I'm sorry."

"You can go back to your nice house in New Rochelle."

"For God's sake, Joe, I said I'm sorry. Leave me alone."

You're left alone and it gets worse. You're not left alone and it gets worse. What are you looking for? You can't stay and you can't go back. But you keep looking. One day it'll burst in your face and it'll hurt more than it ever did before.

"I waited for you last night, Joe."

"I didn't come home."

"I know that."

"I told you what to expect. I went to bed with some babe I picked up and laid with her all night and thought about you and turned her over and laid with her again. I'm no good. Do you want to kill me? Go ahead. Why don't you just get up and leave and maybe someday you'll be happy."

"Don't you understand, you stupid fool, that I can be happy with you. And you can be happy with me if you want to."

"You can't and I can't. We tried and it won't work, Julia. Nothing ever will. I can't help myself. That's the plain and simple truth. I can't live like a human being. I need my castle and I have to count the skirts as they pass by below. I need my bottle and a full bed every night. And every night a different bottle and different bedmate. That makes me feel strong. Maybe someday I'll find another way to be strong? But not now. Do you know what I'm saying, Julia? Does it make any sense?"

"You don't want to try, do you Joe?"

"I can't try. I can't do anything."

"What about the kid?"

"Put me in jail."

"That's why I had him. For you. To get you. To keep you. Now you don't want me."

"It's no good."

"It's funny, Joe. I gave my life away for you and now you don't want me. You know what's even more funny? I don't think I really want you anymore, either. It's not your baby. It never was. It was Ben's. I'll go to Ben. Why should I stay with you when I can have Ben?"

"You're talking crazy, Julia."

"I'll marry Ben. He loves me. They all love me. They always did. Ben's baby. Not Joe's baby."

"For Chrissakes, Julia, stop it."

"Sure, Joe. I'll stop it. Do you want to know something? You're right. You're a sonofabitch. I hate you, but I love you. And I'll probably hate you and love you until the day I die!"

There was no more pretending. Pretending is only good when there's an object to the game. But there was no more object. It was all a blur. It didn't mean anything now. There wasn't even a circle. There wasn't even a deep ditch with high walls to walk into and around and around. Now it was nothing and you had to stop from falling deeper into nothing. Nothing sucked you under into big, wet, sloppy, sweaty hands that belong to something named Walter.

"It's your baby, Ben. I fooled you. It's yours."

"Do you want me to speak to Joe, Julia. I don't know if he'll listen, but I'll speak to him"

"Joe is gone. There's no more Joe. Not ever again. That was the last time. I want you now. It's your baby and I want you now."

"I'm not a fool, Julia. I came to you and asked you. You told me. Jack told me. Now that it won't work with Joe you come to me. I'm not a fool."

"But it is yours. I know it's yours. That last night. After Joe left."

"We went over this before. I know it isn't."

"But I did it for Joe. I wanted Joe. That's why I didn't tell you."

"It won't work, Julia. I don't love you. I'm not going to marry you."

"Ben, you can't say that. Don't you see? It's yours. I'm trying to tell you."

"You're not fooling me and you're not threatening me."

"My God, Ben. What do I do? There's no Joe. No Ben. My God, it's actually funny."

"You've been running away from nothing. You could be happy with Walter. You have Joe's baby, what's left of Joe. Remember him as you knew him. You've got money. You're getting older. You'll get used to Walter. "

"Do you get used to an octopus? It is funny, Ben. This is where I started. This is the beginning. Like it was … how many years ago? Years and years and years ago. Now I'm back where I started. No life, no love, only the baby. That's funny, Ben. But it's not a joke."

Once you step out of the circle you either know where you were going or you don't. Sometimes people know where and there is a straight line that takes them there. But sometimes they're afraid and they step right back into the circle and keep going around and around again. Sometimes they find it easier to step into another circle and the same thing happens. If you stand back and watch these people you wonder which road they are going to take. And where they are going. And where they stop.

Julia stopped the Cadillac, walked into the house in New Rochelle. She went into the living room, opened the cabinet and poured a drink. Then she poured another. And another. Her husband would be coming home soon and she hated the son of a bitch.

She thought about a child upstairs named Joe, poured another drink and thought about Walter again and wondered whether she really hated him.